CW00641196

As she turned over to sleep she heard the sound again. It was a footstep, heavy and resolute, followed by another. Pippa sat upright, reaching for the light switch. Once the room was flooded with soft light and no further sound came, she began to relax. The housekeeper was sleeping not far away, along the corridor, but there was no need to disturb her just because she felt uneasy in her new surroundings.

Then the sound came again, clear and echoing, and Pippa stiffened. It was hard to tell where it was: either in the room, outside or overhead. A quick glance outside in the corridor revealed no one there. Who could it be? Mrs Purvis was asleep, and there was no one else in the Hall.

Pippa trembled, remembering her mother. Whose were the restless steps disturbing the peace of Cambermere on the night she came to it for the first time?

Recent Titles by Aileen Armitage

CEDAR STREET
JERICHO YEARS
TRICK OF THE LIGHT

ANNABELLA*

available from Severn House

For my lovely Anne

'When thy seeing blindeth thee
To what thy fellow-mortals see;
When thy sight to thee is sightless,
Their living, death; their light most lightless;
Search no more —
Pass the gates of Luthany, tread the region Elenore.'

Francis Thompson: *The Mistress of Vision*

1

In the corner of the train compartment a young woman dozed, her fair head leaning against the window pane. Outside, trees and farmhouses sped by as the train rattled on, and now and again the solitary traveller sighed in her sleep.

All of a sudden the slim figure stiffened and cried out, and her green eyes opened wide in alarm. She stared anxiously about her in an effort to recall where she was, and then leaned back against the upholstery again. Three deep, slow breaths and she began to relax.

That nightmare again. Ever since her childhood the recurring dream of darkness — complete and utter blackness, where unseen terror stalked her steps — had haunted Philippa Korvak. She felt angry with herself for letting it happen again, after an interval of years, on a train of all places, where she might well have appeared an utter fool if anyone had chanced to be there when she cried out. She looked out and found comfort in the sight of sunlit Berkshire fields. Darkness and nightmare were quickly banished in the soothing view.

It was too silly for words, she thought as she took a mirror and lipstick from her handbag. Always it was the same dream: the slowly-thudding footsteps coming nearer and nearer while she cowered in some labyrinthine underground place where not a chink of light penetrated the oppressive blackness that threatened to choke her in its intensity. And always she awoke with a cry, bathed in sweat, at the very moment when the menacing footsteps at last reached her. Ridiculous that a childhood dream should recur now, when the reality was already far more catastrophic than any nightmare.

She was a fool; she must be, or she would have seen it coming. But that night when Clive came to her Paris apartment, poised and self-possessed like the man of the world he was, she had been unaware of any difference in him. She must have been blind. His averted cheek when she reached up to kiss him should have warned her, but even after she had poured out a pernod and water for him, just as she had done for the past two years, she still sensed nothing wrong. It was only when she went through to the little kitchen to dish up the ragoût and he followed her, leaning diffidently against the doorframe to watch her, that she began to sense a subtle change in him. Normally Clive left the mysteries of the kitchen severely alone, preferring to wait with his drink until she carried in the evening meal. His grey eyes were unusually sombre.

'There's something I must tell you, Philippa,' he had said, and only then, at the sight of his eyes and the tone of his voice, had her heart leapt in apprehension. As he went on speaking she had watched the steam rise from the dish of ragoût in her hands, the misty swirls vanishing swiftly before her gaze as she felt her hopes shrivel and die.

'Believe me, my dear, it's better this way,' he had said at last. 'Better for both of us,' he added, and the calmness in his voice angered her, but she stayed silent. Diplomat though he was, Clive had had to struggle to find the right words.

'I was taken by surprise, Philippa. I did not expect this, but now Joyce has decided to come and join me here, you must realise it would be very difficult for us to go on as we were . . .'

Difficult, but not impossible, she recalled thinking fiercely. Her first impulse had been to fight, to re-attach to herself that part of her which was about to be severed, but the look in Clive's eyes told her he was already gone from her, already in spirit with his wife. Instantly she made a decision; if she could not have Clive, then amputation, however painful, was the cleanest and most sensible solution. She could remember even now the involuntary expression of relief on his handsome face when she told him that she would go home to London at once on a long-overdue leave. But after he had gone, the meal still uneaten, she had been able to feel nothing but a vast, swamping sense of desolation.

So it was that Pippa was now speeding from London to Cambermere, far from the scent of garlic and Gauloises, of steaming French coffee and croissants, away from Paris and Clive. She was glad she was alone in the compartment as she fought to keep back the tears that brimmed behind her eyelids. A girl jilted in love usually fled home to mother, she supposed, but Pippa had neither mother nor home to run to. It was over twenty years ago that Mother had died, when Pippa was still only six, and now all she could recall of the legendary Carrie Hope, idol of millions, was a mass of Titian-red hair and warm arms and a haunting scent of perfume.

Pippa stared at her pale-faced reflection in the train window. The tawny hair and oval face bore little resemblance to the striking beauty whose face smiled seductively from the magazine and newspaper cuttings Pippa had stuck lovingly into a scrapbook all those years ago. In fact, thought Pippa ruefully, she was not really very pretty at all and she had often wondered what Clive had seen in her. Intelligent, yes, but no match for his debonair charm and complete self-assurance. He could have had his pick of all the women in Paris, but he claimed it was her mind which had attracted him.

'We are soul-mates, Philippa, you and I,' he had murmured. 'We share a common interest in art and music and all things beautiful. We aesthetes are rare creatures. A marriage of true minds, as Donne says. That is what we have, my dear, something unique and special.'

But marriage of the minds had not precluded his interest in her body, cultural attaché at the British Embassy or not, Pippa thought bitterly as the train sped on. Was it because she was the child of a mourned film idol and a world-renowned film producer that she had first evoked Clive's interest, or was she being savagely unfair to him now he had cast her off? She must try firmly to put it all out of her mind and think only of Cambermere and the future. Perhaps in time she could face going back to the Sorbonne and Professor Garnier, to pick up her secretarial work for him

9

again, but right now all she wanted was a haven of peace to forget and try to regather her scattered mind.

Engrossed in her thoughts, Pippa barely noticed when the train pulled up at a small station and the door of the compartment opened. She looked up to see a young man climbing in, his hand on the steel harness of a large golden labrador dog. The dark spectacles confirmed that he was blind.

'Let me take your bag,' Pippa said shyly. She was conscious of not knowing how much help a blind person would accept without feeling patronised. He held out the bag with a mumured thanks, and she was aware of his free hand groping for a seat as she reached up to the rack. Once he was seated, the dog lay down at his feet and Pippa re-seated herself. To her relief the young man did not seem disposed to begin a conversation so she was able to revert to her own private thoughts.

How dreadful it must be to be blind, to be perpetually in the dark, she thought compassionately. His was a nightmare far worse than any of her dreaded dreams, and yet his expression was composed, even cheerful. He must be gifted with far greater courage than she was, running away from life because it had dealt her a blow. She should learn from his fortitude, put the past behind her and think positively.

She tried to visualise Cambermere and the house she had not known her father owned, until today. Alexis Korvak owned flats and villas all over the globe, many of which Pippa had visited, but Cambermere was a surprise to her. It was only when she landed from the Paris plane and headed for Father's luxury flat in fashionable West Kensington that she first learned of it.

'Sorry, miss, the flat has been stripped and closed for redecoration,' the elderly janitor had told her. 'I reckon Mrs Purvis wasn't expecting you. She's gone down to Mr Korvak's place in Buckinghamshire.'

True, the housekeeper had not expected her because Pippa had left Paris in such a hurry, but then she often used Father's flat since he so rarely came to England these days. After some little time turning over the papers and ledgers on the desk in his dusty little office, the janitor had finally unearthed the address.

'Cambermere Hall, near Marlow,' he had announced. 'That'll mean a train from Paddington. Shall I ring Mrs Purvis to expect you?'

It would be a country gentleman's residence, Pippa decided, a house that befitted Father's standing as an international film-maker. Strange he had never mentioned the place, but then there was no reason why he should. He and Pippa were comparative strangers; since Mother died they had only met during Pippa's school and college vacations, and then only briefly because he was always flying off to some far location for a new film.

It was a sad admission to make, even if only to oneself, Pippa thought. At her age still to know her father only as a passing stranger somehow seemed an admission of failure. She was shy of him and his powerful presence, but he had always been generous and she could have made more effort to get to know him better, sought his company more often and made a friend of him.

'Are you going far, miss?'

She was jerked out of her reverie by the cheerful voice of the blind man opposite.

'Oh, Cambermere, near Marlow,' she replied.

'Then you must change at the next stop too,' he told her. 'We're nearly in Maidenhead.' In a few moments the train slowed and stopped. Pippa reached down his bag and her own suitcase.

'Platform five,' he told her as the labrador led him out. Pippa walked beside him as he moved confidently from platform four to five. He was evidently accustomed to the journey.

'How did you know I was a miss?' she asked him as they stood waiting for the next train.

He smiled. 'Deduction. Your voice is young, the skin of your hand is young and firm, and your perfume is youthful. It's nice, by the way. What is it?'

'Rive Gauche.'

'French? You have expensive tastes,' he laughed.

Pippa smiled. 'Not really. I work in France and perfume is not so expensive there.'

'You're going to Cambermere on holiday, then?'

11

'Yes. I've never been there before.'

'Pretty village. The big house is a curious place, though. Belongs to some film producer, I understand. Korval, or something.'

'Korvak. Alexis Korvak. He's my father,' Pippa said. 'Where are you going?'

'Bourne End. The stop before yours. We live in the village there.'

'We?'

'Shula and I.' He reached down to pat the golden labrador's head. 'Don't know what I'd do without Shula.' There was gentle affection in his voice and she liked the man for it.

'How do you cope?' she ventured shyly. She had always found it difficult to talk to anyone who was physically handicapped, but this man was different.

'We have a routine, Shula and I, and one learns to adapt. It wasn't easy at first, but I learnt to develop other senses to compensate. One can see a lot with one's ears, you know. And you learn to count steps, lamp posts − everything. But the hardest thing to accept is other people's attitudes.'

'What attitudes?' Pippa asked with curiosity.

He shrugged his broad shoulders. 'Some people often seem to think the blind − or any other handicapped people for that matter − are mentally defective in some way. They shout, or talk to us like children. Or they just feel ill-at-ease with us. You can hear the constraint in their voices. We are ordinary people who just can't see, that's all.'

Pippa felt guilty, for she recognised herself. But before she could answer, the Marlow train came in and they climbed aboard.

For a time there was silence and the man appeared to doze. Then he awoke and reached down again to pat the dog's head affectionately. 'Cambermere, eh?' he remarked. 'And you're Miss Korvak?'

'That's right.'

'Your father doesn't go to the Hall very much these days, I believe. At one time he was often there.'

'He's a very busy man. He's in America now.'

'Strange. I was in a pub in Marlow only last week and I heard someone mention his name. I gathered from the conversation that Mr Korvak is not a very popular man thereabouts. But then, I don't suppose that troubles you. Famous people are no doubt used to being either admired or disliked.'

Pippa's eyebrows rose. 'Why should he be unpopular? Father is a very charming, agreeable person.' She felt irritated with him now.

'I'm sorry. I was only repeating what I overheard. You know him best, Miss Korvak. I did not mean to offend. Ah, the fourth stop,' he went on as the train began to slow. 'This is Bourne End, and yours is the next stop. Good day to you, Miss Korvak. It was nice meeting you. I hope you have a pleasant stay at Cambermere.'

She watched him follow the dog down the steps and stride away along the little platform, wishing belatedly that she had asked him what he meant about Cambermere Hall being a curious place and just what these people in the pub had said about Father. He's got it all wrong, of course. Or if unkind words had been spoken it was probably only out of envy.

Very soon the train began to slow down again and Pippa gathered her suitcase and handbag. So far as she knew no one would be awaiting her at the station in Marlow since only Mrs Purvis, the housekeeper, now remained in Alexis Korvak's employ. So it was with surprise that she heard a man's voice address her.

'Miss Korvak? I have the car waiting for you outside.'

Sure enough there was a large gleaming Daimler standing in the evening sun. She looked at the man's grey head and bland face curiously, as he took her suitcase.

'I'm Carson, the jobbing gardener,' he explained. 'Mrs Purvis sent me to meet you.'

'It's very kind of you but there was no need to bring the Daimler,' Pippa murmured as she climbed in beside him.

'Mrs Purvis says Mr Korvak would have wanted it,' he replied briefly, and drove away out of the village and along darkening country lanes. Pippa knew her father would have insisted on all the signs of status, but she and her father were very different people. On the rare occasions they met he seemed to be surrounded by gay, exciting people, laughing and drinking and living life at a furious pace. Pippa preferred peace and a gentler more ordered way of living. At Cambermere, with luck, she would find quiet solace where she could forget the scar of Clive.

'Here we are,' said Carson, turning the car off a tree-lined lane and up a long gravel drive. Through the avenue of trees bordering the drive Pippa caught sight of the house in the dusk and drew a deep breath of pleasure. It was beautiful. Its marble colonnaded terrace was reflected in the purpling waters of the lake before it, as it lay, tranquil and splendid, a magnificent Georgian house, its beauty enhanced by its elegant simplicity. Here was a building after her own heart, and she congratulated her Father's good taste. Usually he was given to opulence and exaggerated magnificence, but Cambermere showed he had an eye for genuine beauty too. Pippa felt reassured. Here was the perfect place to lie low and lick one's wounds.

She ascended the marble steps of the great double doors while Carson drove the car round the back to garage it. Mrs Purvis's familiar thin figure opened the door and her angular face permitted itself only the thinnest glimmer of a smile.

'So you found us. Come on in, Philippa. There's a nice hot cup of tea ready in the kitchen.'

Mrs Purvis was one of the few people apart from Clive who called her by her full name. It was as though she was prepared to admit a certain degree of intimacy with her but not presume too far. Philippa she had been in the nursery all those years ago, and Philippa she was to remain. Not that she wanted Mrs Purvis to be too friendly with her, for the housekeeper's thin features and pursed lips indicated a cold nature, and in any event Pippa wanted no close acquaintance to pry into her reasons for being there. All she wanted was to be left alone.

She watched Mrs Purvis's figure as she moved about the kitchen, fetching cups and pouring tea. She must be nearing sixty now, Pippa thought, despite her jet-black hair and sharp gaze. And she still wore the same kind of dress, Pippa noted, dark and high-necked like a Victorian governess. Her neat, deft movements and reserved manner completed the picture. In a modern kitchen that gleamed with stainless steel and futuristic equipment she looked oddly out of place.

'A lovely house,' Pippa commented as she took a cup of tea.

'Nice enough,' Mrs Purvis replied crisply.

'Funny I did not know of it before, though.'

'Not really,' the housekeeper said firmly. 'Your father kept this place as his private hideaway. Few people know of it.'

Not even his daughter, Pippa thought. Still, even he had need of retreat from the world on occasions, so why should he not indulge himself in such a country paradise? He had a villa or apartment in every European capital as well as in California and he could well afford to have a rural hideaway.

'Do you think Father will mind my being here?' she asked.

The housekeeper shrugged her thin shoulders. 'Your father sent word he would not be using the place this summer. He's not well again.'

'Is he back in hospital?'

'Yes. For several weeks, I understand.'

The news did not shock Pippa, for it was common knowledge that Alexis Korvak drank far more than his constitution could cope with, and periodically he was taken into hospital for a lengthy stay to be 'dried out'. He always intended to keep off alcohol thereafter, but the habits of a lifetime die hard. Pippa was not unduly alarmed to hear he was having the cure once again.

After a simple meal of cold chicken and salad in the kitchen with Mrs Purvis, the housekeeper offered to show Pippa up to her room. As they passed through the great marble-floored entrance hall with its graceful pillars and climbed the wide staircase Mrs Purvis questioned Pippa.

'How long will you be staying, Philippa?'

'I have two months' leave,' Pippa replied.

'Two months?' Her thin eyebrows arched. 'You've not stayed in England so long before.'

Pippa sought an excuse. 'Paris in the summer is very hot and very dull. All the inhabitants leave for the country, and my boss at the university was going abroad. And I had two months due to me, so I've no need to go back until the university reopens.'

Without comment, Mrs Purvis opened a tall white door to a bedroom and stood back as Pippa entered. It was enchanting: deep-piled pink carpet and lush rose-pink velvet drapes, a huge rose-canopied bed and draped dressing table. The whole room was in muted shades of pink and cream, and it was just what Pippa might have chosen for herself.

'It must be hard work for you, running such a huge house after the London flat,' she commented.

The housekeeper shook her neat dark head. 'We only keep part of Cambermere open. The wings are closed off, and I have help in from the village, Carson and a cleaning woman. It's many a year now since the whole house was in use, when your father held house parties here and the place was thronged with people. Those were the old days . . . '

Pippa frowned. So she was wrong to think he came to Cambermere to hide and rest. It had been, after all, just another venue for his countless banquets and revels.

'Your mother hated it,' Mrs Purvis went on. Pippa could see her lips pursed in a thin, hard line. 'She must have had some kind of presentiment about the place, for it was here she died.'

The housekeeper had closed the door and left before Pippa could answer. She stood motionless, taken aback. She had always understood that her mother had died in a nursing home. She could remember, child of six though she was, that Mother had gone away, and then the day came when they told her she would not be coming back to their home in Kent.

That was when life changed dramatically for Pippa. Suddenly there was no longer a home with a bright, gay father and ethereal mother who came and went, but a boarding school and the unaccountably guilty feeling that one had done something wrong in losing one's mother when all the other girls still had theirs. Pippa went through her schooldays feeling inadequate. When she went to university and later to Paris, she had learnt to live and cope alone. But why had she never known until now that her mother had died at Cambermere?

16

Having unpacked her case. Pippa put her things away in the drawers and looked about for a wardrobe. There was none in the bedroom. She opened a door in the corner of the room and found it led into a smaller room, a dressing-room evidently, for it was lined with sliding doors. Beyond it lay a bathroom, and she smiled. Father's restraint had given way to his customary ostentation here, for the sunken bath was of white marble with glistening gold taps and so were the washbasin and shower cubicle. Over a vast white dressing table, triple gilt mirrors surmounted by cherubs gleamed in the subdued lighting. Pippa became aware that she was not alone; Mrs Purvis was standing in the doorway watching.

'I see you have found your bathroom. Is there anything else you need, Philippa?'

Her expression was so severe that Pippa felt obliged to make an agreeable comment in an effort to please her.

'Thank you, no. This is a beautiful suite, Mrs Purvis. My father is to be complimented on his taste.'

Mrs Purvis's expression did not soften as she answered. 'Your father? This suite was designed and decorated to your mother's taste, Philippa. She always had excellent taste.'

Pippa turned to her. 'My mother – yes. You told me she died here at Cambermere. I did not know that. Was it here?'

Pippa indicated the bedroom. The housekeeper turned away sharply. 'No, not here. You can sleep in peace. My room is along at the far end of the corridor if you need anything. Goodnight then, Philippa.'

Pippa refused to allow herself to cry as she switched off the light and settled down to sleep. After all, she had two months in England ahead of her in which to forget Clive. She was 26 years old and she had an excellent job as a secretary to return to at the university. She could travel – she was fluent in French and German and Italian and could surely find a similar post far from Paris if she chose. And Clive had done her morale a power of good; he had proved to Pippa that a man could find her attractive even if she had not inherited her mother's incredible beauty. And he had taught her depths of passion she had never known before.

She rolled over, thinking sleepily of Mother and Mrs Purvis's words. Had Mother really died here at Cambermere and not in the nursing home? If so, why had they always told her otherwise? Pippa shuddered. Out in the darkness an owl hooted.

She did not know whether it was the thought of Mother's death here, or the death of the affair with Clive that gave her a sudden sense of chill. Perhaps it had something to do with the blind stranger on the train telling her of Father's unpopularity in the area too. Whatever the reason, she had a distinct feeling that however beautiful Cambermere was, it held a quietly ominous air. Ridiculous, she told herself sternly. It was remote and tranquil, that was all, and a place so lovely could not possess the sinister air she was attributing to it. By September she would have regained her peace of mind and be in a better position to plan the future. Just now, so soon after leaving Paris, she was still upset and vulnerable, but she must not let her vivid imagination spoil the peace of Cambermere . . .

Pippa must have slept, for the hands of her wrist watch were nearing four o'clock when she awoke, clammy with sweat. Something had roused her for she could vaguely remember a pounding sound. Probably her own heartbeat, she reassured herself, for she recalled the childhood nightmares which often woke her in tears, terrified by the sound of her own heartbeat throbbing in her ears. Recent events must be causing a return of the old childhood terror.

But as she turned over to settle down to sleep she heard the sound again. It was a footstep, heavy and resolute, followed by another. Pippa sat upright, reaching for the light switch. Once the room was flooded with soft light and no further sound came, she began to relax. The housekeeper was sleeping not far away, just along the corridor, but there was no need to disturb her just because she felt uneasy in her new surroundings. A cigarette, perhaps, and then she would go back to sleep.

But as Pippa reached for the cigarette packet she heard the sound again, clear and echoing, and she stiffened. It was hard to tell where it was: either in the room, outside or overhead. A quick glance outside in the corridor revealed no one there. Who could it be? Mrs Purvis was asleep, and there was no one else in the Hall.

Pippa trembled, remembering her mother. Whose were the restless steps disturbing the peace of Cambermere on the night she came to it for the first time?

2

Cambermere Hall lay like a pale jewel amid the deep green fields of high summer, early morning sunshine bathing it and its surroundings in crystal-clear light. The air was heavy with the rich sweet scent of elder flowers. It was a perfect English summer morning.

Pippa awoke, not to the sound of Parisian sparrows chattering excitedly to each other on the eaves, but to the mellow cooing of English wood-pigeons in the nearby trees. For a moment she lay wondering, until reality asserted itself.

She was here, in England and far from Paris. Sternly she reproached herself for thinking of the past as soon as she awoke when she had promised herself not to think of it at all. Activity — that was the best way to banish thought.

Sunlight streamed in upon her when she swished back the heavy drapes at the window, and instantly she felt glad to be alive. The sky was Wedgewood blue with cloud-puffs trailing gently across it, a beautiful morning, as delicate and soul-refreshing as she could wish. Pippa's tremors and fears of the night melted like morning mist over the soft green fields, and she determined anew to begin life again positively. No nostalgia, no regrets, no haunting memories were going to mar the future.

The scene below took her breath away. Somehow she had expected a stately terraced garden, in keeping with the impressive façade of the mansion, but she was wrong. Between the two projecting wings at the back of the hall lay a vast marble terrace with an irregularly-shaped swimming pool, and around the pool white tubs containing leafy palms. Gaily-coloured tables and sunlounging chairs were scattered between the foliage and the whole scene looked far more like a Riviera hotel than a rural English retreat. Or like a Hollywood film set, Pippa thought. That was it. The palm trees were surely plastic imitations. This was undoubtedly another of Father's extravagant notions, like the push-button panel in the bedroom of his London flat where a touch could draw the curtains, turn on the lights or the television, or bring forth a concealed cocktail cabinet.

Instead of her customary shower Pippa decided she would have a dip in that beckoning pool below. It was more than time she broke her old habits. She put on a swimsuit and a towelling robe over it, then hurried downstairs and unlocked the glass door leading from the back of the vestibule to the terrace. No one else seemed to be up yet.

Flinging her robe over one of the sunchairs Pippa stepped gingerly down into the pool. The water was invigoratingly cool but not too cold, and in seconds she was swimming leisurely, enjoying the caress of the water on her skin. How beautiful it was, she thought contentedly. As she climbed out and pulled on her robe again she felt positively glad to be alive. Just at that moment she caught sight of a movement at an upstairs window, and stopped to peer against the sunlight. Something moved suddenly behind the curtain in an upper room in the east wing, but she could not be sure what it was. Maybe it was a trick of the morning sunlight, but it had appeared to be a lightning glimpse of a blond head. Carson was greying and the housekeeper decidedly dark, and so far as Pippa knew there was no one else at Cambermere. Suddenly she recalled the footsteps in the night, and wondered. But the steps had been in the main wing, not in the closed down east wing. No, the blond head must have been a trick of the light, after all, she decided. She hurried back up to her room to rub herself down and dress for breakfast.

The succulent smell of frying bacon reached her nostrils as she came down again to the kitchen and found Mrs

Purvis busy at the cooker.

'Lovely morning, Mrs Purvis,' she said cheerfully. 'I've been for a swim.'

'I saw you,' Mrs Purvis replied without looking round.

'Were you up in the east wing?' Pippa asked as she sat down at the table. 'I thought I saw someone up there.'

The housekeeper still did not turn round. 'In the east wing? No. I told you that's not open. Now, do you want boiled eggs?'

Pippa was about to reply that she was used to only a light breakfast, coffee and buttered rolls, when she remembered her decision not to stick to outworn routine. 'I'd love eggs, or bacon, or whatever you have, Mrs Purvis. That swim gave me quite an appetite.'

Mrs Purvis placed two boiled eggs in front of her. 'I remember, you see. Always, right from your nursery days, you liked two boiled eggs, soft and with a pat of butter on. You can have bacon too if you like.' The words were kind, but the housekeeper's voice remained cool and distant.

'No, that's fine, thanks,' Pippa replied, wondering. Mrs Purvis was right: Pippa had forgotten she used to ask for eggs but was usually given porridge. Eggs were only for holidays and birthdays or when she behaved well. Fancy Mrs Purvis remembering that! The thought warmed Pippa, but the tight, uninviting expression on her thin face did not encourage Pippa to talk about the past. She remembered in silence as she ate. Pippa recalled that Mrs Purvis, looked exactly the same as she did now when Pippa was small. She had seemed a very stern, forbidding character then, yet Pippa could recall how she fussed over her mother.

'Hush now, Philippa! Go out and play in the garden quietly. You're mother has a headache and wants to rest,' she would admonish Pippa. Or, 'No, Mother can't come and read a story to you tonight. Go to sleep and perhaps she'll come tomorrow if you're a good girl.'

But Mother rarely came. Pippa had a misty vision of an angel with creamy skin and russet hair that fell in tumbling curls on her shoulders, a delicate creature who languished often in her room on the rare occasions she was at home, and the flurry and scurry of packing trunks when she and

Father were off on their travels again. And for a time there had been Irma too, a young woman she had seemed, although they said she was Pippa's sister, but she had gone away to marry and never came back. Pippa remembered little of her, only that she was always cross with her, and Pippa had not missed her angry scowl when she vanished from her life.

And then Mother had gone away for ever too, and Pippa had only Gwen for company. Mrs Purvis had been most vexed. 'You must not talk to imaginary friends, Philippa, or people will think you are mad,' she had scolded, but Gwen was dear to Pippa and Pippa needed her. Now, looking back with the wisdom of years, she could see what a lonely, frightened child she must have been to need a friend who existed only inside her head. Loneliness is an inexplicable terror to a small child, and she could not understand why her father was always away on business, her mother dead, and her sister presumably dead too. No one troubled to explain to a child of nearly six.

'Coffee?' asked Mrs Purvis, holding out the steaming coffee pot.

'Please,' Pippa said, pushing her cup forward. The aroma of coffee reminded her instantly of Paris. 'With milk,' she added quickly. Pippa always drank her coffee black, but habit must be broken and tamed. Concentrating on altering all the minutiae of her life would give her less time to look back, she reasoned.

Mrs Purvis fetched hot milk from the stove. 'Nice pool, isn't it?' she commented. 'Your father had it built years ago. The back of the hall faces south and he said the terrace was a natural sun-trap and the perfect place for a pool.'

'I thought perhaps it was his idea,' Pippa replied. 'And the plastic trees too. Did he make many other alterations?'

The housekeeper shrugged. 'Some, but then he wasn't here often. Not like the London flat. Now, what would you like to do this morning?'

'Oh, nothing special,' Pippa answered. 'Just laze about, inspect the hall and the grounds perhaps.'

'It's too fine to stay indoors,' the housekeeper replied promptly. 'I'd go down to the village if I were you. Or go for a ride — you used to like horses, as I remember.'

Pippa pricked up her ears. If there was one sport Pippa loved it was horse-riding. 'Does father have horses here then?'

'Two. He keeps them at Walters' livery stables down the road, just before you reach the village. Mr Walters will saddle up for you — he'll be glad of someone to help exercise them.'

Having no jodhpurs with her, Pippa dressed after breakfast in grey jeans and a pale blue shirt she had bought at the Galerie Maréchal in Paris specially to have dinner with Clive . . . Fiercely Pippa banished the thought of the dinner that never came about, put on a pair of strong walking shoes and set off down the gravel drive and out along the country lane towards Marlow. It was a magnificent morning, the birds singing and the hedgerows scented with wild columbine and honeysuckle as she walked along under the interlaced branches of the old oaks. Pippa was young and healthy and free and she was going riding over the rural peace of this lovely countryside.

As she neared the cluster of cottages which evidently marked the outskirts of the village, Pippa saw a white five-barred gate to her right, and alongside it a painted sign. *Cambermere Riding Stables. Proprietor, Geoffrey Walters*, it read. Pippa pushed open the gate and walked up the lane towards the low outline of stable roofs. A dark-haired man, probably in his thirties, was mucking out one of the stalls.

'Mr Walters?'

He turned at the sound of her voice and straightened. He was darkly good-looking but there was no trace of a friendly smile as he answered, 'Geoff Walters, that's me. What can I do for you?'

He leaned his tall frame against the rake and surveyed her curiously. At that moment a young boy of about nine or ten came out of a nearby stall with a leading rein in his hands and stood watching.

'I'm told there are some horses belonging to Mr Korvak at livery here,' Pippa said to Walters, 'and Mrs Purvis thought you'd be glad of someone to exercise one of them. Could I see them, please?'

He did not move, but the boy sidled round Pippa. 'The big chestnut is probably too big for you,' Walters commented slowly, 'but the grey gelding might be about your size.' He was surveying Pippa's five-foot-five critically, too intently for her liking.

'I'm used to a big horse,' she told him. 'Show me them both.'

He straightened slowly and walked towards another stall. Pippa followed him.

'You're staying up at the Hall, I presume,' he remarked as he unlatched the door. 'Friend of Mr Korvak's perhaps? Get on well with him, do you?'

'I can't say. I hardly know him,' Pippa replied as she peered past him into the gloom. A grey horse raised gentle eyes to inspect the intruders. He was beautiful and Pippa would have been glad to ride him but the man irritated her with his casual questioning. Pippa wanted to see the other horse before making her own choice.

'That's Alouette, and Copper is over here,' he said, crossing the cobbled yard to unlatch another stall door. 'Fetch him out, Robin, will you?'

The boy went inside and emerged in a few moments leading a magnificent chestnut. The horse snorted at the sight of Pippa.

'Not keen on strangers, our Copper, is he, Robin?' the dark man smiled. The boy shook his fair head vigorously. 'Alouette seems much more your style, miss,' he added with a patronising smile which irritated Pippa. She was about to retort defiantly that she would ride the chestnut when the beast bared its teeth at her, and she decided that discretion was the better part of valour. She nodded. Walters strode back across the yard to Alouette's stall and Pippa watched as he saddled the grey.

'Copper is a bit sharp, you know,' he remarked. 'An ex-racehorse and rather temperamental. Not like Alouette here – he's a real schoolmaster, as gentle and wise a cob as anyone could wish.' While Walters adjusted the girth Pippa watched the boy. He grinned at her sheepishly and led the big chestnut back into its stall. Then Pippa heard the sound of regular brushing. Robin was evidently grooming him.

Walters watched her as she climbed into the saddle and

rode off down the lane, and Pippa guessed he must be appreciating her style, for the one thing she knew she could do well was to ride. The grey was a pleasure, docile and quick to respond, and he and Pippa cantered along the lane, away from the village and up towards the woods. Below her the Thames snaked lazily through the trees.

For half an hour or so Pippa rode, revelling in the beauty of the morning and feeling the contentment that the serenity of the Thames Valley could bring to a tired soul. Then she turned the grey gelding towards the woods on the upper slopes of the valley, sensing that Alouette too was content. Pippa and the horse would soon become friends.

A breeze rustled through the branches of the bushes and trees when they reached the woods, and Pippa saw Alouette's ears twitch. A horse disliked wind, she knew, for it disturbed his perception, relying as he did more upon hearing than sight. But the gentle horse trotted on along the moss-grown path at Pippa's bidding.

Suddenly, and without any warning, Alouette uttered a strange shriek and reared up on his hind legs. For a split second panic seized Pippa as she caught sight of a pair of blue jeans flashing down from the low branches of a tree in front of her, and then Alouette turned and bolted. Alarmed, Pippa crouched in the saddle, giving the horse rein and as her brain began to function again murmuring words of reassurance. Within a hundred yards Alouette recovered, slowed and stopped.

Pippa turned in the saddle. A tall figure in blue jeans, broad-shouldered and with blond hair was running away across the fields.

'You! Come here!' Pippa called out after him. 'Come back here! You could have killed me!'

But the fair-haired man vanished among the trees, either deaf or too alarmed to listen. What on earth was he doing up a tree over the path she was riding, she wondered. And whatever it was, why on earth should he decide to drop down right in front of Alouette, startling the poor gelding out of its wits and putting Pippa's life in danger?

The idiot. He evidently knew nothing about horses. It was a pity she had not caught sight of his face so that she could give him a piece of her mind if she chanced to see and recognise him again. He was young and of a fine athletic build and he was blond. There could not be many men answering to that description in the area. Unless he was a holidaymaker and only passing through Marlow, of course.

Alouette and Pippa had both fully recovered their good spirits when they turned back at last for the stables. At the sound of hoofbeats on the cobbled yard Walters emerged from the tack room. He watched Pippa critically as she dismounted.

'Alouette is a beauty,' Pippa remarked as she handed over the reins. 'I look forward to riding Copper next.'

'At your own risk,' Walters said, his good looks marred by a scowl. 'Copper is very choosy.'

'And so am I,' Pippa retorted levelly. 'I shall come again soon to ride him.'

She was turning to leave when Walters spoke. 'I've been thinking. You must be the writer they've been talking about.'

'Writer?' Pippa echoed as she turned to face him.

'Well, journalist or whatever. Someone told me a writer was coming to Cambermere. I'm not surprised. There's plenty to tell that even the gossip-columns didn't get to know about. Funny, though, I didn't think it would be a woman.'

Pippa was about to deny it when she stopped, her curiosity aroused. What was it that Walters considered of such interest, she wondered. Suddenly she recollected the blind man's remarks about her father.

'Do you mean gossip about Korvak?' she asked casually.

'To be sure. Who else but the renowned Alexis, jet-setting multi-millionaire.' Walters replied coldly. Pippa's curiosity was aroused further. Her father's activities often reached the newspapers, but why should Walters speak so scornfully of him?

'What is there about Alexis Korvak to interest the press?' Pippa asked coolly but Walters was quick to note the interest she tried to conceal.

'Ah, you scent new material, do you? Well, there's a lot I *could* tell you if I wanted, but why should I? Would your newspaper pay well? Is it to be an exposé in one of the Sunday papers?' he demanded.

Pippa hesitated, reluctant to admit she was no journalist but Korvak's daughter. Walters would probably tell her nothing then. For the time being she would have to curb her impatience to know more.

She turned away. 'I'll come again soon,' she called back over her shoulder. After all, if he was going to be mysterious she could play the game too. Keep him guessing, that was the trick. She did not like Geoffrey Walters.

Skirting the lake, Pippa reached the top of the drive and caught sight of Carson, bucket in hand, disappearing round the side of the house. She followed him and saw him leathering the Daimler, which was parked outside what was evidently once the stables and coach house.

'Morning,' he grunted as she approached, and went on rubbing energetically. He was a strange little man, with a grey fringe surrounding his glistening bald pate and a silvery moustache on his pudgy top lip. He was small, plump and insignificant, but industrious. The Daimler shone almost as brightly as the less ostentatious green saloon parked nearby.

'How many cars are there?' Pippa enquired.

'Three. And all neat as a new pin, the way Mr Korvak likes them kept.' Carson replied proudly. 'The little Fiat's in the mews.'

'Is Mrs Purvis in?' Pippa asked, starting towards the kitchen door.

'Gone down to the village. She'll be back any minute,' Carson replied, bending to inspect the gloss on the paint-work. Pippa went into the kitchen.

Mrs Purvis had evidently been busy too since Pippa left, for the floor gleamed and not a pan was out of place. It looked like a model kitchen in an exhibition ideal home. Curiously Pippa opened the refrigerator and the deep freeze and the pantry. Mrs Purvis was a good housekeeper, for there was an abundance of provisions − there must be at least five dozen eggs in the larder and six pounds of butter. Ample provision for such a small ménage.

Anxious for a cup of coffee, Pippa found the percolator and some coffee and switched on. As she sat down the door

27

opened and Mrs Purvis came in, her thin features aglow from the walk.

'Oh, Philippa, back already? I've just been down to the farm. We needed eggs and I fancied you might care for a fresh chicken − free range, none of your battery or deep frozen birds. You'll have forgotten the taste of fresh chicken, I'll be bound.'

She took the chicken and eggs from her basket and left them on the table while she saw to the coffee, which was now beginning to bubble. Momentarily the thought flitted through Pippa's mind that an extra dozen eggs was hardly necessary when there was already a huge tray of eggs in the larder, but the thought was quickly driven from her mind when the housekeeper asked about Walters.

'How did you find Mr Walters then, Philippa?'

'Curt, not very friendly,' Pippa replied.

Mrs Purvis sighed. 'Ah well, that's a reaction I'm afraid you'll have to expect hereabouts. Your father is not very popular locally and you are your father's daughter. In time perhaps, they'll come to know you better.'

Pippa eyed her curiously. 'Why should Father be un-popular here? What did he do?'

Mrs Purvis raised her thin shoulders in a shrug. 'Oh, you know film people. He used to bring many of his film friends down here at different times, and I suppose their noisy parties scandalised the local worthies.'

'Is that all?' Pippa queried. 'From what Mr Walters hinted I suspected there was more than that.'

'Walters?' the housekeeper said sharply. 'What did he tell you?'

Pippa put down her cup of coffee. 'He didn't actually tell me anything, just hinted darkly that there was a lot he could say if he had a mind to. Actually, he thought I was a journalist or something, and wasn't prepared to talk until he knew how much my newspaper would pay.' Pippa chuckled, but Mrs Purvis's face remained set.

'I'm not in the habit of warning folk about others,' she said quietly, 'but I'd advise you not to get too friendly with that man. He can be malicious if he's a mind to it. Pay no heed to what he says.'

'I shall not. I promise you. I don't care for Mr Walters.

28

Actually, I'm going to ride Copper because he told me not to. He's not going to dictate to me.'

A hint of a smile curved the housekeeper's thin lips. 'You haven't changed much, Philippa. Still as defiant as ever, I see.'

'I? Defiant?' Pippa echoed in surprise. She thought she had always been a meek, submissive child.

'Oh yes,' Mrs Purvis said firmly. 'You were always a handful, as I remember. Whenever you did anything and I found out about it you used to flare up angrily and say she did it, not you — you know, that imaginary little friend you used to have. I forget what you called her.'

'Gwen,' Pippa said absently. She could picture her still, blonde and fragile, and with the innocent expression of an angel.

'That's right. You used to rage with injured innocence, I remember. Stubborn as a mule, you were.'

Carson interrupted her at this point, pushing open the back door and trudging in across the kitchen. Mrs Purvis stared in horror at the trail of muddy footmarks he left behind him on the sparkling floor.

'Carson!' she cried, putting down her cup with a clatter and pursuing him out of the kitchen. 'Where do you think you are going?'

Pippa smiled. Poor little man. She put down her empty cup and strolled out into the sunlit stable yard. The Daimler was now as brilliant and immaculate as a showroom car. Pippa walked on round the coach house and behind it, half-screened by a clump of laurel bushes, she saw the Fiat. It was yellow, or should be, but beneath its coating of mud and grime it was more grey than yellow.

Pippa walked closer to it. It was hardly in the condition Carson had claimed, she mused. He must be slipping. And on its seats Pippa could see various oddments scattered about — an old trench coat, a heap of untidy papers, a cigarette packet and a half-eaten bar of chocolate. And the keys were in the ignition. Curiously, Pippa opened the door and slid in behind the wheel. She could go for a short spin in this car and not feel guilty that she was spoiling Carson's hard work.

But before she had reached for the keys her gaze alighted

on the blue cardboard folder lying on the passenger seat beside her. She might have taken no notice of it but for the bold capital letters inked on it: ALEXIS KORVAK.

Her curiosity was aroused. Why should Carson have any papers belonging to her father? She lifted the folder and opened the flap. Inside were a bunch of photographs, newspaper cuttings and a sheet of handwritten notes.

The photographs she barely glanced at. Some she had seen before in gossip magazines, pictures of Father in his younger days looking extraordinarily handsome and with that devastating smile of his which could out-rival the most debonair of his leading men.

The newspaper cuttings bore such lurid headlines as SCANDAL AT MALIBU BEACH or FILM PRODUCER CITED and these Pippa dropped on her lap. She had no time for the lies that always surrounded a person of world repute. It was the sheet of paper that interested her. She scanned the closely-written words and felt a sense of disappointment. Though she received letters from Father only very rarely, she knew this was not his handwriting.

'Hungarian Jew – early life in obscurity – exiled because of oppression. Industrious, opportunist, made good use of looks and charm – weakness – obsession with women. Disastrous marriage. Hints of blackmail, corruption, even murder.'

Pippa could read no more. Her blood was thundering in her ears. Whoever had written this libellous pack of lies ought to be punished! However indifferent he might be as a father, Alexis Korvak was none of the things someone had written down here. Pippa tore up the sheet of paper, fury boiling in her veins.

But who could it be? Mrs Purvis had worked for Father for years – she would never betray him. But how could papers belonging to someone else have come to be in Father's car at Cambermere? Pippa threw the torn notes on the car floor, stuffed the rest of the papers back in the folder and got out of the car. As she marched back into the kitchen Mrs Purvis was alone.

'Whose is this file?' Pippa demanded loudly, tossing it on the table. Mrs Purvis stared at it for a second. 'Tell me,' Pippa thundered. 'Who wrote those scandalous lies about

30

my father? You must know, Mrs Purvis, and I demand to be told.'

The housekeeper drew herself up to her full height, a clear two inches taller than Pippa. Without taking the file from Pippa she scanned it for a moment. 'Where did you find that?' she asked quietly.

'Does that matter? In the Fiat, as it happens.'

'What colour was the car?'

Pippa felt riled. 'What does the colour matter, for heaven's sake? Yellow, or rather it would be yellow if it were clean.'

'I see,' Mrs Purvis turned calmly towards the cupboard. 'Then it is none of your business, Philippa.'

'What do you mean?' Pippa demanded. 'Someone wrote this vicious calumny, and I want to know who it is.'

The housekeeper eyed her coolly. 'Jumping to conclusions again, Philippa? It could be an outline, a synopsis of a film, for all you know. Why should you demand to know what is none of your business?' she asked quietly.

Her manner infuriated Pippa. 'Because you, of all people, should be loyal to him and not allow anyone to do this!' she said firmly. 'He has been a good employer to you, hasn't he?'

'He pays well,' Mrs Purvis agreed calmly. 'And I obey his orders.'

'Then why do you condone this? Did you know about this file?'

'I did.'

At that moment an elusive thought came back to Pippa. Walters had spoken of a journalist coming to Cambermere.

'It's the journalist, isn't it?' Pippa said in excitement. 'That's it, you've agreed to his coming here, haven't you? Well, I'm not going to let him, and that's that. You can forget the whole thing, Mrs Purvis,' Pippa said emphatically. 'No writer is coming here to make up lies about my father. As his daughter I have a duty to protect him.'

The housekeeper smiled thinly and turned away again. 'Orders are all very well, Philippa, but I already have my orders,' Pippa heard her say. 'You are too late. He is already here. That is his car.'

'Here? In Marlow? In Cambermere?' Pippa exclaimed.

Then she remembered the footsteps in the night and the face at the window. 'Are you telling me that the man who wants to blacken my father's name is here — in this house?' The housekeeper inclined her head. Her coolness infuriated Pippa. 'Then please get him out of here, Mrs Purvis. If you don't, then I will.'

Pippa turned to march to the door, but the housekeeper's quiet voice stopped her. 'You can do that if you wish, Philippa, but I fear you'll make a fool of yourself. He has every right to be here — more so, in fact, than you have.'

'What?' Pippa turned incredulously.

The housekeeper smiled that infuriating humourless smile again. 'That's right, Philippa. He is here with your father's consent. Mr Korvak does not know, however, that you are here. So you see, it is you who are the intruder at Cambermere Hall, not he.'

3

The girl stared at the older woman in disbelief. How could she be an intruder in her father's house? And more than that, she did not care for the tone of pleasure in the housekeeper's voice. Pippa glared at her.

'How can you say that, Mrs Purvis?' she demanded icily. 'To imply that a stranger has more right to be here than a daughter in her father's home is sheer nonsense. So the journalist has Father's permission, but are you saying my father would not have allowed me here if he knew?'

Mrs Purvis gathered up the empty cups and clattered them into the sink. 'He would probably not be very pleased with me for allowing you here. The London flat he didn't mind you using for a week or two, but Cambermere is different. As I told you, this was his private retreat.' She turned and met Pippa's gaze directly. 'But I had little choice. I must confess I did not think it would be for two months. I was stripping the flat for six months, so where else could you go?' Her sharp eyes narrowed. 'It's not like you to arrive so unexpectedly, Philippa. Were you in trouble, a disagreement with the professor, perhaps?'

'Indeed I was not,' Pippa retorted sharply. 'I just felt in need of a holiday. But I did not expect to share my holiday with a snooping journalist.'

Her acid tone was due, she knew to the fact that Mrs Purvis was too shrewd for her comfort. She wanted no further questioning.

'No need for you to see him,' Mrs Purvis replied smoothly as she turned on the tap to fill the sink with suds. 'Just keep out of his way and let him get on with his job. The Hall is large enough for you to avoid each other.'

'A good idea,' Pippa muttered in agreement. 'I have no wish to meet a man who has come here muck-raking. Keep him well out of my sight, Mrs Purvis, for his own sake.'

Mrs Purvis lifted a finger. 'Listen! Isn't that a lorry I hear? That must be the rest of the staff arriving from the flat. I must go and see to the unloading.'

She dried her hands quickly and hurried out. Pippa followed her into the vestibule. Two men in overalls were carrying in a packing case. The housekeeper watched for a moment, her thin arms folded.

'I want these crates stored in the east wing,' she said finally, and Pippa saw her go to the far side of the vestibule beyond the marble pillars and unlock a great double door. As she opened it Pippa could see a vista of long, dusty corridor, arched and vaulted. Not having any interest in the storing of crates she turned away and went up the wide staircase to her room.

Having changed out of trousers into a crisp linen dress, she loitered in her room, undecided. If she went downstairs to lunch, she reflected as she brushed her hair before the dressing-table mirror, she might be obliged to come face-to-face with that journalist fellow before Mrs Purvis had time to tell him to leave. He might even be brash enough to think he could elicit some material about Father from her,

33

and the last thing she wanted was an unholy row with the man. Once he had gone she could forget he existed. She looked at her reflection in the mirror. Judging by her appearance he probably would never guess she was the daughter of the illustrious Alexis Korvak and the beautiful Carrie Hope. With her roundish, snub-nosed face inclining to freckles and her reddish-gold hair she was like neither parent. She had inherited neither Father's dark, flashing-eyed vitality and charm, nor her mother's russet fragility.

Mousy, that's what I am, Pippa thought sadly, fingering her shoulder-length hair. It was soft and with a tendency to curl, and Clive had once described it as leonine; tawny as a mountain lion, he had said. Abruptly Pippa rose from the dressing table and went downstairs.

Carson was alone in the kitchen, munching sandwiches at the table. He wiped the back of a horny hand across his mouth and indicated the plate of sandwiches, some fruit and a bottle of cider on the table before him. 'Mrs Purvis says to help yourself. She's busy unpacking the stuff.'

Pippa sat down opposite him. 'Has the writer-fellow had lunch?' she asked.

Carson shook his grey head. 'He eats out, not with us. Down in the village, I reckon.'

That was a relief. Carson tossed off the glass of cider and rose, trying to muffle a belch. 'Got to get back and clip the hedges,' he muttered by way of an excuse, and trudged out. Pippa ate leisurely and then debated what to do with a whole sunny afternoon before her. Explore, yes that was it. She would investigate the gardens and the Hall.

She caught sight of Carson in the garden in dungarees clipping hedges as she strolled round the lake with its lily pads and darting fish, but on the far side of the Hall, in the shady walks between the lawns she saw no one. It was a stately garden of formal flower beds and terraced lawns, with a delightful herb garden and an orchard where young damsons and apples ripened in the sunshine. For a time Pippa sat in a latticed arbour far from the house and listened to the birdsong, but she found the peace and stillness too nostalgic to bear. It recalled all too vividly the secret moments alone with Clive in the Bois, and the memory was painful to her wounded soul. Pippa left the

34

arbour and retraced her steps quickly towards the Hall.

The great entrance hall was deserted as she entered. From the direction of the kitchen came the sound of men's voices laughing and the clink of cups. Mrs Purvis was evidently entertaining the workmen. As Pippa crossed the hall she noticed that the double doors to the east wing were open, and she could see that one packing case stood in the dusty corridor, its lid off and a heap of what looked like papers lying beside it on the floor.

Curiosity prodded her to go and have a look. She picked up some of the papers and found that they were a collection of old movie magazines, yellowing with age. Through an open doorway leading into a room, Pippa could see more opened packing cases, more papers and folders. She went in and idly picked up more magazines. Flicking over the pages, she was amused by the quaint swimsuits the pin-up girls of yesteryear were obliged to wear, and then suddenly she stopped.

The luscious redhead in the white swimsuit on the centre pages was Pippa's mother. *'Carrie Hope, the sweetheart of the nation,'* the caption read, and Pippa stared at the pouting lips and half-closed eyes. It was her mother as she had never seen her, a siren's face half-veiled by the russet mass of wavy hair. Pippa turned to the next magazine and flicked the pages. Betty Grable, Dorothy Lamour, Esther Williams – and Carrie Hope, this time in a slinky black satin evening gown beaded with diamanté and her head thrown back in a seductive laugh.

Then Pippa realised what all this collection of magazines and papers was. It was a storehouse of photographs and newspaper cuttings from the late 1940s, about the legendary Carrie Hope. Her father's treasured collection of memories, she thought guiltily, his personal mementoes of an adored wife. Pippa was replacing the papers as she had found them when she caught sight of a newspaper cutting dated the year before Mother died.

'WILL CARRIE HOPE MAKE A COMEBACK?' the headline demanded. The paragraphs below hinted that it was unlikely:

'After five years in almost total seclusion Carrie still sees few visitors. It has been rumoured that she has been

suffering from a nervous illness ever since the birth of her child, the daughter of Alexis Korvak. Once the glamour queen the nation adored, Carrie will find it increasingly difficult to make a comeback unless she yields soon to her husband's persuasions. Now in her mid-thirties, Carrie's virginal charms will elude her unless she steps back into the studio lights very soon . . . '

Voices in the hallway interrupted Pippa's reading. She pushed the magazines back as they were when she heard Mrs Purvis showing the workmen out. Then she stood quietly, unwilling to be found prying in Father's papers, as the front door closed.

'Now listen, Carson,' she heard the housekeeper say, 'I've got to go out again, and then I'll finish the unpacking. But you must make certain that Miss Korvak is kept in ignorance of what is going on. Do I make myself clear?'

Carson grunted some reply about having to cut the hedges and Pippa heard their footsteps fade away. She stood there, curious. What was she to be kept in ignorance of, she wondered? About Father's papers? No, that was unlikely, for Mrs Purvis had said she was not to know 'what was going on'. What *was* going on? The journalist's activities, perhaps?

Then she had an idea. Could it be Mrs Purvis's activities she was not to know? After all, she was going out again, and she had made a flimsily transparent excuse for going out this morning. What was her errand? To meet the journalist who always ate down in the village? To supply him with information about Father that she knew would make Pippa angry?

Well, she decided, if Mrs Purvis proposed to give him access to this collection of Father's memorabilia she would be disappointed. After all, Pippa was custodian of his welfare in his absence, and mistress of Cambermere. Pippa returned to the double doors to the vestibule, closed them after her and locked them with the key which was still in the lock. Then purposefully she put the key in her pocket and went out into the grounds. Now no one else could gain entrance to the east wing but herself, unless there was another key. She looked across the smooth, serene expanse of the lake with a feeling of satisfaction.

Far away beyond the lake, where the gravel drive skirted it towards the stone-pillared entrance of the Hall, Pippa caught sight of a diminutive navy-coated figure in the distance hurrying along. It was Mrs Purvis. On an impulse Pippa hastened after her, anxious to know her destination. But by the time she rounded the lake and reached the foot of the drive, there was no sign of the housekeeper in the leafy lane.

To the left there was only a mile of dense woodland, so she must have turned right towards the village, Pippa decided, although she could not see her brisk little figure on the long lane ahead. Pippa walked rapidly, almost running, but by the time she reached Walters' riding stables she still had not seen her. She must have cut off the road and across the fields.

Pippa loitered by the gate, undecided what to do. Suddenly she heard the sound of an engine and saw the Land Rover coming towards her. Behind the wheel Pippa could see Geoffrey Walters' dark head. He drew up at the gate when he saw her, and Pippa could see the horse-box behind him.

'Any luck so far with your story?' he called out. 'Can I give you a lift?'

'Thanks,' she said. 'Going far?'

'Only up to Lane End to collect a horse for livery,' he replied. 'Like to come along for the ride?'

She was mildly surprised at his hospitable tone, far less provocative than his unfriendly tone that morning. Perhaps, he regretted his churlish behaviour. Pippa settled back to enjoy the ride. Country lanes on a hot summer afternoon were undeniably peaceful.

'Haven't you brought your little boy along?' she enquired.

'Robin? He's mending the chicken run. Very clever with his hands. And he's not my son but my nephew.'

'Oh, I'm sorry.'

'Understandable mistake,' Walters said smoothly. 'He's my sister's boy, but as he's an orphan now he lives with me. Bright lad.'

'I'm very sorry,' Pippa said quietly. 'Your sister must

have been young.'

'She was.' Walters' voice was quiet now and she thought she detected an edge of bitterness. 'But that's in the past. Robin's crazy about animals so I guess I now have someone to inherit my stables. I can't grumble. It's only fair the lad has something to inherit. By the way, I hear you have competition.'

'Competition?'

'Well, they tell me there's another journalist fellow in the village who's asking about old Alexis. I'm not surprised, mind you. He was a real swine and no mistake. He caused more trouble than any other ten men I've ever known. About time someone blew the lid on him.'

'What do you mean?' Pippa asked sharply.

'Well, everyone hereabouts knows what a bastard Alexis Korvak is, and I bet many others do too, here and in America. But he's too rich and powerful to challenge. So far no one has ever dared to tell the truth about him for fear of litigation, or worse. Now if you and this other fellow spill everything . . . '

Pippa was about to interrupt, to retort acidly that she had no such intention, that he'd got it all wrong, when Walters suddenly pulled up.

'Here we are,' he said. 'Do you want to get out or wait here?'

They were outside the neatly-painted five-barred gates of a farm. As she made no answer, fuming as she was, Walters strode away, unlatched the gate and went in. After some moments he returned, followed by a greying man in dungarees who was leading a roan. Pippa heard the clatter of the horse-box being unlocked and the coaxing words of the older man to the horse. Within a few more moments she heard the men saying their farewells, and Walters climbed back into the Land Rover. By this time she had managed to control the anger bubbling inside her.

Sunlight flickered through the archway of trees, dappling the lane ahead of them as Walters put the vehicle into gear and set off on the homeward journey. He drove more slowly this time, so as not to jolt the roan she guessed. She sat without speaking, pondering over Walters' words. At length she broke the silence.

38

'It seems to me that Alexis Korvak is a misunderstood man,' she remarked quietly.

Walters looked at her in sharp surprise. 'Misunderstood? Whatever gives you that idea?'

'Well, he lost his beloved wife at a very early age. Doesn't it occur to you that a man grieving as deeply as he must have done may act rather oddly at times? Perhaps he was not really accountable for his actions, if he really behaved as badly as you say.'

'Behaved oddly?' Walters repeated in a tone of disbelief. 'He behaved outrageously, in a way that would have put a poorer man in prison, but Korvak appeared to be beyond the law. And grieving? You must be mad to believe that! Korvak never felt a prick of emotion for anyone in his whole life except himself. He must be the most selfish, egocentric man that ever existed.'

'You can't say that!' Pippa exploded. 'Did you ever meet him and get to know him?'

'I did, to my sorrow. To my dying day I shall regret holding out the hand of friendship to that fiend. He betrayed me, and my sister's life was the forfeit for my mistake. I hate the man and so, you will find, does everyone else around here.'

'Hate? That is a very strong word.'

'Not too strong for Alexis Korvak. The only excuse I can find for his cruelty is that he must be crazed. Only a lunatic could take all from life and give nothing the way he does. It would be a mercy for everyone if he were dead.' There was no doubting Walters' sincerity, for the hatred in his voice was as sharp and cold as ice. Pippa was shocked by the intensity of his feelings.

The Land Rover drew to a halt and Pippa realised they were back at Cambermere. Walters pulled on the handbrake and grinned at her. 'So you see, you have a lot to uncover about Korvak if you plan to write the whole truth about him, and even I don't know it all. I'll bet there's a whole heap more crimes he's committed in the States.'

'You don't know him,' Pippa argued. 'You're prejudiced by what you've experienced.'

'And another thing you'll have to learn, it seems to me,' Walters went on, 'is objectivity. You appear to be determined not to believe what I say. If you are going to write truthfully about Korvak, you will have to learn to be more dispassionate, more objective.'

Pippa made no answer as she climbed down. Walters leaned out and called after her. 'By the way, you haven't told me your name, young lady. Do tell me your name, or at least your pen-name.'

Pippa paused. Sooner or later he was sure to discover his mistake anyway. She turned to face him. 'Philippa Korvak.'

The teasing smile on his handsome face fled and an angry look of suspicion filled his eyes. 'Korvak? His daughter?' She nodded. 'Why the hell didn't you tell me?' he snapped.

'You didn't ask. You shouldn't jump to conclusions. I'm no writer but a secretary,' she replied levelly. It gave her satisfaction that this arrogant young man's confidence should be deflated. 'Thank you for the ride,' she added, turning to go.

'Miss Korvak,' Walters' voice cracked like a whip. She hesitated, then turned.

'Yes?'

'I made a mistake once in befriending a Korvak. I shall not do the same again. I just want to make it clear that I hope our paths do not cross again.' The scorn on his face chilled her, for he was evidently transferring his hatred from Father to herself.

'Have no fear, Mr Walters, I shall not seek you out,' Pippa replied calmly. 'But whether you like it or not I shall come to the stables to ride Copper as I promised.'

'Don't bother,' he snarled.

'But I shall. Have someone else saddle up if you prefer to avoid me, but I shall be there. Don't forget, those are Korvak horses and I shall ride them whenever I choose. Good day, Mr Walters.'

Pippa could feel his eyes boring into her back, penetrating her thin linen frock like daggers as she marched up the drive to the Hall. But he could feel no more fury than she did. Who was he, this arrogant Walters, to set himself up as judge on her father and on her?

For a time she sat on the terrace, unwilling to go indoors while she still felt so angry. When she finally did get up to go in, she realised that for a whole four hours together she hadn't once thought of Clive.

From the hallway she could hear Mrs Purvis's agitated voice in the kitchen. 'Are you *sure* you haven't got it in your pocket, Carson? You must have locked the door because it was open when I left, and you know how absent-minded you can be. Look again.'

'I haven't been in the house all afternoon, I tell you,' Pippa heard Carson grumble. 'I've been cutting hedges. That damn maze goes on for ever and ever. I haven't finished it yet.'

'Well the key's not in the door so you must have it,' Mrs Purvis snapped. It was unusual, thought Pippa, for the usually calm housekeeper to sound so agitated.

Pippa smiled to herself as she went towards the stairs, fingering the key in her pocket. 'For heaven's sake, Carson, you *must* remember,' the housekeeper cried angrily. 'You know there's no other key and the master would be furious if Philippa discovered what's in there. Here, let me turn your pockets out.'

Pippa's curiosity rippled. Whatever Mrs Purvis was trying to hide from her, she would discover it the very next time the housekeeper was out of the way.

4

Pippa declined Mrs Purvis's rather distant invitation to play cards after dinner. The housekeeper was seated at the table with a pack of cards before her.

'Cribbage is quite a good game, Philippa. I'll teach you, if you like,' Mrs Purvis offered.

'Not tonight, thanks. I'm no good at cards anyway,' Pippa replied.

But the night was far too close and sultry to sleep yet, and in any case Pippa felt restless. She was not welcome here, she knew. Mrs Purvis was polite and efficient but hardly welcoming. She had never been warm towards her in the past and now it appeared she was being even more distant. Secretive was the word, and Pippa did not like the feeling of being deceived. Whatever it was she was trying to keep from Pippa, out of defiance she now wanted to know what it was.

Pippa fingered the key in her pocket again. It was no use trying to evade the housekeeper's keen eye and get into the east wing unobserved right now. It would have to be later, when she had gone to bed.

Pippa fidgetted about her room, opening the casement window wide to try to cool the stifling closeness. Outside, the garden lay still and ethereal in the twilight of evening. Something caught her eyes. For a second she thought she glimpsed a movement under the trees beyond the lake, no more than a fleeting shadow. Then it was gone. She must have been mistaken. A cat, perhaps, or a rabbit.

But still Pippa felt edgy. The encounter with Walters had made her irritable, she thought as she undressed. She could not help being her father's daughter and Walters had no right to dislike her so intensely for her accidental parentage. And more than that, she felt he had accused Father unjustly, implying he was a villain of the worst kind. Father was not like that; he was charming and gay and carefree, casting a sunny radiance all about him, a little forgetful and possibly even inconsiderate at times, but no more than that, Pippa was sure. It was true they were comparative strangers, she and he, but from their few encounters and from his TV appearances Pippa knew how vital and glowing he was. Walters must have some personal axe to grind against him, but for what reason, Pippa wondered?

A cool shower, that was what was needed to calm and freshen her. This thick heat had made her sticky and uncomfortable. Pippa walked naked through to the dressing room, switched on the light and opened the shower cubicle. It was a larger shower than she was used to, with many gleaming steel pipes running up the walls. She turned on the water, and watched with pleasure the myriad tiny jets of water that played through countless outlets. Stepping into the cubicle was like standing under a fast-flowing waterfall, caressing and stimulating every inch of her body at once. Trust Father to have such a superb shower. It was just a fraction too warm for her, however, so she adjusted the control to her taste. Evidently it had not been altered for some time for the knob was dusty and stiff to turn.

Having towelled herself down with one of the luxuriously thick bath sheets on the rail, Pippa put on a crisp cotton nightdress and felt infinitely cool and comfortable. She lay on the bed and listened to the owl in the elms outside, trying to keep her mind clear of thoughts of Walters and Clive. She would think of nothing that would disturb her. But the question kept returning to her mind — what was in the east wing that Mrs Purvis did not want her to discover?

At last Pippa heard the sound of footsteps and a closing door. Mrs Purvis was going to bed. Pippa picked up her wristwatch. Ten past eleven. She would wait until midnight to make sure she was asleep. To pass the time she brushed her hair with slow, methodical strokes, just as she had been taught as a child by Mrs Purvis. By midnight her hair was a glossy mane and her right arm ached.

Pippa put on a cotton housecoat and transferred the key to her pocket, together with a tiny torch from her handbag, then opened her door quietly and crept barefoot along the dark corridor to the main staircase. Not a sound stirred the silence. The marble of the stairs was cold to her feet as she went quickly down and crossed the vestibule. There she switched on her torch momentarily to find the lock.

Unlocking the great doors Pippa pushed one of them open with caution. Fortunately the hinges were well-oiled and it made no sound. She pushed it to behind her and switched on her torch again, for the corridor was pitch dark, but when she opened the door of the room where the packing cases were, moonlight streamed in across the floor from the high windows. Outside the owl began its dismal hooting again.

Switching off her torch Pippa deliberated. It would surely be safe to switch on the lights even with the curtains undrawn, for no light here would be seen from the main wing. It would be safe so long as she did not switch on lights in the rooms across the corridor, where the east wing overlooked the terrace and the swimming pool. Here, on the outer side, she would remain undetected. She switched on.

In the light she could appreciate for the first time how elegant and handsomely-furnished the room was: a long, graceful chamber in Regency style with a plush red velvet couch and drapes to match. But Pippa was eager to investigate further the contents of the cases on the floor by the table. She knelt beside them, pulling out a wad of glossy photographs. There were many film stills of her mother: Carrie Hope in all kinds of costume from period fashion to the slick, sophisticated styles of the 'fifties. Only one was not a promotion photograph, but evidently a snap from a family album. It showed the young Carrie Hope smiling shyly at the camera, while beside her Mrs Purvis, looking exactly the same as she did today, held a dark-haired infant in her arms.

A dark child? Pippa frowned, puzzled. At that moment an unexpected sound alarmed her, and without thinking she thrust the snap into her pocket. She froze, listening, but no further sound came to her ears.

After a moment Pippa rose, crossed the room and switched off the light. She opened the door cautiously but in the corridor all was silence. She moved along, away from the vestibule, in the direction whence the bump had come. Outside the next door Pippa paused and listened intently. Only the owl's distant howl broke the stillness. She opened the door and went in, reaching up the wall for the light switch and finding it, she pulled it down.

A gentle glow of light suffused the room and Pippa saw, to her surprise, not the elegant Regency style of all the other rooms she had seen in Cambermere, but a replica of a mid-Victorian parlour complete with horsehair sofa, chenille-covered table and draped mantelshelf over an iron grate. Staid, upright furniture, heavy and cumbersome, filled the room. A rocking chair stood beside the hearth with its dog-irons and countless miniature pictures in frames arrayed along the shelf. Pippa fingered the leaves of the aspidistra in a brass pot and found it to be imitation. The solitary lamp above the table appeared to be a gas lamp, though she knew it was really electric. It was a strange, stifling room, completely out of character with the spacious elegance of the rest of Cambermere Hall. She was puzzled.

Then she caught sight of the dull sepia portrait, larger than the others, on the mantelshelf and went closer to inspect it. The prim woman with demurely clasped hands and hair neatly piled into a bun on top of her head was Pippa's mother. And then she realised it was Mother in one of the roles she had made famous, the heroine of the Victorian film whose title Pippa could not recall, and this room was a replica of the one where the terrified heroine had listened to the menacing footsteps above and watched the lamp dim.

It came to Pippa in a flash that Father had had this room designed in memory of Mother and her triumph. A shrine, in a way, to commemorate her skill and beauty, that's what this room was. A sad and beautiful gesture. Pippa went out and closed the door, feeling like an intruder on Father's private grief.

If that was what Mrs Purvis had not wanted Pippa to discover, then she need not have feared, Pippa thought. There was no reason to keep the room a secret unless Mrs Purvis thought Pippa might consider Father over-sentimental, but Mrs Purvis should have known Pippa would be the first to respect his privacy. Actually, Pippa was rather touched that a man could feel such sentiment. It made her Father seem somehow more human and real to her. She went on along the corridor and opened the door to the next room.

A touch on the light switch revealed a totally different scene this time, one belonging neither to Cambermere nor to England even. It was at first glance a gambling casino, complete with shaded lights and baize-covered tables and roulette wheels and deep-piled Turkey carpet. Then Pippa noted the false walls with circular windows — portholes — and the sepia photographs on the walls. Each one displayed a bare-shouldered lady in evening dress and Edwardian coiffure. None of the beauties appeared to be Carrie Hope, but Pippa recognised that this was the set of a Deep South gambling-boat, probably the scene of yet another of

Mother's triumphs. Idly she rolled the roulette wheel and watched the ball rattle into one of the dust-filled niches. Black three. She felt a shiver touch her spine. Whether it was because the summer night was chillier than she had thought, or because she felt an intruder here in a dusty shrine, or because three was her unlucky number, she refused to ponder.

For a moment she stood in the doorway, then switched off the light and went out again into the corridor, closing the door behind her. Then suddenly she had the strangest feeling, the certain sensation that she was not alone. She leaned against the door and held her breath.

The torch in her pocket — she closed her fingers on it but could not for the life of her force herself to take it out. Whoever was there in the dense blackness of the corridor was close to her, for she heard an indrawn breath. She felt the back of her neck begin to prickle with fear.

'Who's there?' she demanded sharply, in a voice so thin it sounded like a child's. No one answered, but she felt the movement of air as someone moved quickly past her towards the vestibule. She heard the soft pad of footsteps and then the door open and close, but no light relieved the gloom, not even a silhouette as the figure went through the open door. She took several deep breaths in an attempt to recover her composure.

Why should she be frightened? she asked herself. She was in her father's house, and therefore unnecessarily afraid of being caught down here in the middle of the night. Her actions could be construed as snooping, but why should that disturb her? It was only natural curiosity about her Father and his way of life, since he was a comparative stranger to her. And curiosity about her long-dead mother too. In over twenty years facts became magnified myths and it was hard to know what kind of woman she was. A six-year-old child's hazy memories were hardly to be trusted. Was Carrie the ethereal fairy-princess she remembered, and Father the handsome prince on a dashing charger who came to rescue her from poverty and sadness? Pippa wished she knew more about her parents, apart from the lurid tales the press presented to the world.

And who could it be who surprised her in the dark and yet was unwilling to be recognised? Without warning the lights snapped on and the corridor was flooded with light. By the double doors stood a tight-lipped Mrs Purvis in a woollen dressing gown and with her hair no longer coiled but falling to her shoulders.

'May I ask what you are doing, Philippa?' she asked coldly.

'Just having a look around. I was curious.' Mrs Purvis still managed to make her feel like some miscreant school-girl even after all these years.

'Then if you don't mind, I'll lock up again now and we can all get some sleep,' she said, standing back to allow Pippa to pass. She did so sheepishly. Mrs Purvis re-locked the doors, put on the hall light and pocketed the key. Pippa felt resentful at being made to feel guilty, and turned to the housekeeper.

'Was that you who passed me in the corridor just now, in the dark?'

Mrs Purvis's eyes narrowed. 'Indeed it was not. I've just come downstairs because I thought I heard sounds. Can't be too careful, you know. There's been a lot of burglaries in these parts, and Cambermere is very remote.'

'Then who was it?'

The housekeeper shrugged. 'How should I know? Not Carson, that's for sure, because he's snoring in his own bed in the village by now, where anyone in his right mind should be. Come now, Philippa, upstairs with you.'

Pippa stood her ground. 'And what is there worth steal-ing in any case? So far as I could see everything in that wing is false − wax fruit, plastic plants − even the Victorian bric-a-brac is probably only copies. They're film-sets in those rooms, aren't they?'

Mrs Purvis nodded as she headed towards the staircase and Pippa was obliged to follow her. 'Some of the rooms are film-sets, yes. Some are copied and some Mr Korvak had flown from Hollywood. But other rooms contain real objets d'art and are worth a lot of money, so you see vigilance is essential.'

In silence Pippa followed her upstairs and along the bedroom corridor. 'Are the film-sets in memory of my mother, Mrs Purvis?' she added as she paused at her own doorway. She saw the hard light in the housekeeper's eyes soften.

'Some of them are, like the Victorian one. She was magnificent in that. And in *Salome*. Your father worshipped her then.'

'And kept the sets in memory?' Pippa asked.

Opening her door Mrs Purvis turned away. 'You could say that. Those sets were the scenes of his great triumphs more than hers. Now goodnight to you, Philippa, and no more wandering about in the middle of the night, if you please.'

'I'm sorry if I alarmed you,' she said contritely, then added, 'but I should like to have the key again tomorrow and investigate the rest of the wing. Goodnight, Mrs Purvis.'

Pippa walked quietly away towards her room before the housekeeper could argue. After all, it was Pippa's home and she was going to have the freedom of it, and the sooner the housekeeper realised, the better.

Father's triumphs she had said, Pippa mused as she got into bed. As a producer, she guessed. He had kept the sets of the films he had produced which had been box-office successes. Perhaps not all of them were ones in which Mother had starred. That would account for no picture of her being in the gambling saloon. She must ask Mrs Purvis about that tomorrow.

A thought crossed Pippa's mind as she settled down to sleep. The unseen person who brushed by her in the darkness — of course, it might have been the journalist. He could have broken in and been snooping, but at least the thought that it was a real live person removed the chilly feeling she had had. Not that she was foolish enough to believe in the supernatural, but that wing of Cambermere did hold a haunting strangeness that was not quite of this world.

Carson was unbolting the front door as Pippa crossed the vestibule next morning. He grunted an acknowledgement of Pippa's cheerful 'Good morning.' Mrs Purvis was already in the kitchen, beating eggs.

The housekeeper paused in her brisk beating and glanced at Pippa curiously. 'You're up early, Philippa, considering your late night. Breakfast isn't ready yet.'

'No matter. I'll go down to the stables to ride Copper and eat when I get back,' Pippa told her, then added, 'By the way, could it have been that journalist fellow in the east wing last night?'

The housekeeper shook her head firmly. 'It could not. He moved out to the village inn when I told him how you felt. He said he'd come back in a few days when you were settled. I haven't seen him since.'

'Could he have broken in?' Pippa asked.

'Not he. He's a straightforward young man. I told you, he'll come back to ask you if he can carry on. What wild ideas you still have, Philippa.'

Pippa frowned, puzzled. Then who could have been in the house last night? And who else but an inquisitive journalist could be interested in the east wing? The packing cases, that was what he was after, she felt sure, and the stories they could reveal. Perhaps he had had a tantalising glimpse of the contents before he was obliged to leave, and somehow had contrived to get back into the house just at an opportune moment when the wing chanced to be unlocked. Pippa asked Mrs Purvis if he had already had access to the cuttings and photographs.

The housekeeper's keen eyes regarded her penetratingly. 'So you've seen what's in the cases. Well yes, he's seen some of them, not all. Those relating to Mr Alexis.'

'That reminds me,' said Pippa. 'Do you remember this?'

She took the snap from her pocket and handed it to the housekeeper, who laid aside her whisk and inspected it closely. Pippa saw her thin lips soften into a hint of a smile.

'Why, yes. That's my Miss Carrie before she became ill. That's the real Miss Carrie, shy and kind and not all seductive like the films made her look.'

'And the baby? It isn't me, is it? The baby is dark,' Pippa commented. Mrs Purvis's lips snapped into a straight line again.

'Red, not dark. Irma's hair was as red as her mother's, natural Titian. Miss Carrie didn't need dye like the others. All the blondes used bleach and even Rita Hayworth wasn't really a redhead. She was black, you know, Spanish. Had to have electrolysis to give her a higher brow line, and her hair bleached out and then dyed. But not Miss Carrie. She was a natural born beauty.'

There was no doubting the love in her tone as she spoke of her dead mistress. Pippa turned to leave. 'I see. Well, I'll be back by nine.' A ride over the fields in the cool morning air was just what she needed to clear her brain.

She was setting off down the drive to skirt around the lake when the scent of woodsmoke caught her nostrils. Over to the left she could see Carson's stocky figure leaning on a rake beside a tall hedge. And he was not alone; a young man in blue jeans stood chatting to him, tall and broad-shouldered and with fair hair that gleamed in the morning sunlight. Carson caught sight of her and nodded. Pippa set off across the lawns towards them.

'Morning, miss,' said Carson gruffly. 'I were collecting all these hedge-clippings to burn and Mr Lorant here were kind enough to offer to help.'

Pippa looked up at the stranger. His keen eyes were regarding her with an air of interest. 'Good morning. I'm Pippa Korvak.' She held out her hand and felt him take it firmly. 'Haven't we met somewhere?'

He smiled, and his tanned face became decidedly good-looking. 'A pleasure to meet you, Miss Korvak. My name is Stephen Lorant, and so far I don't think I've had the pleasure.'

Blond. And blue jeans. For a moment she had taken him for the stranger in the woods nearby who almost caused Alouette to throw her. But this man's accent was slightly American; no doubt he was a tourist passing through Marlow.

'I'm sorry. I just felt you were somehow familiar,' she murmured in embarrassment. He was smiling still, a hint of amusement in his hazel eyes.

'No matter, we've met now,' he remarked. 'And may I compliment you on the very fine grounds you have here, Miss Korvak. The lawns are beautifully kept, the roses magnificent and, if I'm not mistaken, this is a maze here, isn't it?'

Carson's normally expressionless face lit up. Pippa

smiled. 'I take no credit, Mr Lorant. Mr Carson here is responsible and as you say, he has reason to be proud of his handiwork. Is this indeed a maze, Carson?'

He nodded. 'A copy of the one at Hampton Court they say, Miss. Trouble is, it makes a lot of work clipping and burning the clippings.'

The stranger turned away from Pippa to look at the maze. 'But well worth the effort, Mr Carson. I'd like to have a go at finding my way to the centre one day.'

Carson was positively beaming. Pippa admired the easy way this young man could talk to him and draw him out. Perhaps he seemed familiar because he gave people a feeling of being relaxed and made them seem old friends. But as he stood there, his broad back towards her and his hands on his hips she suddenly started. She *did* know that back! It *was* the man who had dropped from the tree and then raced off across the fields, she was sure of it. He was talking about the trees and that gave her an opening.

'Have you been in the wood up alongside the north wall of Cambermere?' she asked quietly. He turned to face her. 'Were you by any chance up there yesterday?'

'As a matter of fact . . . ' he began hesitantly.

'I thought so!' Pippa broke in. 'Mr Lorant, I have a bone to pick with you.'

'Ah, excuse me, miss,' Carson muttered, 'but I'd best get back to my bonfire. Not safe to leave it for long.'

Picking up his rake he left them. Pippa turned to the stranger. 'It was you up in the tree, wasn't it? It was you who jumped down and frightened my horse.'

He cocked his head to one side and shrugged apologetically. 'I'm sorry. It wasn't on purpose, I assure you. I fell, and that's the truth. After all my misspent years as a boy climbing trees there's no excuse for such clumsiness, but I lost my hold and fell. On my feet, fortunately, but I'm sorry I scared your horse.'

'And you didn't even wait to see if I was hurt!' Pippa exclaimed. 'You just ran off like a boy caught stealing apples! Not only clumsy, but thoughtless, Mr Lorant!'

'Unforgivable,' he murmured, and his contrite tone added to the faint American drawl made him sound as appealing as a small boy caught red-handed. 'Truth is, I was

51

scared stiff you'd discover me when I was trying to track you down.'

'Track me down?' Pippa echoed. 'Why?'

A slight flicker of a smile illuminated his rueful expression. 'Two reasons, really. One, curiosity to see the daughter of the famed Alexis Korvak, and two, to ask a favour of you. In the circumstances, however, I think I'm no longer in a position to do the latter. I admit I was in the wrong. I confess it unreservedly, and I won't object if you think fit to order me off your property. Shall I go, Miss Korvak?'

He stood there, towering a clear head above her with such a penitent expression that Pippa was tempted to laugh. Abject contrition looked so incongruous on the face of this tall, lithe man. At once she felt guilty.

'No, of course not. I've said my piece and you've explained and apologised, so now that's over. Please feel free to walk in the grounds whenever you like since you obviously admire Carson's handiwork — I'm sure he'll be delighted.'

'But you will not,' he murmured.

'No, please, don't misunderstand me,' Pippa hastened to assure him. She did not want to make this warm and likeable young man feel so uncomfortable. 'And you mentioned a favour — what was it you were going to ask?'

He smiled quizzically. 'You mean you would forgive me enough to consider it?'

'It depends what it is. Tell me.'

His hazel eyes challenged hers directly. 'Allow me access to your father's papers so that I may continue my work.' His tone was level, his gaze calm, but Pippa's heart leapt.

'Papers? You mean, you are the journalist?' Of course, she thought angrily, she should have guessed. Loitering near the Hall yesterday, hiding in the trees when he saw her — she ought to have realised. She held her chin high. 'No, I see no reason why you should pry into private documents. If you must write about Father, you can research in the normal way. I cannot help you.'

'You have not forgiven me or you would not refuse before asking me more,' Stephen Lorant remarked. 'Hearing about me has prejudiced you, and my clumsiness yesterday has steeled you against me. That is hardly rational.'

'Rational?' Pippa retorted. 'Your behaviour – snooping around the Hall and then hiding up that tree is hardly rational, or commendable for that matter!' She felt herself shaking with anger, and knew the extent of her anger was unreasonable. She was angry because she had allowed herself to warm to this young man before discovering what he was. She was tense, but he still stood, relaxed and completely at ease, a tolerant, undismayed expression on his handsome face.

'Miss Korvak, I have already apologised and I think I should add that I have your father's permission to look through his papers. It seems your housekeeper omitted to tell you that.'

Pippa blushed. She had completely forgotten, but now he reminded her she remembered Mrs Purvis's words – that he was invited, whereas she was an intruder at Cambermere. With difficulty she searched for words.

'I see,' she murmured, unwilling to admit she had forgotten. 'You have a letter of introduction, no doubt?'

'Which I gave to Mrs Purvis. You do not doubt my word, surely?' His face remained composed, not unfriendly despite his words.

'No. Then you'd better come up to the Hall. Would this afternoon suit you?' She could not help it. Anger still prevented warmth from entering her tone.

'Fine. I'll come up after lunch. So long, then, Miss Korvak. I look forward to seeing you.'

He strode away across the lawn towards the gates. Pippa watched his long, easy stride and his broad back until he was lost to view behind the rhododendron bushes. Then she sighed. No time to ride now – she would go in for breakfast.

Mrs Purvis barely glanced at Pippa as she came into the kitchen. 'There was a telephone call for you, Philippa. Mr Bainbridge asked if he might call to visit you.'

'Bainbridge?' repeated Pippa. 'I don't know him, do I? I don't recall the name.'

'He owns the estate adjoining Cambermere Hall. He used to visit your father sometimes, a long time ago. I expect he wants to welcome you, and one must accept such courtesy with grace.'

Pippa smiled to herself as she began eating. Mrs Purvis sounded like a governess as well as looking like one. Her tone was always equable and patient as though humouring a child.

'What is he like, this Mr Bainbridge?' Pippa enquired.

Mrs Purvis thought for a moment. 'Nearing fifty, I would say, very rich and a bachelor.'

That was the housekeeper's summary of him, concise but outlining only what she considered relevant.

'No, I meant what is he like as a person?' Pippa persisted. 'Pleasant? Argumentative? Generous? That kind of thing.'

'I hardly know the gentleman, Philippa. He's a north-country man, sometimes a little abrupt as I recall, but he's highly-respected in the area. A churchwarden, I believe, and perhaps a magistrate too.'

'I see. Then I suppose I'd better receive him, in the best English country lady tradition,' Pippa said with a smile. The housekeeper cast her a quick glance.

'I've already told him you will be at home this afternoon,' she announced calmly. 'He will be here at two-thirty. I suggest you receive him in the drawing room, and I will bring you tea at three.'

Pippa looked up at her in surprise but Mrs Purvis appeared unaware. Really, thought Pippa, this is taking matters too far, to decide for me and give me instructions as if I were incapable of deciding for myself. But then another thought struck her − Bainbridge's presence would probably prevent her from seeing Stephen Lorant when he came, and she wondered at the feeling of disappointment it caused her. Still, there would be other days . . .

At half-past two precisely there was a knock at the drawing room door and Mrs Purvis entered, followed by a thick-set man with greying hair and a moustache. His face remained expressionless as the housekeeper introduced him.

'Mr Bainbridge, Philippa,' she said, and then withdrew discreetly.

Pippa rose, her hand outstretched. 'How kind of you to call, Mr Bainbridge,' she said warmly. 'You are a near neighbour, I believe.'

'Next door,' he grunted as he touched her hand briefly. 'I only heard last night when I were down at the George and Dragon that you were here.'

'I came unexpectedly,' Pippa explained, wondering if he always spoke in that staccato way or whether he was uncomfortable in her presence. She made an effort to put him at ease. 'I believe you were a friend of my father's,' she commented, indicating a chair for him to be seated.

'Not really. More a business acquaintance.'

Pippa observed him unobtrusively. He was unprepossessing in appearance, inclining to corpulence, with a hard, uncompromising voice and little red veins in his eyes. 'I see, you did business together.'

'Tried to, but his mind was always on films, not interested in business. Never would give me a straight answer, and that's not my way. Where I come from we pride ourselves on forthrightness. Saves time in the long run, and time's a very valuable commodity.'

'I do so agree.' By now Stephen Lorant would be in the east wing, going through those packing cases. Pippa would dearly like to be down there too.

'Then I'll waste no more time but come straight to the point, Miss Korvak,' Bainbridge said leaning forward in his chair, his cheeks flushed. 'I've come here not for idle chat, but for serious talk. I've come to make a proposal.'

'Proposal?'

'Aye. A proposal of marriage. I want you to marry me, Miss Korvak.'

5

Pippa jerked upright in her chair, incredulous.

'I beg your pardon?' she stammered. Bainbridge spread

his thick fingers in an apologetic gesture.

'There, I've blurted it out and taken you by surprise, I can see. But I've always found that's the best way to do business — come straight to the point and no beating about the bush. I fancy it would be an advantage to both of us if we were wed. If you'll bear with me, I'll explain.'

Pippa cut in. 'There's no need, Mr Bainbridge, because however good your reasons, I'm afraid I'm not contemplating marriage at the moment, not to you nor to anyone else. Your bluntness does you credit, but I fear you are wasting your time.'

She rose to indicate she had done, but Bainbridge held up a restraining hand. 'Hold hard a moment, Miss Korvak. Hear me out, at least. I know we're total strangers — why, you don't know me from Adam any more than I know you from Eve, but at least let me explain.'

'If you insist,' Pippa said in a weary tone, 'but really it is a waste of time.'

'I've sprung it on you too sudden. You see, I'm a land-owner first and foremost — I've got land up north as well as here, land I inherited from my mother. Came south years ago. Splendid farming land here. I wanted more — I tried to buy some from your father.'

'And he would not sell?'

'He wouldn't discuss it much, but I wanted to extend my farm. Whenever I thought I'd get an answer at last, off he'd shoot to Istanbul or Fiji or somewhere for a new film.'

Pippa smiled, recognising the truth of what he said. 'That's my father, all right. As hard to pin down as a ball of mercury. Does he have a lot of land here then?'

'Several hundred acres — more than he needs. He could have let some of it go without missing it. Walters was after some too, at one time, to extend his stables, but he got nowhere.'

'I'm very sorry, Mr Bainbridge, but I'm afraid I can't help you there. My father is a law unto himself.'

'Too right he is,' Bainbridge muttered. 'But you could help me all the same.'

'I could? How?'

'Well, if you've come back here to settle down . . . '

'But I don't know that I have. I may only stay briefly,' she corrected him.

'That's as maybe. But in any event, as Korvak's only living child, one day you'll inherit.'

'Ah well, perhaps. But I hope that day is a long way off. When it comes, then you can talk to me again.' She waved the matter aside with a smile, but Bainbridge was not to be deterred.

'I don't see as we need wait,' he said urgently, leaning forward again and fixing Pippa with his keen gaze. 'That day may not be so far off as you think, and in the meantime it seems to me as we could solve both your problems and mine by acting now. One neat and simple solution would solve the matter for once and for all.'

Pippa sat up, intrigued. What was the man talking about? What did he know of her problems? The only way to find out was to encourage him to continue in a subject she would really have preferred to drop.

'You mean our marriage, I take it. But I fail to see how that would help, Mr Bainbridge.'

'Arthur, please. Well, that way I'd be sure of the land once you inherit. And what's more it's high time I was wed if I'm going to have an heir to succeed to my land and my money, and looking at you I guess you must be thirty already . . .'

'Twenty-six,' she corrected him stiffly.

'Well, old enough to be classed as a spinster if you've not had a proposal yet. Seems to me you should be glad to get off the shelf.'

Pippa stared in amazement at his insolence, and he seemed to realise he had been hasty and abrupt. He spread his hands and grunted.

'I don't think I expressed myself too well, Philippa, but I'd no intention of being rude. Regard it as a business proposition, if you like. I need a wife and an heir − '

'And Korvak land,' she could not help interrupting.

'Aye, and the land too. But I'm not asking you to make a free gift of it. I'd see you had all you wanted − a fine house, cars, furs, jewels − whatever a woman wants. I'm not short of a pound or two.'

'I hear you're a wealthy man,' she commented.

'Wealthy enough to give you all you're accustomed to as

57

a rich man's daughter, I can promise you,' he agreed.

'Everything except what I want,' she murmured.

'What do you want that I can't give? Money can buy anything.'

'Except love. When I marry I want to feel secure in the love of a man,' Pippa said. Her tone was light, but the sentiment was sincere. Recent experience had taught her the hard way the difference between being loved and being used.

'Aye, well, it doesn't come easy to me to talk about feelings,' Bainbridge muttered. 'But I reckon as we'd come to like each other well enough.'

'That's not enough.'

'Enough for me. I won't ask you to feel what you can't.'

Pippa rose and crossed the room to ring the bell. Bainbridge watched her, his eyes betraying his anxiety for an answer, but she was in no mood to hasten to satisfy him. What a nerve he had, proposing marriage to a total stranger in the hope of acquiring Father's land, and under the pretext that he was doing her a favour!

'What are you doing?' Bainbridge asked. It amused her to think that perhaps he suspected she was going to have him thrown out.

'Ringing for Mrs Purvis to bring tea,' she replied coolly. 'Or would you prefer coffee?'

'Tea's fine,' he grunted.

Mrs Purvis's sharp eyes surveyed both Pippa and her visitor curiously as she came in, and Pippa guessed she was wondering what had been said. When she returned a few moments later with a tea tray Pippa could not resist a sudden impulse.

'Mr Bainbridge has proposed to me, Mrs Purvis,' Pippa said and saw his startled look, but the housekeeper remained placid.

'Indeed?'

'What do you think, Mrs Purvis?' Pippa asked her.

She shrugged. 'It's not for me to comment, I'm sure.'

'But I need your help and guidance,' Pippa teased. Arthur Bainbridge looked downright embarrassed.

'There's no need for an immediate answer, Philippa,' he said jerkily. 'Take your time and think it over.'

'Oh, I will. But I'd like to hear what Mrs Purvis thinks all the same.' It was wicked of her, she knew, but she felt his importunate behaviour warranted it. She was enjoying the game.

The housekeeper poured out the tea, and as she handed a cup to Bainbridge she said, 'Well, it's a bit sudden, when you've only just met, but it seems to me you could do worse, Philippa. Mr Bainbridge is a respected gentleman.'

'And wealthy,' Pippa added.

'So it's perhaps not an idea to be dismissed lightly,' the housekeeper concluded, and then she left them.

Decidedly she must be feeling better than she did a few days ago, Pippa thought, to be in such a wilful, capricious mood. Only a week ago, still sorrowing at the loss of Clive, she could not have undergone the ordeal of having a proposal of marriage from a man she did not even know, let alone like. Now she could face the situation with comparative equanimity.

Bainbridge drained his tea and put down the cup. 'Well, I'd best be off,' he said laconically, rising from his chair.

'So soon?' Pippa said. 'Then let me see you out.'

In the hallway he shook hands with her. 'Let me know your decision when you've had time to think it over,' he said gruffly.

'By the way,' she said on the doorstep, 'I'm curious about what you said. You said marriage would solve my problems as well as yours. Do I have any problems, apart from being an old maid left on the shelf?' she smiled at him, and he coloured slightly.

'Aye, well, you need looking after, don't you? You're not liked hereabouts as you probably know, but I doubt as anyone would dare to harm Mrs Bainbridge. You'll be safer with me.'

'Not liked? Harm me?' Pippa echoed in surprise. 'The people here hardly know me, and I've done no harm to anyone.'

'You're Korvak's daughter, aren't you? That's enough for them. And as you'd well find out, they'll stop at nothing.'

'I know no such thing. What are you talking about?'

He looked at her keenly for a moment and could see she

59

was genuinely mystified. 'You mean you don't know about your father? They haven't told you?'

'What should they tell me?'

'Nay, it's not for me to tell tales, but I'd have thought your housekeeper would have done well to warn you before letting you come here. Must be loyalty to her master that she's held her tongue. We must give her credit for that at least.'

Pippa felt hurt and angry. 'What are you hinting at, Mr Bainbridge? I do not care for your insinuations.'

'Like I said, I'll let them who have reason to hate Korvak for the way he's deceived them tell you for themselves. It's not for me to say.'

'No. So you should have held your tongue. My father has not deceived you, has he?'

A veiled look came into Bainbridge's bloodshot eyes. 'As a matter of fact — but then, it were a long time ago. I'll say good day to you, Philippa, and let me know when you make up your mind. My proposal stays open.'

He nodded and went out. Stunned, Pippa stood in the doorway and watched his stocky figure receding down the drive. What an overwhelming man, and how insolent! How dare he suggest Father was some kind of cheat or fraud — but then, she recollected sadly, it was not the first time there had been hints. First the blind man, then Walters, and now Bainbridge. There must be some kind of misunderstanding if several people believed ill of Father.

Across the green sward Pippa caught sight of the tall, rangy figure of Stephen Lorant. He was standing where she had met him this morning, by the maze. Pippa's spirits lifted as she walked across the lawns to him.

'Hello, Stephen.' The warmth in her voice added to her smile was meant to show him that she intended friendship with him, past misunderstandings forgotten.

His tanned face creased into a smile in response. 'Hi. That was Arthur Bainbridge I saw just now, wasn't it?'

'You've met him? A strange man,' Pippa remarked.

'Saw him in the pub, that's all, and heard people say he was a rich landowner.'

'Have you been to look at the papers?'

'Not yet. I wanted to have a go at this maze and put a theory to the test. If you've got an hour or so to spare, maybe you'd like to take a chance on getting completely lost in there with me?'

'Not just now, thanks. To tell the truth, mazes frighten me — I get so disorientated and confused at having lost my sense of direction that I begin to feel quite dizzy.'

'Pity,' he murmured. 'I wanted to try out my friend's theory. He tells me that if you chalk a line on the right-hand wall continuously, whatever corners you turn, you'll eventually arrive at the centre and then find your way out again. I wonder if it really works.'

'You can hardly chalk on hedges,' Pippa pointed out.

'No, but I could keep touching the right hand side. Never mind, I guess I'd better get down to work anyway.'

Together they walked back towards the house, and again Pippa felt a sense of ease in his company. In the vestibule she was reluctant to leave him. She hesitated, about to suggest that they looked through the papers together, when Mrs Purvis emerged silently from the kitchen quarters.

'Good afternoon, Mr Lorant. I have the key for you here,' she said quietly, offering him the key to the east wing. 'Was there a particular subject you wanted to cover today?'

'Yes, as a matter of fact, I wanted some details about Mr Korvak's leaving Hungary and coming to the States,' Stephen replied. 'Do you happen to know if there is a diary or something of the kind?'

The housekeeper thought for a moment. 'I think there is very little on that subject, so far as I remember, but what there is will be in the crate labelled number two. When you have finished perhaps you would be kind enough to return the key to me personally,' she went on, with the briefest of glances at Pippa. 'In the meantime, Philippa, perhaps you would care to iron your silk blouses — I've just washed them by hand for you.'

She was gone again, quickly and silently, before Pippa could demur. Stephen was already unlocking the double doors.

'Perhaps I'll see you later?' he said, and then he too was

61

gone and the doors closed behind him. With a sigh Pippa went to the kitchen. The ironing board was already set up and the iron heating, but Mrs Purvis was not there.

She came in some minutes later. Pippa looked up from her work. 'Did Mr Lorant bring a letter of introduction from Father?' she asked.

'He did, otherwise I would not have allowed him here?'

'May I see it?'

The housekeeper looked at her with a trace of annoyance on her normally serene features. 'Don't you believe me, child? Of course I don't have the letter now – it came to the London flat. I only stored and kept what was essential.'

'I see. Well, what exactly is he writing about Father?'

'A complete biography, I understand. You'd better ask Mr Lorant for yourself.'

'I shall.'

So it was that when Stephen Lorant eventually emerged from the east wing Pippa was waiting for him. 'Come and have a cup of tea with me,' she invited. 'There are questions I want to ask you.'

'Great idea,' he replied. 'Dusty papers have given me quite a thirst.'

'Now,' she said, as she handed him a cup from the tray Mrs Purvis had set ready in the drawing room, 'tell me who commissioned you, and to write just what.'

'Your father did. To write his life story.'

'How a penniless Hungarian emigrant became a re-nowned producer? But surely that's been done before.'

'Not the whole of it,' Stephen said quietly. 'His life in Hungary before he left, and much of his private life after-wards. Much of that has been kept quiet.'

'We all have parts of our lives we prefer to forget,' Pippa commented with feeling. 'So why should my father change his mind now and ask you to uncover it all.'

'He didn't exactly ask me – he challenged me,' Stephen replied. 'And I am a man who can't resist a challenge.'

'Challenge? Yet he laid all his private papers at your disposal? You expect me to believe that?' Pippa exclaimed.

'I can prove it. In my car I have a tape of a conversation with Korvak,' Stephen said quietly. 'Shall I fetch it?'

'Do.'

When he had left the room, Pippa remembered the dirty little yellow Fiat with the file on the seat about Korvak. That must have been Stephen's car. And the notes in the file had hinted at some unpleasant facts about Father. There was more she must ask Stephen Lorant.

He came back with a small tape-recorder in his hands. 'Wait a moment until I find the place,' he said.

Pippa poured more tea while he ran the tape back and forth and odd snatches of incomprehensible speech issued from the machine. More clicks and a whirring sound, and then suddenly the room was filled with the sound of a voice which made her start.

'That's Father's voice!' she murmured. There was no doubt of it — the lazy American drawl superimposed upon but not disguising the gutteral accent of his native Hungary. It was a rich, resonant voice, which latterly she had heard over the transatlantic telephone more often than in person.

'Listen,' said Stephen. 'Hear what he says.'

The rich voice rolled on. 'So you want to print my whole story from the beginning, do you, Stefan? From the start in Budapest to England and then to the States? The whole truth like it's never been done before, warts and all? Then go ahead, I won't stop you. You can check out what you will — it will do no harm to me. And when you've done, let me see it, to confirm that it is the truth. I want no distorted picture of me to go down to posterity.'

'You'll allow me to check any of your papers?' Stephen's voice on the tape asked crisply.

Korvak gave a deep, rumbling laugh. 'You are determined to prove me an *ördög,* aren't you, Stefan? Go on then, prove it.'

There was a click, and her father's voice vanished from the tape.

Stephen cocked his head to one side. 'Do you believe me now, Miss Korvak?'

'Yes, of course. And do call me Pippa. Tell me, what did that word mean that Father said?'

'You mean *ördög?* It means a devil in Hungarian.'

'You know Hungarian?'

'We spoke it as well as English at home. I think I told you

63

my father too was Hungarian.'

'Why does my father accuse you of wanting to prove he is a devil?' Pippa pressed him.

'He did not accuse me — he challenged me to do so. His life is a very eventful one, to put it mildly,' Stephen replied. 'And he himself is to vet the story when I have completed it. Are you satisfied now?'

'I suppose so,' Pippa admitted. 'Tell me, it has been suggested he was hated — have you uncovered any reasons why he should be?'

Stephen looked away, replacing the cassette in its case. 'I haven't yet done very much research. After the papers, I shall have to cover all the ground he travelled and ask many questions. Since I arrived in England I've been busy mostly on another assignment, about bats, for a naturalist magazine. Fascinating creatures, bats. Didn't know a thing about them until I started this assignment.'

Pippa was barely listening as he launched into an enthusiastic account of his meeting a couple in Hertford-shire who were bat experts and had convinced him that bats were not the sinister, repulsive creatures superstition had led people to believe. 'They're tiny, harmless creatures, very poor-sighted but with an incredibly efficient echo-location system, like radar. They can catch their prey in the dark and find their way unerringly — it's a fallacy that they get stuck in people's hair.'

Although she was not listening, Stephen seemed un-aware. 'I never knew they were so interesting. Did you know that apart from living high under roofs like old churches, some bats burrow underground, like the Daubenton? I was given a baby Pipistrelle to hold in my hand.'

'Pardon?' said Pippa, her attention arrested by the word, so like her own name.

'You weren't listening,' Stephen accused her. 'It was such an appealing little thing, so small and helpless and vulnerable. I shall think quite differently about the genus *Chiroptera* from now on, and I hope my readers will too.'

Despite his smile and obvious enthusiasm Pippa had the distinct impression that she was being side-tracked, but before she could attempt to pick up the thread of her enquiries about her father, Mrs Purvis glided into the room.

'Mr Bainbridge is on the telephone. He wants to speak to you, Philippa.'

Pippa rose. 'Excuse me a moment,' she murmured.

Stephen rose too. 'It's time I was going anyway. Thanks for the tea.'

He followed Pippa out into the hall, where she picked up the 'phone.

'Hello?'

'Ah, there you are, Philippa,' Bainbridge's voice rasped. 'Now about that Dormobile on the edge of my land — is it yours? I want it shifted, otherwise trippers will get the notion they can all park there and I don't want my fields covered with litter.'

'Dormobile? Where? I know nothing about it,' Pippa remarked. Stephen paused in the doorway. 'Where is it anyway?'

'By the copse, where there's a handy stream. Just where your land reaches mine — that's why I thought it might be yours. Sorry. I'll have to go down and speak to them. Sorry I troubled you. And by the way, don't forget, my offer is still open.'

Stephen was still waiting when she turned away from the telephone. 'What was that about a Dormobile?' he asked. She told him. Stephen frowned. 'It wasn't there when I came by this morning. As he says, it's probably a cheeky camper.'

Pippa smiled. 'Well, I wouldn't like to be him when Bainbridge gets there — he'll make short shrift of the fellow.'

'I don't doubt it. Cheerio, Pippa. Be seeing you.'

Impulsively Pippa followed him out on to the doorstep.

'Stephen,' she called after him before she had time to think what she was saying, 'Why don't you move back into the Hall? After all, it would make your work so much easier and I'm sure Mrs Purvis hasn't stripped your room yet. Whereabouts was your room?'

Stephen was regarding her quizzically. 'Upstairs in the east wing. Are you sure you don't mind?'

'Not in the least, now I know you. I acted hastily when I

65

said you had to leave — I was just angry at the thought of a snooper. But now it's different — I'd be glad to have you back here.'

'That's very kind of you. I'll move my things back this evening, if you're sure.'

'I'll tell Mrs Purvis to expect you.' Smiling, Pippa was about to turn back into the house when a thought struck her. 'Upstairs in the east wing? Then it must have been you I saw at the window that morning I was swimming,' she murmured.

Stephen grinned. 'So you spotted me. I have to confess — I was prying then. It was a lovely sight — you looked like a water-nymph, Pippa, so graceful and relaxed in the water. You have a very trim and shapely figure, if I may say so.'

Pippa felt a blush of pleasure begin to tingle on her cheeks, and then another thought came. 'And it was also you who brushed past me in the dark that night in the east wing? Was that you?'

Stephen shook his fair head. 'I left that day and didn't come back into the Hall until you invited me.'

Pippa smiled. 'Well, one mystery is solved anyway. I daresay the other will be too in time. Shall we expect you after dinner?'

Mrs Purvis's thin eyebrows rose fractionally when Pippa announced the news to her. 'So you've changed your mind?' she remarked drily. 'You do not change, Philippa. Unpredictable and impulsive still, I see.'

Her tone was cool and Pippa wondered if she had annoyed the older woman. 'I'm sorry — does it inconvenience you, Mrs Purvis? I'll make up the bed again if that will help.'

'No, no inconvenience at all,' the housekeeper replied. 'The bed is still made up so Mr Lorant may return as soon as he wishes.'

It was curious, Pippa thought privately, how Mrs Purvis always said the right words yet at the same time managed to sound as if she meant the opposite. Her unsmiling expression and cold eyes made it clear she did not like Pippa's invitation to the young man but could not criticise her right to do so.

After dinner that evening Pippa heard Stephen's car pull up outside the Hall and his voice in the vestibule as he talked to Mrs Purvis. She kept her distance while he unloaded his belongings and carried them upstairs, glad he was here but reluctant to appear too eager for his company. To her disappointment, however, he remained upstairs for the rest of the evening, and when the housekeeper announced that she was going to bed, Pippa had no choice but to retire too.

Of course, she thought as she undressed, the footsteps in the night when she first arrived — he was still here in the Hall then. It must have been Stephen's footsteps she had heard. That was another small mystery solved. She went through to the bathroom and turned on the controls of the shower, then went back to the bedroom to fetch her robe.

On re-entering the bathroom Pippa let her robe fall to the floor and slid aside the cubicle door. Instantly she leapt and screamed — a myriad tiny red-hot needles seemed to be piercing and burning her naked flesh while a vast white cloud of steam enveloped her. Horror and disbelief swept through her. Another step and the skin would have been boiled away from her bones.

Incredulous, she switched off the control and then inspected the heat control knob. Stiff and resisting to her touch, it was clearly set at maximum. With an effort she managed to turn it down to cool.

She was shaken. It could be no accident, she thought as she stood under the cool, refreshing spray. Even the cleaning woman could not have moved the control by chance as she polished. Someone must have changed it purposely, using some effort to set it to high. But why? There was no reason for it — unless someone had wanted Pippa to be severely scalded. Surely not; no one had any reason to want to harm her. And yet — there had been many hints of the hatred for Korvak. Could it be that someone hated him so much they were malicious enough to transfer that hate from father to daughter?

No, she told herself firmly as she prepared for bed. There was some other, simpler reason for the near-accident, and she would doubtless find out in the morning when she told Mrs Purvis about it. She must be careful not to let the strange and subtle air of mystery in the Hall influence her, simply because it was night and she was slightly excited.

She had to be honest with herself and admit that it was Stephen Lorant's proximity which disturbed her. Pleasure filled her at the thought — and it proved she had driven all lingering desire for Clive out of her mind. She fell asleep and dreamt peacefully until suddenly, and for no apparent reason, she awoke. Pippa lay still, wondering, and then an uneasy sensation filled her that she was not alone. She sat up slowly, staring into the darkness.

'Hello? Who's there?'

No answer came. Pippa was aware only of a perfume, a heavy scent that filled the room. It was a strange scent, like none she had smelt before, and the silence in the room was oppressive.

'Hello?' she said again, in a whisper. Her fingers reached for the light switch. Before she could reach it she heard a click. The room filled with light, and there was no one there.

Pippa leapt from the bed and darted to the door. The corridor outside was in total darkness and not a sound disturbed the stillness of the house. For a moment she stood there, and then returned slowly to her room.

Either she had dreamt or imagined it, she told herself. But no, the lingering scent hovered in the room still. It must have been a woman, and so it must have been Mrs Purvis — who, to Pippa's knowledge, never wore perfume. And why on earth should the housekeeper visit Pippa's room in the middle of the night and not speak?

Purposefully Pippa climbed back into bed. Mrs Purvis would have several questions to answer in the morning.

6

Pippa was down in the kitchen early the next morning, anxious to put her questions to the housekeeper, but to her surprise it was Stephen's tall figure that stood by the stove, not the thin, angular figure of Mrs Purvis. He smiled at Pippa.

'Hi, there. Want a cup of coffee, Pippa? I've just taken the liberty of brewing up for myself since Mrs Purvis doesn't seem to be about yet.'

'I'd love some.' Pippa felt disappointed, not at seeing Stephen so early in the day but in having to contain her curiosity a little longer. It was a ridiculous question, but as Stephen handed her a steaming cup of black coffee she looked him straight in the eye. 'Did you by any chance go to my room last night, Stephen? I have a reason for asking.'

He showed no sign of shocked amazement, but only buttered one slice of the toast he had just lifted out of the toaster. 'Not guilty, but why do you ask?'

'Because someone seems to have tampered with my shower in an attempt to scald me, and someone came in while I was sleeping. I'm determined to find out who it was.' Her voice was as level in tone as his, betraying no sign of her eager curiosity. He placed the toast on a plate and put it before her on the table.

'I never moved from my room all evening or in the night,' he assured her. 'But I'm disturbed to hear about it. Perhaps someone does have it in for you after all, though Lord knows why. We'll have to keep a close watch from now on.'

She liked the quiet, possessive way he took her problems on to his own shoulders. It gave her a warm, comfortable feeling of being protected, a sensation she had never felt before. But then suddenly he shattered the reassuring feeling of closeness.

'Well, I'd best be off — a lot to do,' he muttered, and tossing off his cup of coffee he left the kitchen.

Shortly afterwards Pippa heard the front door close, and felt oddly disappointed. She had thought he was going to work on the papers, but he had evidently gone out.

Five minutes later the housekeeper appeared. She looked at the used cups on the table and then at Pippa. 'Is Mr Lorant up?'

'He's gone out,' Pippa replied. 'Mrs Purvis, did you alter the control on my shower?'

'Why on earth should I do that? Now, what will you have for breakfast?'

'I've already eaten. And did you come to my room during the night?'

The housekeeper stopped and looked at her curiously. 'During the night? Of course not. Now what is this, Philippa? Questions about your shower and midnight visitors — are you up to your imaginative games again? If so, I must warn you that I have no time for such nonsense. I'm much too busy with you and Mr Lorant to look after.'

'It's not my imagination, Mrs Purvis,' Pippa said firmly. 'Someone altered my shower to high, so that I was nearly scalded. Could it have been the cleaning woman?'

'She hasn't been in since you arrived. Dear me, at high that shower could have flayed the skin off your back. You must be more careful in future.'

Pippa could have throttled the woman. In her cool, detached way she was implying that Pippa herself had carelessly set the control too high. She had to resist the impulse to snap at her. Instead, she rose from her chair.

'I'm going to have a dip in the pool,' she announced.

Mrs Purvis glanced up. 'Ah, you haven't swum yet today. I thought you might have while I was out.'

Out so early? Pippa mused as she changed in her room. She and Stephen had both thought she was late getting up, and had overslept for once or had forgotten to set her alarm clock. The idle thought faded from her mind as she went out on to the terrace and felt the sun's warmth on her skin. She sat on the lip of the pool and lowered herself into the water, revelling in its cool caress. A water nymph, Stephen had called her, she thought with pleasure as she swam with leisurely grace. It was so warming and comforting to receive compliments from a man like him. It was a pity he was not here now, to share the pleasure of the pool. She must remember to invite him to make free of the Hall's facilities, and to ride the Korvak horses if he had a mind to.

She turned over to float on her back and was so relaxed, with her ears under water, that at first she did not hear the housekeeper calling to her. Mrs Purvis was standing at the open doorway, shielding her eyes with one hand against the sun.

'Philippa! Here a moment! I'd like a word with you!'

Pippa swam smoothly towards the shallow end of the pool. The housekeeper disappeared back inside the Hall. Pippa made for the steps in the corner of the pool and as she came to them, she put a hand on the highest step. Her fingers slid off, unable to grip the smooth surface. She tried again, curious, and again her hand slipped off. The surface of the step was unnaturally smooth and slippery, as though it had been coated with an oily substance.

It was far too unsafe to attempt to walk up the steps, but tentatively Pippa tried. The steps under the water were perfectly easy to climb, but the top three were impossible. Had she not discovered their state by touching them first, she could have come a nasty cropper. Pippa heaved herself up over the lip of the pool and put on her robe, then went in to the kitchen. Mrs Purvis handed her a large towel.

'I thought I would go into Reading for some shopping, Philippa. I shall need Carson to drive me and to carry the groceries, so I just wanted to be sure you'd be all right on your own and had no need of a car this morning.'

'No, I'll be fine,' Pippa assured her. With luck she might manage to have Stephen's company all to herself while they were gone. 'Oh, by the way, would you tell Carson the pool steps are very slippery. They could be dangerous,' Pippa remarked, and at once she saw the light that leapt into the housekeeper's eyes.

'Slippery? You didn't fall, did you?'

'Luckily, no. I found out in time, but they'd better be attended to before someone has an accident.'

The light in the older woman's eyes puzzled Pippa. After the housekeeper had driven off, Pippa went back to the pool. She had made no mistake: the top three steps were treacherous and the substance looked and smelt like engine oil. No one but she used the pool . . . and someone had tampered with the shower yesterday. Was it too ridiculous to believe that someone was trying to cause an accident? To Pippa, who had no enemy and had never hurt anyone in her life? Of course it was ridiculous. She must have been reading too many Agatha Christie novels lately. She ran back into the house and upstairs to dress.

The Hall seemed strangely quiet and empty now that Mrs Purvis, Carson and Stephen were gone. Pippa made up her mind to walk into Marlow and look around.

Going down the lane, she soon found the road that led into the little town. It was a pretty place, full of picturesque charm and items of interest. The grammar school, she noted as she passed its mellowed brick, bore a plaque which dated its origins in the seventeenth century, and next to it was a small row of Georgian houses, one of which carried another plaque bearing testimony to the fact that the poet Shelley once lived there. A little further along she came to a small obelisk marking the town centre, the old market square, and from it a busy high street leading towards the Thames.

Sunlight rippled on the river's surface, furrowed by the pleasure launches and cabin cruisers of the holidaymakers. Shrill cries of children filled the air as she leaned over the parapet of the suspension bridge to watch. It was a lively, bustling scene, far different from the calm, strange quiet of Cambermere. Girls in summer frocks giggled on the towpath below, watching with covert glances the passing youths evidently unaware of their presence. A dog leapt from a launch moored on the quayside and fell with a splash into the water, sending a squad of marauding ducks squawking away over the flashing waters. Pippa was so engrossed watching the ever-changing scene that she did not notice someone approach.

'Hi, there! Beautiful, isn't it?'

Pippa started, and then felt a rush of pleasure. She

responded warmly.

'Indeed it is. Have you seen the weir down there, and the lock? I think I'll walk down that way and take a closer look.'

'I'll come with you. There's a road down behind the church,' Stephen said, turning in step beside her. She did not ask why he was here or what he had been doing. She was content to have his company.

Crossing the green with its war memorial by the slender-spired church, Pippa and Stephen turned down towards the river bank. Stephen was in high good humour.

'It's a fascinating town, with quite a history. Did you know that in the Catholic church they had a relic claimed to be the mummified hand of St James the Apostle? The town was once surrounded by a ring of monasteries and nunneries and the Knights Templar and Knights Hospitaller had houses here — in fact, Spittal Street is a relic of the Hospitallers.'

They walked down a small street to the water's edge.

'This is the wharf,' Stephen went on. 'The old wooden bridge used to cross the river here before the suspension bridge was built.'

Pippa breathed a deep sigh of pleasure. From here she had a superb view of the weir with the water tumbling over it and a magnificent backdrop of woods on the Berkshire side of the river. Stephen was silent now, staring into the distance, the sunlight gleaming on his fair head.

'It's lovely,' Pippa said softly. 'And the pub there looks very old.'

'The Two Brewers? It is, and there's always been an inn there. Can't you imagine the Roundhead or Cavalier soldiers quaffing their ale there after a skirmish on the bridge?' He glanced at his wrist watch. 'Let's go and have a drink there too.'

Pippa was enchanted by the oak panelling and low raftered ceiling which gave atmosphere to the bar, and also by Stephen's words about the Cavaliers. It showed that he too was an imaginative person. Clive would never have thought of the past. But then, Clive was long ago and far away, part of the past now himself.

'There is so much more I could show you,' Stephen said

as he returned from the bar and set two glasses down on the table in the corner. 'I must take you to the two headstones in the graveyard, back to back. It seems a Marlow man who was a showman, some time in the eighteenth century, bought an African child for his show because the boy was piebald — part of his skin white and part black. He grew very attached to the little thing, possibly because he'd been born in a workhouse himself, and when the boy died as a result of the English climate, he had him buried in his own family mausoleum. Master and boy, they lie together back to back now.'

'Curious,' Pippa remarked. 'You know a great deal about Marlow, Stephen.'

He shrugged. 'Read it up in the local library. Journalist's training — learn about the background of your subject. I can't write about Alexis Korvak at Cambermere if I don't know something about the area.'

'You're very thorough,' Pippa said thoughtfully. 'Are you always so meticulous?'

He leaned back in the small wooden chair, his long body appearing far too large for it. 'I guess so. That's just my way.'

Inwardly Pippa approved of all she was learning about Stephen Lorant. Meticulousness showed professional pride and conscientiousness, yet he was not fussy and critical like Clive used to be. She was pleased with herself too. Already she could look back on the past with critical objectivity, and that argued well for the future.

'But tell me about yourself, Pippa. You hardly ever talk about your hopes and fears, your likes and dislikes. You interest me. Tell me about your job.' He was leaning across the table now, his bronzed forearms reflected in the high black gloss of the varnish and his blue eyes eager. Pippa found herself talking easily to him about Paris and the Sorbonne and Professor Garnier, but making no mention of Clive. Stephen's keen gaze never moved from her face as she spoke, and Pippa sensed herself blossom and come alive, feeling an unaccustomed sensation of being an attractive and interesting woman. A sudden breeze flicked her hair as the door opened and a group of strangers entered.

'Gee, that was fascinating,' a vivid blonde woman in her

forties exclaimed to her two men companions. It was evident from her accent and from the exotic shirts the men wore that they were American tourists. 'I'm so glad we decided to moor here overnight or we'd never have seen those fabulous caves.'

'Yes, they must have been quite some group, those Hell Fire men,' her balding companion drawled. 'What are you drinking, Ida — Scotch, or some more of that warm English beer?' He headed towards the bar, and the woman and the other man followed. As they passed under the low lintel into the inner bar, Pippa heard the second man's voice trail back over his shoulder. 'I reckon Korvak must have been forming a new club of his own to compete with Sir Francis, don't you, Ida? Remember all those stories?'

'I sure do, honey. Mine's a Scotch, Ben.'

Pippa looked at Stephen with wide eyes. 'Did you hear that, Stephen? They were talking of my father.'

Stephen leaned back. 'I guess so, but forget it. He was, and still is, always the subject of gossip and speculation.'

Pippa frowned. 'No one seems to have a good word for him, though, and that troubles me. Who is Sir Francis, anyway, and what was this club they mentioned?'

'Ah, now that I have read up, though somewhat hastily, I admit,' Stephen replied, and she could see his momentary stiffness relaxing instantly. 'Sir Francis Dashwood was an eighteenth century nobleman who had estates near here. He was your proverbial rake, wild as they come, and he and his group of rich, pleasure-seeking companions held their secret debaucheries in this area. At first they took over the ruined Medmenham Abbey and held strange rituals there — not black magic, you know, but certainly anti-Christian. They used to row up river to the abbey by barge from London. Then later they transferred their activities to Sir Francis's estate at West Wycombe.'

'West Wycombe?'

'A small village not far from here, just outside High Wycombe. Sir Francis had the grounds of his hall laid out specially, with underground caves where they conducted their rites. The Hell Fire Club's activities were the terror of the neighbourhood.'

'Terror? Why, what did they do?'

Stephen smiled. 'I didn't read all the details, but I gather the local peasant girls who were virgins were in demand for their destructive purposes. Sir Francis was a cruel, relentless man when it came to pleasure. The club's motto was "Fay ce que voudras." '

'Do as you please,' Pippa murmured. 'And was that their aim, then, gratifying their own pleasures?'

'Totally, and the villagers hated and feared them as a result. Peasant folk had no redress against the rich. Whatever the Hell Fire men wanted, they took.'

Pippa mulled over the information for a few moments. From what the American tourists had said, it seemed they were comparing Father to this historic villain, and the thought hurt. Suddenly she could tolerate the close atmosphere of the inn no longer.

'Let's get out of here,' she said abruptly, rising from her chair.

Stephen followed her out without question.

Outside, with the cool breeze fanning her face, Pippa found her tongue. 'Do they really believe my father is as wicked as Sir Francis was?' she asked quietly as they climbed the narrow street back to the church. 'Can they really believe he is such a monster?'

Stephen was silent for a moment, his sun-bronzed forehead furrowed in a frown. 'It seems from what I've heard that some people have reason to believe that, yes. He hasn't treated everyone as generously as he has you.'

'But he wouldn't deliberately hurt anyone either,' Pippa protested. 'He's a sick man, in hospital again now. You can't speak of him like that!'

'He may be failing now, but he was vigorous and active once and he too took what he wanted,' Stephen said quietly, but with a firmness that appalled her. 'I know of several instances of his misdeeds.'

'Like what?' Pippa stopped and turned to face him, her expression at once angry and challenging. Stephen's answering gaze was equally resolute.

'He has lied, cheated and stolen. As a young man he killed another man.'

'In self-defence, surely? There must be an explanation!'

'The evidence indicated otherwise, but in the event he

was acquitted. The fight was over a woman.'

'There you are, then,' Pippa said hotly. 'A *crime passionnelle*, and that's always been regarded leniently, in French courts at least.'

'The woman was a whore in a brothel,' Stephen said levelly, as though determined to spare her nothing. 'And women have figured largely in his life.'

'Who would attack an impulsive lover?' Pippa demanded.

Stephen's laugh was dry, ironic. 'Korvak love? He never loved anyone. He used women as pawns – charmed them, used them and abandoned them. Charmed money from the rich ones to further his career. He's an exploiter, Pippa, but I can't expect you to understand that. You don't know the man; you only believe in a fantasy picture you have built up of him.'

'He's my father, and he's always been kind to me!'

'Your family loyalty does you credit, my dear, but he has behaved cruelly to others nonetheless – cheated and deceived them, betrayed their trust and used them diabolically. This I know for a fact, and the more I learn of him the more I know it to be true, and there are many who positively hate him.'

'Like Walters, you mean, and Bainbridge? But why?'

Stephen sighed and took her elbow to lead her into the churchyard. 'He cheated one out of his land and the other of his sister. But that's all in the past now. Let me show you those two back-to-back headstones I told you about.'

Pippa's mind was racing with a confusion of tangled thoughts as they walked along the tree-shaded path of the graveyard. It was impossible to believe her father was as ruthless as Stephen said – a hard bargainer and relentless in business, perhaps, but then any man who reached the height of success he had achieved had to be so. And apart from her angry disbelief, she regretted too the shadow that had fallen on the warm closeness which had been blossoming between Stephen and herself until a few moments ago.

Stephen was pointing at the two headstones, but Pippa could only look on with disinterest. 'What did Father do to Bainbridge?' she persisted quietly. Stephen looked away as he answered.

'Bainbridge wanted Korvak land to extend his farm. Your father would not sell but in the end agreed to gamble a piece of land against an equivalent plot of Bainbridge's — he was like that, enjoying the danger of a gamble rather than a straightforward deal. However, the cards fell in Korvak's favour.'

'So why did Bainbridge object? He agreed to the wager, presumably?' Pippa asked in puzzled tones.

'Yes, but Korvak cheated, he said. He kept an ace up his sleeve. There was no way he could prove it, however, so he lost his piece of land. Years later Korvak let it out while drunk, bragging about his cleverness, so I know it was true.'

'Were you there? Did you hear him admit it?' Pippa challenged.

'No, but my father was.'

There was no retort Pippa could make to that. But Walters — what had father done to him? Something to do with his sister, Stephen had said. In the dappled shadows cast by the trees over the grey slabs in memory of the dead, Pippa looked up at him hopefully.

'And Walters? What of him?'

Stephen smiled ruefully. 'Worse, I'm afraid. Korvak caught sight of Geoff Walters' sister Nina and desired her instantly. He seduced her.'

'Is that so terrible? I imagine she must have wanted him to,' Pippa argued. 'I expect it was when he was still a bachelor, for I know he was devoted to my mother — his mementoes of her at Cambermere show he loves her still.'

Stephen's eyes were solemn as he looked down at her. 'No, Pippa. It was only ten or twelve years ago. Nina Walters gave birth to a child and shortly afterwards killed herself.'

A child! Pippa drew in her breath sharply. 'Robin? Is the boy Nina's child?'

'And your half-brother.'

For a few minutes Pippa could not speak. The revelation had shattered the last illusion about Father. 'Would he not acknowledge her — or the child?' she ventured tremulously at last.

'He cast Nina off. She never told him of the boy.'

'But surely Father knows now?'

'No, Geoff Walters is a proud man, but he will never forgive your father's heartlessness. If it had not been for him, Nina would not have committed suicide.'

Pippa could take no more. 'I've heard enough. I'm going back to the Hall,' she said, and turned sharply towards the gate. Stephen followed.

'My car is here. I'll drive you,' he said.

Pippa slumped in the passenger seat as Stephen negotiated the busy high street towards the obelisk and climbed the hill towards Cambermere. Maybe Father was not the perfect man she had always believed him to be, but time should have mellowed people's attitudes towards him, though it evidently had not. Even his daughter bore the brunt of his misdeeds, it seemed. She thought again about the shower and the oil on the pool steps.

In the front drive of the Hall, Stephen pulled up. 'Look, I'm sorry, Pippa, but you had to know the truth,' he said quietly. 'You could not go on living in a fool's paradise.'

There was compassion in his tone and she responded with a thin smile. 'Stephen, do you honestly think anyone would harm me because of Father?'

'Why do you ask?'

'Because, as I told you, someone tampered with my shower. And then today there was oil on the steps of the swimming pool. Only I use the pool, Stephen, and the oil couldn't have got there by chance, could it?'

His eyes narrowed and the frown reappeared. 'Oil? That's a mean trick. I'll go and see.'

He stepped out of the car, then paused before he closed the door. 'Don't worry, *dragam,* I'll see no harm comes to you.'

Pippa glanced up. 'What was that? That word you said?'

'Oh, *dragam* − it's Hungarian. It means my dear. No offence, Pippa, but endearments come more easily to the tongue for me in Hungarian. I'll just go and have a look at the pool.'

In a few strides he had disappeared around the side of the Hall. Pippa got out and went indoors.

As if by magic, Mrs Purvis materialised as soon as Pippa entered the vestibule. 'Ah, there you are, Philippa. Have you had lunch?'

'No, I'm not hungry,' Pippa said dispiritedly.

'I hope you're not becoming ill, Philippa, going off your food and imagining things as well. I'm not sure that I shouldn't call Dr Ramsay in to have a look at you.' The housekeeper's thin features registered doubt and disapproval and her proprietorial air irritated Pippa.

'I'm not ill and I don't imagine things, Mrs Purvis,' she said crisply.

'Intruders in your room and scalding showers?' Mrs Purvis replied in a tone of patent disbelief.

'Both were real,' Pippa exclaimed, 'and so was the oil on the pool steps. I could have fallen when you called me in this morning.'

'Oil? My dear girl, you don't really expect me to believe that,' the housekeeper said, her tone still cool and level but with an air of vexed impatience. 'You'll be telling me next that someone plans deliberately to hurt you.'

'And how can you be sure they are not? From what I have learnt it would hardly be surprising.'

Pippa and the older woman held each other's gaze for a moment, until the door opened and Stephen entered. He stood looking at the two women and Mrs Purvis turned to him.

'Some coffee, Mr Lorant? I have some bubbling ready in the kitchen.' She walked smoothly to the kitchen door.

Alone with Stephen, Pippa turned to him eagerly. 'Well?' she asked. 'Don't you agree those steps are dangerous?'

Stephen shook his head slowly. 'Pippa, there is not a trace of oil there. I inspected every step carefully.'

'What? But they were thick with oil this morning, I know they were!' She rushed past him to the french windows and out on to the terrace. The waters of the pool rippled with a limpid shimmer. The steps were dry, rough and so easy to gain a footing that even a toddler would have been safe there. Pippa squatted, looking at her dry fingertips disbelievingly, then slowly returned to the Hall. Stephen was sitting in the kitchen. He and Mrs Purvis fell silent as Pippa entered, and she knew she had been the subject of their conversation.

'It was there, I tell you,' she said sullenly. 'I don't know how it's gone, but I know I could have fallen on it this morning.'

'You see?' Mrs Purvis said quietly to Stephen. 'It's always been like this. Imagination working overtime. Philippa certainly is in need of a rest so that her nervous tension is relaxed.'

'I'm not imagining!' Pippa snapped. 'Not the oil nor the shower nor the person who was in my room in the night — someone wearing perfume too, an odd sweet perfume it was. I'd know it if I smelt it again because it was unusual. But I imagined nothing!'

'Imagination,' Mrs Purvis went on smoothly as if Pippa had not spoken. 'In her childhood days it was this imaginary friend of hers, Gwen, who kept getting up to mischief. Are you sure it isn't Gwen who is doing all these tricks now, Philippa?' She spoke to Pippa in an unusually gentle voice, as though humouring a sick child's fantasies. Pippa was angry and frustrated, knowing that the housekeeper presented an image of cool reason in contrast with Pippa's excitedly expressed statements which, in the cold light of day, could only appear paranoid.

'And as to perfume,' Mrs Purvis went on as she poured out the coffee, 'as I told you that was your mother's room. Her things in the drawers probably still retain traces of her scent — she always wore the same one. Come, I'll show you if you like, Philippa.'

She led the way from the kitchen and Pippa followed, angry with herself for appearing the chastened, now-dutiful child in front of Stephen. In the bedroom she watched while the housekeeper opened drawers, revealing layers of fine linen and silk underwear. 'Here,' she said.

Pippa came closer. As she bent to touch the fragile lingerie she caught the scent, and recognised it. 'That's it!' she exclaimed. 'That's the perfume I smelt last night!'

'I thought so,' said Mrs Purvis, closing the drawer again. Her smugly satisfied tone was infuriating. 'That explains away one of your fantasies, Philippa, and I'm sure the others have an equally simple explanation. Now let us get

81

on with lunch, for we're late enough already.'

'What is the perfume?' Pippa asked as they made their way downstairs again.

'Californian Poppy, it's called. Miss Carrie always wore it. In fact, she began the vogue for it in the 'forties, and even years later when every shop-girl in the country was wearing it, she still would not use any other. Ah yes,' she murmured, pausing at the foot of the staircase and looking towards the doors to the east wing, 'just to catch a whiff of it recalls Miss Carrie clearly to me. So beautiful, so kind and gentle, the loveliest creature that ever lived. She didn't deserve to go the way she did.'

For a fleeting second Pippa could swear there was a mist in the black eyes of the normally imperturbable house-keeper, but the glimpse vanished instantly as she turned to the kitchen. Whatever Mrs Purvis's shortcomings towards Pippa, she evidently had one human streak in her love for her dead mistress.

Lunch was a belated and silent affair, neither Stephen nor Mrs Purvis being disposed to talk any more than Pippa. Carson must have been busy elsewhere, for he did not appear. Pippa's thoughts were confused and she ate little. Someone had been in her bedroom last night, despite Mrs Purvis's explanation of the perfume. Someone had altered the shower control – and put oil on the steps – but were they all one and the same person? And why? Was it because of Father, unreasonable as it might seem?

If so, was it Arthur Bainbridge, cheated out of his land? It seemed hardly likely. No more likely than Geoff Walters, whose sister Nina Father had betrayed, if Stephen's words were true – and Pippa had no reason to disbelieve him. After all, Stephen was an outsider; he had no axe to grind over Alexis Korvak, only a commission to fulfil.

Nina Walters. Her son, the young boy Robin, was Pippa's half-brother. It was a shock to discover a sibling she had never heard of until now. And more than that, he was an unacknowledged bastard, poor thing. Father should know of his existence and surely then he would do something for the boy.

She must get in touch with Geoffrey Walters and apologise to him for her behaviour. Had she known the truth she would have been far more considerate and understanding. She made up her mind to telephone him straight after lunch.

Pippa declined the cheese and biscuits Mrs Purvis set on the table, saying she had eaten enough. Stephen was still munching thoughtfully when she excused herself and left. In the vestibule she found the local telephone directory, looked up Walters' number, and dialled it. Walters' voice crackled over the wire.

'Mr Walters? Philippa Korvak here. I just wanted to have a word with you . . . '

'Miss Korvak?' he interrupted in surprise. 'What a coincidence! I was going to ring you this afternoon to apologise. You were quite right. The horses are Korvak horses and you have a perfect right to ride whichever you choose, whenever you choose. I'm sorry I spoke so sharply to you. Very uncivil of me, and I hope you'll forgive me and call again soon.'

'That's very courteous of you, Mr Walters,' Pippa replied, warming to him for his gracious apology. 'As a matter of fact it's for me to apologise to you. I've since learnt that you had good reason to distrust the Korvak name and I'm truly sorry that I spoke so hastily.'

'Not at all, Miss Korvak. You held to your rights and one can only admire a young woman of spirit.'

Complimentary as well as gracious, Pippa thought. Her earlier dislike of the man faded altogether. Her response was equally gracious. 'Mr Walters, if you will forgive my touching upon what must be a painful subject to you, I think it would be fair that my father should know about Robin. I believe he knows nothing.'

'No.' Walters' voice was almost a bark. 'We want nothing from Korvak. It's best he should continue in ignorance, though I can't claim to want to spare him any discomfort or inconvenience. But no, I want him to have no part in Robin's life — he's better off not knowing about a father like that.' There was a pause, and then he added gruffly, 'I do appreciate your concern, Miss Korvak, but I'd rather you left things as they are.'

'But you don't see,' Pippa said as a fresh thought struck her, 'Robin is a Korvak, and is entitled to some share of Father's inheritance one day, just as much . . . '

She never reached the end of the sentence because a hand suddenly appeared in front of her and cracked down on the receiver rest. She turned to see Mrs Purvis's face, set and cold − so cold that her dark eyes glittered like icicles.

'What do you think you are doing, Philippa?' she demanded quietly. 'I did not know you knew about the boy but even if you do, why do you presume to interfere? He is your father's affair, not yours.'

'But Father doesn't know,' Pippa countered. 'I was only suggesting that he should be told so the boy can be treated fairly.'

'And by that you meant to apportion part, at least of the Korvak inheritance to him. How impulsive you are, child! And don't you realise that people could see you as a vulture, waiting to pounce along with the boy the moment your father dies? He is already a sick man, and appearances could be against you if he were to worsen.'

'Oh no, you couldn't think that!' Pippa cried. 'I don't want that at all! I was only trying to see Robin was fairly treated!'

'By giving away to him what is not yours to give,' Mrs Purvis pointed out. 'It is fortunate that I overheard. And you should know that the child is already well provided for, as his uncle's heir. He will want for nothing.'

'Maybe not, but in justice my father ought to know he has a son,' Pippa argued.

Mrs Purvis eyed her closely. 'And possibly disinherit yourself? No, Philippa, he must not be troubled with the news, not when he is already so ill too. Now come along, no more of your rash gestures, if you please. I know you meant well, but in your usual way you have allowed your impetuosity to rush you headlong into foolish actions. Let us talk no more of it, and with luck Mr Walters will forget it also.'

'He would have none of it anyway,' Pippa admitted lamely. 'He is too proud to want Korvak charity, he told me so.'

'There you are, then. That's the end of the matter,' the

housekeeper remarked with obvious satisfaction. 'Now if you'll excuse me I have matters to see to.'

She glided smoothly away. Pippa went gloomily out on to the front terrace. Mrs Purvis was probably right. She had no business to interfere, especially as Walters was so opposed to her suggestions. Gloomily she sat on the stone balustrade and looked out over the lake. Over the scent-laden air, heavy with the perfume of roses, she could hear the whir of a motorised lawn-mower. Carson must be cutting the lawns on the far side of the maze. A dragonfly fluttered up from the water's edge and hovered momentarily before Pippa, its azure wings irridescent in the sun's rays.

At that moment Pippa became aware that someone was standing close behind her and she looked up with a start. It was Stephen. His proximity, so close she could catch the scent of his sun-warmed arms, threw her off balance and she blurted out what was on her mind.

'Oh, Stephen, I feel such a fool! I misjudged Geoff Walters, I misjudged even my own father, and now you and Mrs Purvis both think I am lying about the oil. But I'm not lying, Stephen, and I'm not mistaken − it *was* there this morning! Someone must have cleaned it off, and that would be easy for anyone to do since you and I and Mrs Purvis were all out most of the day.'

He looked down at her gravely, his hazel eyes penetrating hers as though he could read her soul. Pippa looked away quickly. He seated himself beside her on the balustrade. Then, to her surprise, he covered her hand with his.

'I do believe you, *édesem*. I know you speak the truth.' His quiet tones thrilled her.

'You do? Even though the oil is gone?'

He nodded. 'Whoever it was, was able to remove the oil from the steps, but I've seen the detergent in the pool, and the thin film of grease on the surface. They didn't have time to empty and re-fill the pool to remove all traces of the evidence.'

Pippa digested the information. It gave her a degree of pleasure to be proved right and she returned the pressure of Stephen's hand. 'Then perhaps you will believe the rest too

— about the shower, and about someone coming into my room in the night? Oh, Stephen, I'm so glad! You can't know what pleasure it affords me to know I have a friend here at Cambermere, someone who believes in me! Until you came I felt so alone.'

His hands still lay over hers but the smile had faded from his handsome face. Pippa began to feel gauche. She had cried out with the unbridled lack of inhibition of a school-child. Perhaps she had embarrassed him with her clumsiness. Shyly she began to withdraw her hand, but Stephen's closed tightly over it.

'Pippa, let's go for a walk this evening after dinner,' he murmured. 'Away from Cambermere Hall where we can talk more freely.'

She looked at him, surprise in her eyes. 'Of course. I would enjoy that,' she replied.

'By the way, did you get your letter?' Stephen went on. 'I saw it in the vestibule this morning.'

'A letter for me? No,' Pippa said slowly. 'I wonder why Mrs Purvis didn't tell me. But how strange, since no one knows I am here.'

When at last they went indoors Pippa went to the vestibule. No letter lay on the hall table. It was at dinner that she remembered to put the question to Mrs Purvis.

'A letter? No, Philippa, there was no mail for you,' the housekeeper replied coolly. 'How could there be since you have told no one you were coming to Cambermere?'

Pippa would have been satisfied with the answer if she had not glanced up at that moment and seen Stephen looking in disbelief at Mrs Purvis, and the housekeeper's coldly challenging stare. Pippa was aware of the sudden hostility that screamed across the silent air between the older woman and her guest.

7

The sun had spread its last saffron rays along the western horizon and finally sunk from view. The low crescent moon had not yet gathered sufficient strength to illuminate the shadows of the wood where the figure of a tall young man bent attentively towards the slighter figure of the girl beside him.

They strolled in leisurely fashion, deeply engrossed in each other and with a strong bond of intimacy between them despite the twelve or fourteen inches that separated them. Suddenly the young man stopped and ran his fingers through his thick blond hair.

'I can't understand it, Pippa, any more than you can. There was oil there this morning but not this afternoon. Your housekeeper appears to know nothing about it, and yet who else can have cleaned it up? It must have been Carson or Mrs Purvis.'

'Don't forget they were out of the house all morning and so were we,' Pippa said dubiously. 'Anyone could have come up to the Hall while no one was there.'

'But who? Walters? Bainbridge? Or any one of a dozen or more people probably who hate Korvak. But why attack you, Pippa? That's what doesn't make sense to me.' Stephen shook his head, defeated by the bewildering enigma.

'Perhaps it wasn't aimed at me after all,' Pippa remarked, though she did not believe it even as she spoke the words. Neither did Stephen.

'No. Only you swim in that pool. Only you use your shower. They mean to hurt you, Pippa, though heaven alone knows why — unless it's to get back at your father. I'm still curious about Mrs Purvis — why did she lie to you?'

'About the oil, you mean? But it could truly be that she doesn't know . . . '

'No. That letter. There was definitely a letter for you. I saw it. It had a foreign stamp on it. It was lying in the vestibule this morning, and yet tonight she told you there was no letter. Now why should she say that, Pippa? Do you know? Have you ever offended her in some way that makes her want to get even with you?'

'Of course not!' Pippa protested hotly. 'We hardly ever meet and when we do she treats me civilly. And what's more, she makes it plain how much she loved and still misses my mother. If only for that she would bear no grudge against me, certainly not to the extent of wanting to harm me!'

'No, perhaps not as strong a dislike as that, but there's something that makes her less than honest with you if she denies the existence of that letter.'

'Are you sure about it, Stephen? That it was for me? Perhaps it was for her. After all, no one knew I was here.'

Stephen shook his head decisively. 'I saw the name Korvak clearly, and the foreign stamp — French, I think, though I'm not sure. Perhaps a friend in Paris was writing to you.'

A friend? Pippa started. The only people in Paris who would write to her would be Professor Garnier and Clive. The Professor was unlikely to contact her when the vacation had barely begun, and she could not believe it was Clive, after what had happened. She looked up at Stephen's darkly thoughtful face.

'I shall find that letter,' he said quietly, 'if only to prove what I say.'

Pippa smiled, touched by his concern. 'Don't worry about it, Stephen. It can't have been important. Let's not talk about it any more, but talk about you instead. I know so little about you and yet I feel you know all there is to know about me.'

He grinned broadly. 'This is likely to take some time. Shall we find ourselves a comfortable spot?'

The night hung in the sky like a magnificent deep blue tapestry scattered with glittering points of starlight. Stephen selected a grassy knoll in a clearing where the moonlight threw latticed shadows, and sprawled non-chalantly on the grass. Pippa sat beside him, drawing up her knees to her chin and clasping her arms around them to listen attentively.

Stephen's expression grew serious. 'I was joking, Pippa. There isn't really a lot to tell. My father died when I was still young and my mother worked hard to keep the two of us.

She was a wonderful woman, always optimistic and never complaining, determined to do the best she could for her only child. She used to talk to me, I remember, about how clever I would be when I was grown up, how famous and admired, and that would be all the reward she wanted. But she too died young.' There was a catch in Stephen's voice but he went on quickly. 'It was an orphanage then for me, and after that working on a farm out west. I loved the country life — the animals, riding in rodeos — but always there was this thing, this feeling deep inside me. I knew that somehow I had to get to college.'

Pippa nodded but did not speak. She could understand. He had a deep need to fulfill his dead mother's dream for him, and that was commendable.

Stephen sat up. 'Well, to cut a long story short, I got to university in the end, working nights in a drugstore and early mornings in an automobile showroom cleaning the cars, and finally I made it. I graduated from college with a degree in English studies and managed to get a job as a journalist on a local newspaper. From there I moved on to one of the big papers and finally I broke away to freelance. And here I am. Story complete, Pippa, up to today, that is.'

Pippa noticed that he made no mention of a wife or girlfriend. Presumably he had pursued his career so single-mindedly that there had been no room for that. She shied away from the thought.

'And today you are working on my father's story,' she said quietly. 'Where do you go from there?'

'After the Korvak story? I haven't really planned that far ahead. You see this one is going to be big — the most complete, exhaustive story of Alexis Korvak from the cradle — ' He stopped suddenly, as though aware of his maladroit choice of words. 'The definitive work on Korvak, Pippa. It'll sell to the syndicated newspapers and in book form to the publishers both here and back home in the States. It'll make me a fortune. After that, I can choose what I do, if I want to work at all.'

Pippa's feeling of easy closeness with him faded instantly. He no longer sounded like the warm, sympathetic Stephen she knew but a cold, calculating stranger. She glanced up at him.

'You sound as though you mean to exploit my father's story to your gain and profit,' she challenged.

Stephen nodded. 'It's no more exploitive than what he did to others,' he replied coolly. 'Notorious people are fair game.'

It was true. Famous people were open to fair comment, but would a journalist's account be fair, she wondered? Stephen had played the tape which proved that Father knew and approved of this venture, but Pippa felt uneasy, nonetheless. Nothing that Stephen said about Alexis Korvak gave any hint of sympathetic treatment of his subject. To her surprise, Stephen stretched out a hand and laid it gently on hers.

'It's something that's got to be done, Pippa, and after that the future is our own.' His voice was low, his tone sombre, but it was his words that puzzled Pippa. The touch of his hand on hers, however, awoke such a vibration in her that she could not think clearly what it was that puzzled her.

And then a cold tingle shivered in her spine. Pippa darted a quick, backward glance over her shoulder, certain that someone stood watching. But amongst the shadows under the trees nothing was to be seen, nothing moved except, perhaps, a badger or a mole on its nocturnal prowl. Stephen felt her shudder.

'What is it, Pippa? What's the matter?'

She conjured up a smile to reassure him. 'Nothing. I just had a feeling that we were being watched, that's all. You know that feeling that someone's eyes are boring into your back. It's just the darkness and the moonlight stirring my imagination. Mrs Purvis says I'm full of that.'

Without a word Stephen got up and looked about, then strode to the edge of the clearing and paced slowly round it. Pippa watched him, then got up.

'It's time we went back anyway, Stephen. It's growing chilly now.'

Stephen took her arm to guide her down the grassy slope beyond the wood, and Pippa welcomed his warm, comforting touch.

Nearing the Hall Stephen began to talk again of Mrs Purvis. 'Odd how she keeps slipping off. I wonder what she does? She's a very private, even secretive person.'

Pippa remembered the eggs, the way the housekeeper said she had to go out for more eggs when there was already a stack in the larder. 'Yes,' she agreed cautiously. 'Once I tried to follow her, but she vanished in the lane. But honestly, Stephen, what's so odd about that? You're getting as bad as me, looking desperately for a culprit, but I'm certain she's not the one. After all her years of loyalty to the family, why, it's laughable to think so!'

'I guess you're right. Okay, then, let's leave the subject for the moment.' He paused to look across the fields to the stream alongside the woods. 'I see the Dormobile has been moved — it's over there now. Bainbridge must have made them shift. Is it Korvak land they're on now?'

Pippa shrugged. 'I don't know, and if they are I don't think it matters. There's no litter or fire burning. So long as they cause no harm I don't see why they shouldn't be left in peace to enjoy the place.'

Stephen smiled down at her and she felt the pressure of his hand on her elbow. 'You can't tell how glad I am to hear you say that, Pippa. It proves you are not possessive like your father. You're a very gentle soul without a trace of malice in you.'

Pippa was about to retort in defence of her father, and then held her tongue. In the light of all she had learnt recently it began to seem that she really did not know him at all. This tall, handsome man at her side knew him perhaps better than she did. At the top of the long lawn, where the beech trees shaded a gravel walk down towards the Hall, Stephen suddenly stopped and let go of her arm. Pippa stopped too, looking up at him questioningly. Without a word he drew her to him and kissed her lightly. Pippa did not resist, nor did she respond, but when he bent his head to kiss her again, longer this time and with fire, she felt herself react with warmth, sliding her arms about his neck. Over his shoulder she could see the moonlight flickering through the branches of the trees and she began to feel dizzy, intoxicated with the fever he stirred in her.

Suddenly he broke away. 'I'm sorry, Pippa,' he muttered. 'I had no right to do that. Stupid of me. It must have been the moonlight, the magic of the woods, and your warm personality. Forgive me. I won't do it again.'

He was walking on and she had to hurry to catch up and fall in step with him. She felt ashamed and embarrassed. How could she tell him there was nothing to forgive, that she was enjoying it until he stopped so unexpectedly? He did not speak again, striding along with a set, almost savage expression on his face until they reached the terrace.

'I'm sorry,' he muttered again. 'Forgive me.'

'There's nothing to forgive,' Pippa murmured.

'But there is. I promised myself long ago that I would not become − well, involved with anyone − until I had done what I set out to do. There's no excuse, only that I found you too great a temptation for a moment. Goodnight.'

He vanished inside the Hall while she was still standing there bewildered. Forlornly she let herself in, locked the door, and went up to her room. Well, at least he had found her tempting, she consoled herself as she undressed for bed. She had stirred the man in him, however involuntarily, and far from being angered by his uninvited kiss, she was flattered. The first gentle kiss had blossomed into fire, no less ardent on his side than on hers, and for that she was grateful and glad. She could not help nursing a secret hope that perhaps, in spite of his protestations, he might be tempted again . . .

The next morning Pippa was greeted in the hallway when she came downstairs by an eager-eyed Stephen. He brandished a key before her.

'Guess what, *babam,*' he said with an air of triumph. 'Mrs Purvis was ready to go out when I came down. She said she had to go up to London to see to something to do with the redecoration of the flat and before she left she gave me the key to the east wing again.'

Pippa was surprised. Now she would be free to explore in peace. 'Odd she never mentioned she was going away,' she remarked to Stephen. 'Did she say for how long?'

'Only overnight. She'll be back tomorrow.'

Stephen declined to come into the kitchen and drink coffee while Pippa breakfasted, so she ate alone, savouring both the bacon and the prospect of freedom and the next twenty-four hours alone with Stephen. When she went to join him she found him in the first room in the east wing,

92

sitting cross-legged on the floor amongst the packing cases. As she entered he looked up and smiled.

'By the way, Pippa, I forgot to tell you that I found your letter this morning, in the cutlery drawer in the kitchen. I was right; Mrs Purvis must have forgotten she left it there.'

From his pocket he produced an envelope, a crisp, thin airmail letter, and handed it to her. He had been right. It bore a French stamp and Clive's neat handwriting. The address of the London flat had been crossed out and the Cambermere address added in untidy thick felt-tip hand-writing – the janitor's, no doubt. Pippa thrust it in her pocket.

Stephen, apparently immersed in a yellowing magazine, glanced up. 'Not going to read it now?'

'No, later.'

He gave a wry smile. 'From which I deduce it is either from a boring correspondent or a matter too personal to be opened in public.' Pippa darted him a sharp look, which he acknowledged with a shrug. 'I'm sorry, I shouldn't have said that,' he apologised.

Pippa allowed her expression to relax into a smile. 'You're quite a student of human nature, Stephen. But I shan't satisfy your curiosity as to whether you were right on either count. Tell me instead what you have found.'

She settled herself on the floor beside him, both enveloped in the pool of golden sunlight that fell across the carpeted floor from the high window. This was going to be a wonderful day, Pippa thought contentedly, and no intrusive letter from Clive was going to spoil it. Excuses, explanations, an apology even – that was all the letter would contain and she was in no hurry to reawaken the hurt.

Stephen laid aside the magazine and picked up a sheaf of photographs. Leaning close to Pippa, so close that his shoulder touched hers, he looked at the first one. It was a studio still of Carrie Hope, wide green eyes and half-open mouth betraying a childlike innocence despite the clinging black gown, so filmy it revealed the flesh beneath. The Titian hair cascaded in lustrous curls on her bare shoulders and long jet earrings were suspended from her ears.

Stephen looked curiously from the photograph to Pippa.

'You have your mother's eyes,' he remarked.

Pippa laughed. 'And there the resemblance ends, I'm afraid. She was beautiful.'

He was still staring at her closely. 'You have the same gentle air of innocence, and that is where the beauty lies, *szerelmem.*'

Pippa felt her heart flutter at his praise, but she did not know how to answer. Instead she looked over his shoulder at the next photograph. It was Father with a child on his knee in a sunlit garden. The dark child, not herself.

'Is this your sister?' Stephen asked.

'My half-sister, Irma.'

'Ah yes, I remember. Your mother had been married before, to a businessman, hadn't she? And he was eager to get her into films so he introduced her to Korvak.'

'She was a very talented dancer,' Pippa said hotly. 'Her talent and beauty were what got her into films.'

'Added to her husband's ambition. But that was his mistake,' Stephen said quietly. 'He did not allow for Korvak's weakness for beautiful women.'

'What are you saying?' Pippa demanded.

'Only what any gossip column of the time would tell you. Your father wanted her, and Jacobs, her husband, agreed to a quiet divorce in return for a consideration. Don't look so angry, Pippa. It's no reflection on you if your mother's first husband was an opportunist.'

Pippa sat silent. She had known of Mother's first marriage and of the child Irma, but she had never heard before how the first marriage ended.

Stephen was peering at the picture. 'Your half-sister looks decidedly like your mother here,' he commented. 'Did she still resemble her when she grew up?'

'I don't know,' Pippa answered briefly. 'I don't remember. She left home when I was still very young; I haven't seen her since.'

He looked at her in surprise. 'Not seen her since? In how long?'

'Oh, about twenty years. I think she ran away to marry someone Father didn't approve of and no one spoke her name after that. In fact, I rather think she must be dead.'

Pippa rose and walked to the window, vaguely irritated

by his questions. It was unkind to subject her to a form of interrogation about things which the family never discussed. Even now she could recall the way Mrs Purvis's always-reserved expression became decidedly withdrawn, almost melancholy, whenever Mother or Irma were mentioned. And once, when Pippa had chanced to mention Irma's name to Father, his gaiety had momentarily fled, to be replaced a second later with animated conversation about another matter altogether. She had been astute enough to recognise that this subject was one he preferred to ignore.

'Hey, I guess this must be yours.' Stephen's tone was surprised and pleased. Pippa went across to him. In his hand he held the dog-eared scrapbook she had cherished through all her schooldays. Even now she could remember lying face-down on the dormitory floor while the other girls were out on the games-field, lovingly pasting the latest magazine picture of Mother into place. To see it in Stephen's hand seemed an invasion of her youthful privacy. She snatched it from him impulsively. Unperturbed, he reached into the packing case for more papers.

Turning away from him Pippa stood by the window, leafing through the now rather dilapidated pages. The lovely, gentle face of Carrie Hope appeared again and again, once in the arms of a smiling Tyrone Power at a film ball, once at a banqueting table seated between Father and Edmund Purdom. In another David Niven smiled down at her while Ronald Reagan looked on benignly. The illustrious stars of her day were always admiring companions and often Father too looking proud and magnanimous.

'I can see the resemblance between you and your mother here,' Stephen remarked, holding out a glossy film-still he had taken from the case. 'The same long, slender legs.'

Pippa took the photograph from him. It was Mother in fishnet tights and a leotard with a feather boa about her neck, and alongside her the blonde, voluptuous Betty Grable.

'She was a superb dancer, you know, Stephen. She danced with Gene Kelly in one film.'

'Do you inherit her talent? Do you dance?'

Pippa laughed, the first time she could remember laughing in weeks. 'No, not really. I learnt ballet as a child, but I had no aptitude for it. A little ballroom dancing now and again, that's all.'

She stopped abruptly. Formal dances and balls at the Sorbonne were a thing of the past now, a part of a life so far removed from Cambermere that it already seemed like another planet in another time-scale. Stephen did not appear to notice her sudden change of mood. He was engrossed in reading a small notebook. Then he suddenly stuffed it in his pocket and got to his feet.

'Pippa, I've got to go out for a while. Will you be all right by yourself? I should be back by lunchtime. Tell you what, we could take a picnic lunch out into the countryside if you like.'

'Good idea,' Pippa said. 'I'll get it ready while you're out.'

He left her, without saying a word about the key or locking up the east wing. Now she could explore further.

The corridor and indeed the whole house seemed to ring very hollow once Stephen had gone. Pippa would have welcomed his company longer, but he had work to do and in any event there was the picnic to look forward to.

Putting down the scrapbook, Pippa went out into the corridor and walked along it. The first room, the Victorian parlour, looked even more desolate than before with its deepening layer of dust. She closed the door and went on. The Mississippi gambling saloon looked sombre despite its crimson plush, the sunlight outside Cambermere Hall hardly penetrating the small circular portholes. Pippa closed the door.

The third room took her breath away. It was oriental in style, with marble floor and pillars and rich drapes of tapestry and satins. Scattered cushions of rainbow colours trailed up a flight of marble steps to a dais, where a gilded throne bedecked with peacock feathers overlooked the pool in the centre of the marble floor. The water lay placid now, but Pippa could see that the miniature figure of a nymph in the centre was probably a fountain.

The court of an Indian prince or the suite of a sultan,

Pippa concluded. She could not recall any such film in which Mother had appeared but then, as Mrs Purvis had told her, these were sets from Father's films. Perhaps it was from *The Slave Girl and the Sultan*, an exotic picture made in his early years in Hollywood.

The fourth door revealed the set of yet another of his exotic eastern triumphs. It was a jungle setting, with synthetic liana vines hung from ceiling to floor and dense plastic undergrowth. A rubber python lay draped around the foot of a thick tree trunk. If Pippa remembered aright, it was Dorothy Lamour who had slunk sultrily among the scarlet hibiscus in her sarong to Father's directions.

She moved on, curious to discover what the next room would disclose. As the door swung open she saw a scene as sombre and gloomy as the others had been colourful, so dark that she had to switch on the lights. Stone walls and a heavy nail-studded door with an iron grille revealed that it was a prison, and the iron sconces set in the walls bearing unlit torches told her it was a period set. The dungeon of an old castle, no doubt. On a thick oak table lay a metal ring hung with heavy keys. Around the wall stood a variety of metal contrivances, which she gradually realised were instruments of torture − thumbscrews, a bed of nails, a rack, an iron maiden. A torture chamber. Pippa shivered. She could not remember this film, but even on a summer day the air felt cold and clammy in here. She closed the door quickly and retraced her steps to the vestibule.

Back in the main block of the hall Pippa began to feel at ease. Sunlight streamed in between the marble pillars of the hallway and flooded the shining kitchen, filling the house with cheerfulness. The shiver induced by the cardboard stone walls of the dungeon was gone, or was it simply Mrs Purvis's absence that gave her this welcome feeling of freedom? Whatever it was Pippa sliced tomatoes and cheese and cucumber to prepare a picnic lunch as she had promised, humming to herself as she worked. It was only as she wiped her hands clean on a towel that she remembered the letter still unread in her pocket.

'*Dear Philippa,*' the neat, clear handwriting read. '*I do so hope your journey home was pleasant.*' Pippa snorted. What a lame wish after giving her an abrupt brush-off!

She read on.

Clive made a few more statements about his doings since she had left, and then added, as if as an afterthought, that Joyce had decided after all not to disturb the even tenor of her life by uprooting herself and going to live in Paris.

'*So on your return, presumably when the Sorbonne re-opens, perhaps we could arrange to meet,*' he had added coolly. At once Pippa felt angered by his presumption. Now that Joyce was not going to clutter up his life after all, he evidently saw no reason why he and Pippa should not carry on where they left off. What impertinence! After all the pain he had caused her! Pippa crumpled the letter and thrust it back into her pocket. It had been an effort to shut this man out of her mind, and she was not going to let him reassert his domination over her. Clive was finished, and that was that.

It was with a positive leap of pleasure that she heard a car-horn tooting outside and knew that Stephen was back. She hurried out and climbed into the passenger seat of the dusty little Fiat beside him, her face aglow in a smile. Stephen looked thoughtful as he put the car into gear and drove off.

'Here we are,' he said at last, turning off the road down a narrow track. 'Temple Lock. It's a pretty spot for a picnic.'

Indeed it was: a serene stretch of the river where willow trees bent languidly over the water and a group of ducks paddled at a discreet distance from a majestic white swan. Stephen opened a blanket under the shade of a willow and Pippa laid out the food. Stephen returned to the car to fetch a bottle of wine and two glasses. After the meal Pippa lay back on the grass feeling utterly relaxed and content.

Stephen rolled over to look at her. 'More wine, Pippa?'

'Just a little. I'm feeling sleepy as it is. How's the work going, Stephen?'

He refilled her glass and regarded her soberly. 'From my point of view it goes well, thanks.'

She squinted up at him. 'You say that oddly. What do you mean?'

'I mean I've been reading a diary your mother wrote in the year before she died. It proves to me once again what a

98

bastard your father is, so for me it's good but I don't expect you to feel so happy about it.'

Pippa thought for a moment. He was right, of course, but at the same time her curiosity tingled, and within seconds it got the better of her. 'So that's the little book I saw you put in your pocket. What did Mother say in it?'

Stephen looked at her closely. 'Are you sure you want to hear? Wouldn't you rather treasure your illusions, Pippa?'

She sat up sharply. 'You're going to shatter them all when you finally publish your findings, so why be reticent now? Do you have the diary here? I'd like to hear how my mother felt about Father.'

Stephen took a deep breath. 'Well, at the time she was writing this diary she didn't think too highly of him. It seems she could not keep the peace between Alexis and your half-sister, Irma. Irma was sixteen and something of a handful, by your mother's account, and your father had no patience with her.'

'She was fiery, I remember,' Pippa remarked. 'There was always tension and anger. That frightened me.'

Stephen nodded. 'Your mother wrote that she was afraid that her little one would be upset by the frequent rows. She obviously loved you deeply, Pippa.'

'I never doubted it.'

'And Irma too. She tells how beautiful but how tempestuous the girl was, and says she thinks perhaps Alexis had no time for her because she was not his child. There's a part where Carrie comments how much he spoilt you yet was hard with Irma, in an effort to tame her. It's clear Carrie began to hate him for that, and as the diary goes on that hate deepened, especially when she discovered Alexis was carrying on with other women.'

'She must have had a hard time,' Pippa said sadly.

'Harder than you know. The terrible tension came to a head when Alexis not only said he was willing to let Irma go off with the young man she fancied, but insisted she left. He wasn't prepared to shelter her in his home any longer; he told Carrie she must part with Irma or with him.'

Pippa buried her face in her hands, unwilling to believe it. 'Lord, I did not think he could be so cruel,' she murmured between her fingers. 'Poor Mother.'

'Yes, poor Carrie. It seems she had never been well since your birth; not really ill, but on the other hand not in robust health. There are frequent references in the diary to the doctor visiting her. It's obvious that the whole business of Irma made her go into the decline which killed her.'

Pippa could not speak for the lump in her throat. Stephen took the diary from his pocket. 'Would you like to read it, Pippa? She speaks very touchingly and lovingly about you.'

Pippa pushed his hand away. 'No. Tell me no more, Stephen. Whatever else you unearth, please don't tell me about it.'

He put the little book away in silence and then began gathering together the remains of their meal. Pippa sat numb, not offering to help until everything had been packed and put back in the car. Then she got to her feet.

'Let's go home. I feel cold.'

The sun still beat its fierce rays on the roof of the car as they sped homeward. In the driveway Stephen pulled up.

'Look, I'm sorry, Pippa, but I've got my work to do and I can't let sentiment get in the way. I won't talk about it if you prefer.'

'Thank you, I'm glad you won't say any more.' She got out stiffly and mounted the steps to the front door. 'Have you got the key?'

He came up beside her. 'Pippa, I'll take you out to dinner tonight. Dino's in the High Street is a very good Italian restaurant, they tell me. We'll eat and drink and talk about everything except Alexis. Okay?'

'No,' said Pippa sharply. 'I don't want to see you any more today. I want to be on my own.'

Stephen opened the door and stood back. As Pippa passed him he put something into her hand. 'Here, in case you change your mind,' he said quietly. 'I'll stay out for the rest of the day.'

He turned and left. Pippa looked down at the little brown notebook in her hand, then slammed the door and ran upstairs to her room. Through the window she could hear the sound of the car receding down the drive. In a turmoil of rage and frustration she flung herself on the bed and wept.

Life was going crazy again, getting all out of hand and unruly just as it had been beginning to sort itself out in the most pleasant way. A warm and significant relationship seemed to be blossoming between her and Stephen — why did he have to destroy it all with his unwanted revelations. It was bitterly cruel. If she let him go on telling her more and more unpleasant facts about Alexis Korvak, she would have no one left. How could he, knowing she had lost her mother, try to rob her of her father too?

Pippa sobbed unrestrainedly. More than anything she needed someone to love and trust, and she was not going to let a young man, however personable, destroy her faith in her father.

She reached for a tissue on the bedside cupboard and caught sight of the diary. She picked it up and flicked over the pages. The spidery handwriting blurred before her misty eyes, but gradually she began to focus.

'My poor baby Pippa, I fear she is more disturbed than anyone realises by all that is going on, poor lamb. She hides away in the nursery for hours at a time and I sometimes find her holding conversations with a creature who is not there — Gwen she calls her.

'And the nightmares too. Alexis does not understand that he himself causes them, the way he thunders up the stairs to remonstrate with Irma. The baby has been long asleep, but soon I hear her scream in terror. I ran to her again last night, and she told me of the bogey man chasing her in a cellar. Poor darling. I'm sure it's Alexis' footsteps she hears in her sleep. She is terrified of the dark and I put a night light by her bed, though Mrs Purvis often removes it because she fears a naked candle is dangerous in a child's room. She too does not understand the baby. Despite her very evident affection for me and Irma, her patience and conscientiousness in her care of Pippa, she really does not seem to understand or to have time for her childish fears.

'It is strange that a woman can bear two daughters so unalike — one wild and beautiful, the other timid and withdrawn. It must be having different fathers, though one would have expected Alexis' child to be the fiery one

and not my gentle Pippa.'

Tears filled Pippa's eyes again as she read her dead mother's words, and she cast the diary aside and lay down on the bed. In spite of a jumble of confused thoughts about the insensitive, selfish father and the loving, helpless mother, she finally drifted off into uneasy sleep.

Dreams filtered in and out of her sleep, disturbing her mind so that she found no repose. The final dream was claustrophobic. No clear figures emerged in it, only a terrifying sense that something was trying to choke her, to rob her lungs of air. Some thick, nauseous fog seemed to be clawing its way into her nostrils so that she could not breathe.

Gasping, terrified, Pippa awoke with a start. The room was filled with a heavy, cloying scent, a perfume so powerful that it was sickening. That was what had caused her dream and made her waken. Pippa sat up, sniffing.

The square of the window framed a patch of darkness now, not sunshine. Her watch showed it was after eleven — she had slept the whole evening away. But it was the perfume that puzzled her.

She recognised it as the scent on Carrie Hope's underwear, but far more lavishly spread than the subtle scent in the drawer, as if someone had just sprayed it there. Californian Poppy, that was it.

Pippa shivered. It was as though her strong emotions about her mother had conjured her spirit to return, shrouded in her favourite perfume. She got up off the bed. That was silly thinking. There must be some more rational reason for the scent.

In an effort to dispel the clammy, pungent atmosphere which made her feel so uneasy, Pippa went across to the window and opened it. A low, lambent moon hung over the trees, bathing the grey stone of the Hall in a sombre light. Pippa looked down into the shadows, and suddenly caught her breath.

A pale wisp of light drifted across the terrace, miasmic and tenuous, and slowly came to a halt beneath the window. Not a sound stirred the stillness of the night, and as Pippa's eyes became accustomed to the dark she began to make out the shape of a human figure, clad in a pale, diaphanous robe. The figure began to move again, slowly and deliberately, like a slowed-down film-clip, and the light of the moon grew stronger. It was a girl, her pale face turned upwards and her arms held aloft as she moved in a slow, graceful dance. Her hair, dark in the pearly light, streamed about her shoulders. There was no mistaking that beautiful face, and she knew that the hair was only dark because of the feeble light. In the sun it would have shone fiery and red, for the face with its wide eyes and parted lips was unmistakably that of Carrie Hope.

Mother! Pippa gasped, her fingers gripping the window sill and the scent of Californian Poppy choking in her nostrils. Disbelief and horror froze in her veins. The figure below pirouetted in a gauzy swirl, a grey vision that blurred at the edges into the darkness, and drifted as if suspended toward the bushes. In another second it had vanished from sight.

Pippa turned away from the window, the thick miasma of perfume still choking in her throat. Alone in this great Hall, with no one near but the vision outside in the darkness, she felt a chill of dread seeping into her bones.

Was she ill, or had the ghost of Carrie Hope really returned to Cambermere? And if so, why had she come?

To protect her child? Or to warn her? Fearfully Pippa slid under the bedcovers, and wished desperately that morning would come.

8

Pippa, shaken and disturbed by her inexplicable experience barely slept for the rest of the night. Stephen did not return and it was strangely frightening to be alone in the Hall, its air of mystery now charged with menace and the fragrance that lay heavy on the air.

She wondered if indeed she had really seen the figure on the terrace and not just imagined it. She had been disturbed at the time by the dark and the loneliness and Stephen's words, and above all by that heady perfume. But not disturbed enough to hallucinate, surely.

So if the vision was real, what did it mean? Was it truly Mother, drawn back to the scene of her death because her beloved child was in need of her? Or was it some omen, a portent of evil? Pippa shuddered. She had a strange sense of foreboding, and she wished with all her heart that she were not alone in Cambermere Hall. If only Stephen were here, or even Mrs Purvis. If only the welcome sight of dawn would streak the eastern horizon.

When at last daybreak began to spread pale fingertips of light over the trees Pippa rose. Still there had been no sound of the car returning. Stephen had evidently stayed out all night, presumably at the inn he had used before. She dressed shakily and went downstairs to make coffee. As the full light of day began to flood the bright kitchen her fears of the night began to fade. Strange how darkness could breed fear and exaggerate tremors into terrors, and then the sun could banish them all in an instant.

By mid-morning Stephen had still not appeared. Pippa made up her mind to go out, far from the Hall and its claustrophobic atmosphere. But where? Not to the stables, she decided. Walters hated her father, and for that reason alone she would not go near the stables. She needed to get away from anyone and everything which had any connection with the Hall and its occupants.

West Wycombe. Those historic caves the American woman in the pub had mentioned — that's where she would go. A visit to the haunt of those eighteenth-century rakes was just the thing to divert her mind from Cambermere for a few hours. It could not be far from here, and Mrs Purvis would only have taken one car from the garage.

The keys. A quick hunt through the kitchen drawers unearthed two sets of car keys, and in the garage the little Fiat stood waiting. Mrs Purvis had evidently taken the saloon to London. Pippa climbed in, and the engine sprang to life instantly at the turn of the key.

Pippa pulled up in the high street to ask a woman traffic-warden the way. Her instructions were clear and precise, and fifteen minutes later Pippa found herself in a charming old-world village, a cluster of thatched cottages nestling beneath a village church and a rippling stream. She breathed a sigh of pleasure. On such a summer day, warm and balmy although for once the sun was not actually shining, the peace and tranquillity of the hamlet was just what Pippa sought.

Leaving the Fiat in the car-park, she climbed the steps to where the signpost indicated the caves. The way was steep, and at the top she could see a wall of rock facing her and a terrace with scattered tables and chairs, a long low shed which housed a souvenir shop, and a turnstile at the opening into the face of the rock. Intent on savouring the leisure of the day, Pippa went first into the shop and bought a guide book, then sat on the terrace to acquaint herself further with the affairs of the Hell Fire Club before going into the caves. Here, in the peace of the village, she could afford to smile at the account of the ridiculous, often obscene, antics of a crowd of rich eighteenth-century rakes who had little better to occupy their idle minds. Dressing up in monks' habits and coming here with great ceremony to the accompaniment of organ music just to feast and revel and indulge in orgies with maids both willing and unwilling – it seemed so ludicrous and unreal that the whole idea reminded her of a fantasy film-script. Alexis Korvak would have done justice to the theme. Hastily she put her father out of her mind. Nothing to do with Cambermere was to spoil today.

People passed by her table, some British and some European, for she caught snatches of French and German behind her as she flicked the pages of the guide book. The caves were evidently popular with tourists. As she looked up, she glimpsed a dark head in the crowd and caught her breath.

Geoffrey Walters – and he had Robin with him. Swiftly Pippa rose from the table and made for the pay-kiosk. If she stayed at the table he would be bound to see her, but with luck she could get away into the caves unnoticed.

Beyond the turnstile a vaulted passage in the rock curved gently downwards. The instant she set foot in it she felt cold air encircle her, and the further she hurried along the colder and damper the air became. After a moment her eyes became accustomed to the gloom, for the passage was only dimly lit at intervals. Behind her she could hear voices chattering in Spanish, and breathed a sigh of relief.

The passage broadened out suddenly into a chamber. To Pippa's surprise a voice announced, mechanical and tinny, that this was the robing room where the Hell Fire monks used to don their scarlet habits before proceeding. She hastened on to where the passage narrowed, leaving the voice to continue its tale to an empty chamber until the Spaniards arrived.

Even the walls were damp, she realised, as she put out a hand to steady her steps on the uneven ground which still sloped downwards. And there were carvings in the rock walls too. She peered closely. A demon's face leered back at her from the chalk rock. Pippa went on, catching up with a group in the next chamber who were pointing through a steel grille and talking in broad, north-country accents. Beyond the grille Pippa could see wax figures in eighteenth-century costume: two gentlemen standing by a table.

A small boy tugged his mother's hand. 'Come on, Mam. There's a skeleton somewhere I know because Jimmy told me. Come on, let's find the skeleton, Mam.'

Pippa left them behind. A little further on, the passage-way spread itself out into a series of tunnels. She followed one which twisted and looped, intersecting with other passages. She went on, as far as she could from the entrance and Geoff Walters. Another mechanical voice described the labyrinth as 'the catacombs', and shortly after that the passages joined into one again. Presently it opened out into a huge chamber, where twenty or so tourists stood looking about them at the waxwork effigies contained in many small cells which ran around the walls of the huge cavern. From yet another taped voice Pippa learnt that this was the banqueting room, and the cells used to be screened by curtains when the 'monks', sated with gargantuan meals and copious wine, indulged in their lascivious orgies. With a squeal of delight the little north-country boy found his waxwork skeleton beyond the grille in a cell.

Pippa shivered. It was extremely cold and damp down here in the bowels of the earth. She must have walked a quarter of a mile underground, downhill all the way. She tried to visualise silent figures in blood-red robes filing down here in candlelight procession, organ music reverberating through the great subterranean hollow, but it was not easy with so many chattering folk in modern dresses and sandals and shirtsleeves. It must have been eerie once, terrifying even, for those unwilling maidens brought here to be ravished. But she could sense no chill of fear here now, only the cold darkness. Nevertheless she gave a start of alarm when a voice suddenly spoke her name.

'Hello, Philippa.'

She turned to see Walters looking down at her gravely, no hint of a smile curving his lips. She stared in amazement. How could he have caught up with her?

Robin's excited little face broke in on them. 'Aren't you glad I made you run, Uncle Geoff? It's super down here, isn't it? And there's that skeleton, come and see.'

'Say hello to Miss Korvak, Robin,' his uncle reproached him.

'Oh, I'm sorry. Hello, Miss Korvak.'

'Hello, Robin. Show me the skeleton, will you?'

He took her hand and almost dragged her towards the grille. Pippa was aware of Walters coming to stand behind her, and wondered how she was going to get away. Robin was chattering happily, and she could see Walters' face soften at the boy's evident pleasure. When Robin had finished telling her his somewhat garbled version of the Hell Fire Club's activities, he looked up at her thoughtfully.

'Do you like spooky things too?' he asked.

Pippa nodded and crossed her fingers. She did not, and especially the strange happenings at Cambermere Hall, but she could not cloud his happiness by appearing a wet blanket.

Robin was approving. 'I thought you did. I told Uncle Geoff you were a nice lady the day you came to ride Alouette. Are you really going to ride Copper too?'

She glanced at Walters, who looked away. 'Perhaps,' she said. 'We'll see. I'm rather busy at the moment.'

'He can be a bit awkward at times, but I bet you could manage him. Uncle Geoff doesn't think so but I heard him say you were a Korvak and used to having your own way. So you probably could ride Copper, couldn't you?'

'Come on, Robin. Don't forget we've got to get to the dentist this afternoon,' Walters cut in. 'I told you we wouldn't be able to stay here long.'

'Oh, just let me see the river before we go,' Robin pleaded, and the cunning smile on his young face jolted Pippa's memory. *Alexis Korvak:* He wore exactly that look in some of his photographs, a smile calculated to charm and cajole. She felt suddenly sick. Until this moment she had forgotten Robin was her father's son.

Robin skipped away towards the far end of the chamber and Walters strode after him. Pippa began to hurry back the way she had come.

Very few visitors were coming downhill towards her. It was lunchtime, she realised. Her hurried footsteps began to slow after a time, for the return route was all uphill. The way was clear until she reached the labyrinth. Here she hesitated, then chose one passage.

'The reason for Sir Francis' construction of the catacomb is not clear,' the mechanical voice was saying. Pippa turned from one passage to another, and began to realise she was lost. 'Possibly it was meant to confuse intruders, but more likely he was endeavouring to imitate the catacombs of Rome which he had visited.'

The taped voice was growing fainter. She had evidently gone further into the labyrinth, and she began to feel alarmed. Down here, alone in the chill, damp atmosphere, it was eerily frightening. At yet another intersection of the low passageways, she paused.

Suddenly the spotlamps overhead went out, plunging her into utter darkness and Pippa gasped. Don't panic, you fool, she told herself fiercely, they'll come on again in a moment. She reached out a hand to find the clammy rock wall and moved forward cautiously. Seconds passed and still the lights did not come on. Sweat began to break out on Pippa's brow. Suddenly it came to her that this situation was her lifelong nightmare realised: lost in impenetrable darkness, shut in underground. All it lacked was the thud of approaching footsteps.

Even as she thought it, the sound of footsteps came to her ears, distant and hollow but closing rapidly. Recognition that this was the nightmare complete made the perspiration begin to trickle down her neck and fear choked in her throat. Then she heard a voice calling.

'*Philippa!*'

It was Walters! Unreasoning terror made Pippa hurry forward, away from the sound, until her foot caught a rock and she stumbled. Dear heaven, don't let him catch me, here alone in the black void and helpless, she prayed, but at every step the sound of the pursuing footsteps came closer. Pippa leaned back against the clammy rock wall, panting.

'Philippa! Where are you?'

At that second light splashed out, revealing the face of Walters within yards of her. Pippa's fear vanished when she saw he was leading Robin by the hand. With the boy he would hardly dare to harm her.

'So there you are,' he said. 'I guessed you'd get lost and then when the lights went out . . . Well, anyway, now they're on again we'll show you the way, won't we, Robin?'

Walters spoke little after that as they retraced their steps up towards the entrance. He had little opportunity, it was true, for Robin was talking eagerly all the way about his earlier visit to the caves. Once outside the turnstile the heat of the day, although it still remained sunless, struck Pippa forcibly. It was wonderful to be warm again, out in the air where she could breathe and away from the nightmare of the dark. Unwilling to speak to Walters, ashamed now of her earlier panic, she thanked Robin instead for his guidance.

'You will come and see us soon, won't you?' Robin asked shyly. She nodded.

'Yes, I'll see you soon. Goodbye, and thanks again. I couldn't have managed without you.'

The boy was still smiling with pride but Walters' expression remained impassive as she turned away to go down to the car-park. She had been stupidly alarmed by the dark, she thought as she drove away out of the little village, but the doubt still lingered in her mind about Geoff Walters. Had his intentions really been chivalrous, trying to find her to lead her out, or might events have taken a different turn if the lights had not suddenly come on again, and if Robin had not been there?

Speculation was idle, she knew, but she still remembered with a shiver how terrified she had been for a few minutes down there under the chalk rocks of the Buckinghamshire countryside. As she sped away through the lanes thick with elm and beech trees on either side, she realised she was hungry. She would drive into High Wycombe and buy something to eat.

In the town centre she managed to find a parking meter and walked through the Hexagon, the indoor shopping arcade. Here she purchased some rolls, fruit and a carton of apple juice, feeling happier now that she was surrounded by people busily pursuing their errands. For a time she sat on a bench, munching a crisp roll, then went back to the car. She would continue her lunch in the countryside, for the sun was at last beginning to shine.

Nearing Marlow, she swung the car off to the right, in the general direction of Cambermere and the river, to find a pleasant spot on the river bank. The lattice of interlocked branches overhead spattered sunlight on the windscreen in sporadic bursts, momentarily dazzling her, and she realised with a start that there was a figure on the road in front of her. She slammed on the brakes before she recognised it was Arthur Bainbridge waving his thick arms. As the car stopped, he came alongside the open window.

'Recognised the car and saw it was you,' he grunted without even a greeting. 'Wanted to see you anyway. Come along up to the house and I'll get us a drink.'

He turned to go up a drive, which Pippa could see led to a long, low house. He had given her no opportunity to refuse, so she pulled the Fiat up on to the grass verge and then got out and followed him. At the top of the drive she saw a long, rambling farmhouse, whitewashed and neatly painted. Bainbridge stood in an open doorway and beckoned her in.

She found herself in the kitchen, which was large and

110

airy, with a stone-flagged floor and a deal table in the middle surrounded by several wheel-backed chairs. Genuine old farmhouse-style, she thought with admiration, even to the copper pans gleaming on the wall and the Aga range.

'What will you have to drink, Philippa?' Bainbridge asked. His red-veined eyes rested on her in a way that made Philippa feel uncomfortable. 'Sherry? Gin?'

'I'd rather have lemonade or some orange juice, if you don't mind, Mr Bainbridge.'

'Arthur,' he corrected. 'Remember, I told you to call me Arthur.'

So he had, in an attempt at familiarity which had led to an instant proposal of marriage. Pippa hoped he was not going to mention that again. He took a bottle of orange juice from the refrigerator and poured two large glasses, then plopped in several ice cubes.

'Let's drink it in the parlour,' he said, leading the way out of the kitchen. The parlour was an equally pleasant room, sunlit and airy, with chintz curtains and chair covers, a pretty Pembroke table by the wall with an inlaid tracery of brass, a long sideboard which looked decidedly seventeenth century and a lovely brass carriage clock on the mantelpiece and above it a flintlock of ebony and silver. In the passage beyond she glimpsed a grandfather clock, which even now was whirring like an ancient bronchitic as a prelude to striking the hour.

'It's a lovely house,' she commented to Bainbridge. He nodded his thanks of her approval. 'Have you collected all this furniture?'

'Aye, and it's all genuine antique, none of your reproduction stuff. Some of the pieces were here when I bought it. That's why I wanted you to come.'

'I don't understand. You wanted me to see your house and furniture?'

'Aye, I wanted you to see what you'd be getting if you agree to my proposition. You'll have a good home, nowt artifical or make-shift — but the real thing. You can see over the rest of the house before you go, and if there's owt else you want I'll see you get it. I'm a man of my word, Philippa, and for you there'll be only the best.'

Pippa put her glass down. 'Now look here, Mr Bainbridge, you must realise – '

'Arthur,' he interrupted.

'You must realise that a proposal of marriage at one's first meeting is not really something one can take seriously.'

'I meant it seriously, as you should well know. Tell me, has anyone bothered you up at the Hall yet?'

'Bothered me?'

Bainbridge slapped his glass down on the table testily. 'Have you forgotten already? I warned you you'd need protection if you was to stay in Cambermere, and I was willing to offer that protection in return for marriage. Are you telling me that you've been here above a week already and no one has yet shown you how much you Korvaks are hated? Hasn't anyone harassed you or even threatened you?'

Pippa looked away from his challenging blue gaze, reluctant to admit what he wanted to hear. 'So far as I can gather there are a few who had cause to dislike Father,' she replied slowly. 'Is it true he acquired your land by cheating at cards?'

'Who told you that?' Bainbridge's fresh complexion reddened even more. 'Look here, I gave you time to consider my proposal and you've kept me dangling. I'm not used to being messed about, particularly by a chit of a girl. I've shown you you've everything to gain by marrying me and nowt to lose, now give me my answer. Will you marry me?'

'No I will not.' Pippa rose purposefully, angered by his threatening, domineering tone. 'Now good day to you, Mr Bainbridge. Thank you for the drink.'

He stood glowering in the open doorway as she retreated down the drive. 'You'll be sorry, mark my words,' he called after her. 'God help me, you'll be sorry!' Pippa leapt into the Fiat and drove off at speed, angry with Bainbridge and with herself. It was high time she stopped letting people affect her so deeply. Once it had been Clive, now she was letting suspicion and distrust of her new acquaintances lead her into fear.

The intended picnic by the river completely forgotten,

she drove into the grounds of Cambermere Hall, its stately grace imposing in the afternoon sunlight. Funny, she thought, she had left the Hall behind so as to forget its occupants and the threats it seemed to hold out to her, only to run into Walters and Bainbridge. It had not been a very successful outing, to say the least.

The Hall was strangely still and silent when Pippa unlocked the door and let herself in. Then she remembered she had left the remainder of her picnic rolls and fruit in the car, but she simply shrugged. She was no longer hungry anyway. For a time she lingered in the vestibule, noting the way the shafts of sunlight fell between the seven marble pillars grouped in a circle and played vividly on the mosaic pattern in the floor between them. She eyed the door to the east wing, and then crossed to try it. It was locked, and Stephen had the key.

She went first to the kitchen and then called his name up the great staircase. She remembered there had been no sign of his dusty little Fiat when she had driven round to the stable yard. He was taking her at her word and keeping his distance. Pippa began to regret her hastiness. She would have liked Stephen to be here now, to hear his opinion of her exploits. Now, after the way she had spoken, he would be in no hurry to seek her out again.

Suddenly, and for no apparent reason, she had a strange, unpleasant feeling and a tingling at the nape of her neck; the feeling of someone walking over one's grave. Or of being watched. She spun round quickly, the shafts of sunlight between the pillars dazzling her for a moment but not blinding her entirely to the tall black figure at the top of the staircase. With a quick intake of breath she stepped forward, shading her eyes.

'Who is that? Who's there?'

A smooth voice rippled down the stairs, calm and almost sepulchral in the great void: 'Philippa, my dear girl, it's only me.'

It was Mrs Purvis, dressed in black as she almost always was, and looking far taller than usual from this angle. Pippa breathed a sigh of relief as the figure began to glide down the stairs. 'Oh, Mrs Purvis! I didn't know you were back. I didn't see the car.'

'I left the car in the village because the battery seemed to be going flat. I walked up,' the housekeeper explained, her keen eyes inspecting Pippa closely. 'What have you been doing with yourself today?'

'Oh, I went out. To the West Wycombe caves.'

There was something different about her, but at first Pippa could not place it. Then she realised: the housekeeper was wearing a pair of pendant black earrings. It was unusual for her to sport something so feminine, but to Pippa's mind they only added to the woman's funereal starkness. They were long and thin, just like their owner, and with a glittering brittleness about them. Pippa could not help remarking on them.

'I like your earrings, Mrs Purvis. Did you buy them in London?'

For a second the housekeeper's searching eyes were veiled by fluttering lashes. 'In London? Ah, no. They were a gift, from a friend.'

'They're very pretty.'

'Jet, my dear. Real Whitby jet. Victorian, I believe. I've always wanted some although I don't go in for jewellery as a rule. Still, a treasured gift from a treasured friend. My Miss Carrie used to have some just like them.'

That was it, Pippa realised. Mother was wearing long black earrings in that photograph. That was why Mrs Purvis admired them so, because her adored mistress had once worn ones very similar. Pippa softened towards her.

'They're very pretty, and tasteful,' she commented.

'Of course. Miss Carrie always had perfect taste,' Mrs Purvis said with a touch of asperity. 'I'll put the kettle on now if you would like a cup of tea.'

Pippa followed her to the kitchen. Mrs Purvis rattled the kettle under the kitchen tap. 'Did you enjoy the caves, Philippa? I've never been there myself.'

Pippa smiled. Her fears of the afternoon now seemed unreasonable and childish. 'Not really. I got lost in what they call the catacombs, and if it hadn't been for Geoff Walters and young Robin I might have been there still. They led me out.'

'Walters?' the housekeeper repeated. 'I hope you

weren't too friendly towards him. It would be foolish to encourage him, knowing how he feels about the Korvaks.'

'He feels no more strongly against Father than Bainbridge does,' Pippa pointed out.

'Did you see him too?' Pippa could see disapproval shaping in her face again. 'He's an even less desirable character.'

'He asked me again to marry him so as to protect me,' Pippa asserted. 'He can't dislike me too much.'

'He wants Korvak land, that's all. And do you think you need protection Philippa? Against what, and whom?' The housekeeper's cold eyes challenged hers.

Pippa stammered, confused: 'You've just said – Walters hates the Korvaks, and someone *did* put oil on the pool steps. Someone does want to harm me.'

'Nonsense. Imagination, as I said. You must be careful, Philippa, or you'll become paranoid, imagining someone is out to harm you. Paranoid, what your father kept accusing Miss Carrie of being.' She bit her lip suddenly.

'Did he, Mrs Purvis? Why, what did Mother think?'

'Nothing. Forget it. It's all long ago now.'

'But you said it, Mrs Purvis,' Pippa insisted. 'Are you saying my mother's nervous condition was brought about by Father? And if so, how? What did she think he was doing?'

'Nothing, I told you! It's true he was hard on her, true she suffered from her nerves as a result, poor lamb. But she didn't imagine things; she wasn't paranoid or schizophrenic or any of the dreadful things he said. But he wanted her to think she was going crazy so he could get his own way. All I'm saying is that you'd better guard against being driven the same way with your wild dreams of being threatened and all. There was no oil in the pool, no one in your room at night – it's all your fancy, Philippa. Rest and quiet, that's what you need.'

There had been no one in my room at night, she had said, and Pippa remembered suddenly the perfume and the vision in the garden last night. Perhaps the housekeeper was right and she was simply overwrought. But that perfume? The memory of it choked Pippa's nostrils even now.

The housekeeper was standing at the stove with her back to Pippa, waiting for the kettle to boil. The question came unbidden to Pippa's lips and before she could think she had spoken it. 'Mrs Purvis, I keep smelling Californian Poppy in my room. Strongly, and always at night. Did you know how it comes to be there?'

She saw the housekeeper's back stiffen slightly before she answered. 'I showed you the drawer where your mother's things are . . . '

'It's much stronger than that. Almost as if someone sprayed it freely in the air.'

'Well, yes, I do spray it sometimes, but not often. I haven't done it since you came.' The woman's voice was almost defensive. Pippa was curious.

'Why do you do that, Mrs Purvis? Is it because it reminds you of Mother?' she asked gently. Mrs Purvis turned quickly, her dark eyes glittering like her earrings.

'Because it was her room and because for me she will always be there. Because I have to cleanse the air and purify it, the way it was when she was still here. It has to be sanctified after strangers have been in her room, alien, unclean presences who defile her memory! I do it for Miss Carrie, my pure and saintly mistress!'

Pippa stared at her, stunned. 'Alien presences? Unclean? Do you mean me, Mrs Purvis? For heaven's sake, I'm her daughter!'

The housekeeper's eyes blazed from a white face, 'Anyone who invades her room defiles it because no one else can hope to attain her purity and goodness. Oh yes, I know some may say she too was defiled by the way her first husband prostituted her beauty and sold her to Korvak. They both used her shamelessly, exposing her to the lustful eyes of men, but whatever they did to her my Miss Carrie stayed untouched, pure in heart and soul as only an angel can be.'

Her words were quietly-spoken but venom glittered in them like an icicle. Pippa stared at her aghast. Mrs Purvis's fierce loyalty and devotion to her mistress were hysterical to the point of blasphemy.

'But you didn't spray her perfume last night because you weren't here,' Pippa went on quietly. 'But someone did.

Either that, or my mother came back — but why?'

'Came back? What makes you say that?' Mrs Purvis demanded.

Pippa regarded her levelly. 'Because I could swear I saw her, down in the garden, dancing in the moonlight.'

The housekeeper stared hard at her for a moment as though she were trying to lay bare Pippa's soul, and the look in her dark eyes made Pippa quail. 'She did come back, didn't she?' Pippa persisted. 'She did come back — but why?'

The housekeeper's angular face appeared hazy through the cloud of steam as she poured boiling water into the teapot, and Pippa could see a faint smile curving her thin lips. 'You think she too wants to protect you, like Mr Bainbridge?' Mrs Purvis asked, and Pippa could detect the edge of irony in her tone.

'Why not? She would not wish to harm me,' Pippa said defensively.

'You think not? I would not be too sure.'

'Mrs Purvis! What on earth makes you say such a thing?' Pippa was shocked. The housekeeper put down the kettle and eyed her coldly. Pippa rushed on. 'I've seen her diary! I know she loved me!'

'So she did, until your father forced her to part from her elder daughter.' The words were icy.

'Irma? You mean when he made Irma leave? But Mother would not stop loving me just because she lost her!'

Mrs Purvis shrugged. 'Oh, she never said as much. She was too gentle and kind to hurt anyone, but could you blame her if secretly she came to hate the child she was obliged to keep in place of the one she was forced to part with? The child of a man who was a brute to her? If she came back to you, Philippa, I should be concerned if I were you, not too ready to believe it was a sign of good.'

'You're wrong!' Pippa cried, ignoring the cup of tea the housekeeper held out. 'You say that, yet you profess to love her!'

'Profess?' The housekeeper put down the cup and drew herself upright. 'I do not *profess* to love, Philippa. I worship her now as I worshipped her then, with the kind of love you will never know or understand.'

Pippa could only stare at her. She was mad, inhuman, to be so obsessed by a dead woman, and Pippa resented the way she seemed to try to exercise some kind of proprietorial right over Mother. It was no use arguing with her, carried away as she was with her idolatry. Angry and sickened, Pippa rushed from the kitchen.

Tears pricked her eyelids and her first impulse was to rush to her room, but in the hallway she hesitated. It was Carrie Hope's room, not hers, and no doubt when Mrs Purvis had appeared suddenly at the top of the stairs she had just been to that room to tidy it and perhaps even, as she put it, to purify it. Pippa would not go there, not yet.

At that moment the front door opened and Stephen strode in, his handsome face set and unsmiling. Pippa felt a rush of warmth and moved towards him.

'Stephen! Oh, Stephen!'

He stood in front of her, stiff and erect. 'Pippa, I want to talk to you. Come into the music room.'

She followed him, glad at heart to see one sympathetic person at last. Once inside the music room he closed the door and turned to her; afternoon sunlight from the high window surrounded his tall silhouette.

'Pippa, it's no good. I've been allowing myself to be diverted from what I came here to do. Now I've made up my mind to ignore everything else.'

'Of course you must, Stephen, and I won't prevent you. Indeed, I'll help all I can, so long as you don't expect me to hurt my father.' She said the words gently, persuasively, anxious for his friendship at least. He jerked away from her and leant on the grand piano.

Pippa watched him, as anxious premonition leaping in her. The great white piano with its gilt candelabra and the Aubusson carpet seemed to lose their colour and fade as Stephen spoke.

'You don't understand. I must hurt your father — I *want* to hurt him. It's been my plan for so many years, and it kept me and my mother going when times were hard. It was her dying wish that I should carry this thing through, and I will. Pippa I'm going to expose him utterly. He was, and is, a bastard, an *ördög,* and now I think I can prove he was a murderer too. I must and will do it.'

118

Pippa was dismayed. 'But we knew of that — he was tried and acquitted! And it was years ago, when he was a youth.'

Stephen turned slowly. 'Not that, Pippa. I think he murdered again — and I aim to find the proof. I aim to clear my father of the shame that was attached to his name, and to blacken Alexis Korvak's name in revenge. I'm sorry. There's nothing you can do to stop me. My mind is made up.'

Pippa's fingers flew to her lips. 'Oh no! Stephen, no, you can't! You must not! Does our friendship mean nothing to you?'

He smiled wryly, but there was no trace of humour in his face. 'Friendship or any other commitment must give way to justice.'

Fury rose in Pippa. 'Do as you feel you must, Stephen Lorant, but I hope I never set eyes on you again! I never want to see you as long as I live!'

She turned and fled from the music room, tears of rage and frustration blinding her now. Like a crazed thing she ran from the house, down the drive and away, not knowing where she was going nor caring. Flight was instinctive, essential, to escape what her mind refused to accept. Mrs Purvis's declaration, so closely followed by Stephen's insistence, were facts Pippa yearned to disown, to deny, and since that was impossible, to escape.

She ran madly, unseeing and uncaring, until a white gate suddenly appeared before her: Walters' riding stables. She pushed open the gate and rushed up the drive. Ride, that was what she would do, ride in wild, headlong flight where the dizzying sensation of excitement and exhilaration would drive all else from her mind and bring peace, for a few moments at least.

Panting, she reached the stable yard and saw Robin standing outside a stall, his young face full of concern.

'Oh, Miss Korvak! Copper seems to be upset and Uncle Geoff's gone out. I think there must be a mouse in his stall or something.'

She looked through the open upper half of the stable door. Copper, already saddled, was snorting and moving around in agitation, every now and again snorting and

119

whinnying.

'Uncle Geoff was going to ride him, but Mr Bainbridge called him away,' Robin said. 'I don't know where he is now.'

'Telephone Bainbridge. Leave Copper to me.'

The boy ran off obediently towards the house. Pippa laid a hand on the lower door and began murmuring words to the horse.

'There now, boy, take it easy,' she said soothingly. 'There's nothing to get excited about.'

He seemed to grow calmer, and Pippa opened the door cautiously and moved towards him. He backed away nervously, smelling that she was a stranger, but Pippa knew that he must sense that she was calm and in control.

'There boy, there,' she murmured and reached up for his bridle. He let her take it, regarding her with curiosity and distrust. There was no sign of a mouse or a rat, or anything which could have alarmed him. As she peered about in the gloom of the stall, the door suddenly slammed shut and she heard the sound of a bolt.

She turned in dismay, resisting the temptation to shout angrily lest she alarm Copper again. Whoever it was, it was a damn fool trick to shut her in the dark with a capricious, temperamental horse like Copper in his present mood. Any second he could decide to dislike her and start to rear up, and in this confined space she could not escape being trampled. Then alarm leapt in her. Perhaps it was the same person who had put oil on the pool steps . . . Copper pawed the ground restively and Pippa tried to slow her thundering heartbeat as she crooned soft words to him. It was not easy with the anger that blazed in her.

Suddenly she heard the bolt slide back and daylight streamed in again. With a surge of relief she saw Robin's head peer over the stable door.

'Who locked the door, Miss Korvak?'

'I don't know. Let me out, will you, Robin? Is your uncle coming?'

'Mr Bainbridge's housekeeper said he's not there, so he must be meeting Mr Bainbridge somewhere else.'

'Never mind. Copper only needs exercise,' she said as she led the horse out. 'I'll ride him for a while and then bring him back.'

She adjusted the girth and shortened the stirrups and then mounted Copper smoothly, still speaking softly and confidently to him. She saw the boy watching her as she rode away across the cobbled yard.

Once out in the fields she gave Copper his head, both animal and rider eager to give full vent to their emotions. Pippa forgot the horse as she galloped, bursting only with her own anger and frustration. Walters, Bainbridge and Mrs Purvis had all conspired to enrage her, but Stephen was the last straw. Even the ill-wisher who had locked her in the stable with an animal half-crazed with fear seemed of less importance than Stephen's disloyalty. She had come to trust and even to — to like him, she told herself angrily — and he had betrayed her just when she needed him most.

The breeze fanned her cheeks as Copper sped along, tossing her long hair wildly about her, but even the summer wind could not cool her anger. *I hate him, I hate him,* she muttered savagely to herself, and she was so choked with her own fury and sense of betrayal that she did not notice that Copper was heading straight for the wall.

At the last second before he jumped, he suddenly whinnied and reared. Pippa saw the ground flash past her face and then the blue sky racing past her. She knew that she was sailing through the air, clear of the stirrups and over the wall. It all happened with the same slow-motion clarity of a delayed film-run. She could even see, on the far side of the wall, the scattered rocks and pebbles and realised in that instant that there was nothing she could do to avoid falling on them. A million sparks of multi-coloured fire scorched across her brain, and then utter darkness enveloped her.

9

As consciousness returned, Pippa lay there, un-comprehending, and then wished desperately that she could turn back to the womb-like comfort of oblivion.

Voices murmured quietly about her, but at first they were no more real than flickering ghosts in the empty corridors of her mind. Where her head should be there was just one enormous ache, and for a time she lay, eyes closed, trying to overcome the pain and reorientate her disordered brain.

There were also confused sounds of footsteps and metallic clinks. With an effort she sought to remember where she was. Not Cambermere Hall, she thought hazily, for the sounds were wrong.

'Miss Korvak?' a quiet voice interrupted. 'Are you awake?'

Even more puzzling. The voice was totally strange. Pippa nodded, without opening her eyes.

'That's good. There's someone here to see you.'

More footsteps, the ring of a bell, someone coughing, and then at last a remembered sound.

'Philippa? How are you now, my dear?' It was Mrs Purvis's voice, and Pippa's confusion began to slow down from a whirl of something more like normality.

'Where am I?' she murmured.

'In hospital. But don't worry. The doctors say no bones are broken. A spot of concussion, that's all, but you had a nasty fall. It was lucky Mr Walters found you so quickly.'

Walters. Copper. The fall at the stone wall – it all came back. She shuddered as she remembered those strewn rocks on the ground. No wonder her head ached. She heard the sound of a chair being pulled forward, then Mrs Purvis

122

spoke again.

'It gave us all quite a turn, I can tell you, but as I say, you were lucky. You could have lain up there by the woods all day and all night, hidden by the wall, if Mr Walters hadn't gone out to look for you. He warned you that horse was too big and powerful. He got worried when the boy told him you'd gone out on Copper and you weren't back. Very lucky. The doctors say they only need to keep you in overnight for observation. That's the usual procedure for concussion.'

Pippa lay silent, barely listening and only wishing that Mrs Purvis would stop talking and let her fall asleep again. Consciousness brought with it only returning worry about Walters and Stephen — and that vile headache.

'Was there anyone with you when you fell?' Mrs Purvis asked. Pippa moved her head from side to side slowly, and even that hurt.

'Had you been with anyone before? Was anyone in sight?'

'No.' Even that was a tremendous effort.

'So you saw no one after you left the stables until you fell?' Oh, why did the woman persist so.

'No.'

'And do you know how you came to fall? Did the horse refuse, or was it your own clumsiness?'

Pippa hated her. The housekeeper could be cruel in her choice of words, and why on earth should it matter to her how the accident occurred?

'Something startled Copper, I think. A rabbit or something, that's all.'

The effort of replying had cleared the last of the fog from Pippa's brain. She was fully awake now, troubled only by the thudding ache, and slowly she opened her eyes.

'Is it night?' she queried doubtfully. 'Is the room in darkness, Mrs Purvis? I can see nothing.'

She heard the scrape of the chair on the floor. Mrs Purvis's cold fingers touched hers. 'Are you sure, Philippa? Can you see nothing?'

'Not a thing. Is it night?'

Mrs Purvis breathed a slow sigh. 'No. It is full daylight. I'll fetch the sister.' Pippa lay stunned. Whatever fears she had felt before, they were as nothing to the panic that leapt in her now. Full daylight, did the housekeeper say, and yet for Pippa there was only impenetrable blackness? Something was wrong, terribly wrong, and before swift footsteps pattered to the bedside the full horror of the situation had crashed in on her: the fall had robbed her of her sight. *She was blind.*

'Now, Miss Korvak what's this I hear?' It was the pleasant, unruffled woman's voice which had first awoken Pippa. 'Can you see me?'

Pippa groaned.

'Can you see the sunlight at the window?'

Pippa turned and buried her aching head in the pillow. Distantly she heard the nurse's voice. 'Don't upset yourself, my dear. There's probably a very simple reason after that fall. I'll ask the doctor to have a look at you. Until he comes, just lie still and rest.'

Retreating footsteps pattered away down the ward, and Pippa heard Mrs Purvis's murmured questions, then silence. Evidently the Sister had made the housekeeper leave the ward, and for that at least Pippa was grateful. It was terrifying enough to recognise her plight without that thin voice rattling on. Blind panic rose in her. How on earth was she going to cope with life, sightless? The prospect was too horrifying to contemplate, and she felt herself begin to shiver uncontrollably.

More footsteps, and then a deep, masculine voice spoke. 'Let's have a look at you, Miss Korvak. Tell me about it.'

Pippa muttered garbled words and heard a click. 'Look up, towards the ceiling,' the voice commanded gently. She did so, wishing with all her heart that the ceiling would magically appear, but it did not. It was like being back in the catacomb when the lights went out.

The masculine voice was murmuring quiet words at the foot of the bed now and the nurse was answering, but Pippa could not catch their words. She clenched her fists in fear, then a cool hand pushed up her sleeve.

'A little prick, Miss Korvak. It will make you feel better.'

She felt the needle slide into her arm. Of course, they were sedating her to counteract the shock, but that was useless. She felt angry and helpless. Even if she became unconscious again she would only have to face the horror once more when she awoke. It was only delaying the terrible truth. She seized the cool hand as it was about to withdraw.

'Am I blind, nurse? What did the doctor say?' She could not help the fear, the childish tremulousness in her voice.

The Sister's reply was meant to be reassuring. 'He cannot see any reason for your condition so he'll ask the ophthalmic consultant to have a look at you. Now you just lie and rest. That's the best thing you can do right now.'

No evident cause, Pippa thought, as the nurse went away up the ward again. She digested the information, trying to extract a gleam of hope from it. If no physical evidence was visible, perhaps the darkness was only temporary, perhaps a shock-reaction, like a black-out, which would pass. It was only a glimmer of hope, but it was something to which she could cling. Her whole mind rebelled against submitting to perpetual darkness — for darkness was where all terrors lurked for her, and always had done.

Sleep came uninvited, but when Pippa awoke the terror returned. Open or closed, her eyes still saw only deep black velvet. Everyday noises around her told her that life was continuing as usual for others, and she felt desperately lonely. She pulled the bedcovers over her face, trying to find comfort in the warm haven of darkness as she had as a child, but the terrible feeling of fear was not so easily banished. Inwardly she prayed for someone to turn to, and for a moment her thoughts rested on Stephen. His low, vibrant voice and gentle touch would have been reassuring. But he too was an enemy now. There was no one left to calm the way and chase the nightmare.

'Tea, Miss Korvak?' Pippa emerged from the sheets. 'Do you take sugar?'

She must make an effort to behave like a human being, however terrified she was. She nodded in the direction of the cheerful voice. 'Thanks. No sugar.'

Cold china pressed against her hand and she groped for the handle while the nurse waited patiently.

'Bread and butter? There's raspberry jam today. I'll do it for you.'

Moments later she heard a plate being placed before her

on a surface, and her fingertips revealed to her that it was an overbed table. Carefully she placed her cup on it. Metallic sounds came to her ears — a trolley where the tea was poured, she guessed.

After the tea things had been cleared away the nurse came back. 'Mr Hunter-Price, the eye-specialist, is on his way to see you, Miss Korvak. He'll be here in a moment.'

Pippa heard the deep voice at the end of the ward and the firm tread as he approached. His words to Pippa were few, his examination of her eyes brief — almost perfunctory. He breathed deeply.

'I'll need to do some tests. Send Miss Korvak to the ophthalmic department right away, will you, Sister?'

A few minutes later Pippa was transferred to a wheel-chair. The journey from the ward, along corridors and then downwards in a lift was confusing, like being hurtled along in a car at night, without headlights, on an unlit road. Then she was moved from the wheelchair to a seat and asked if she could see lights flashing. Electrodes, the technician told her, would now be placed on her head and face while further tests were done and readings taken. One set of the electrodes were placed on her eyeballs and though not painful, it felt unnatural not to be able to close her eyes. The whole proceedings had an unreal quality about them and Pippa wished heartily that any second she might awake to find it had all been a ghastly dream.

When the tests were at last concluded, the technician told her cheerily that Mr Price would see her again.

Once more the specialist spoke little, and as she rose from the examination couch Pippa could contain her anxiety no longer.

'Well?' she asked timidly. 'How bad is it?'

'I can't tell you yet. I've still to see the results of the tests when the calculations are complete. Don't fret, my dear. We'll let you know in the morning.'

The morning? A whole long night still to endure the agony of not knowing whether this fearful darkness was only temporary? Pippa could hardly bear the thought of it. The nurse, helping her out of the wheelchair and back into bed evidently noticed her stricken face.

'Cheer up, love. It's nearly visiting time and your friend

will be back to see you then.'

Mrs Purvis. The thought of her spare, angular frame and unsmiling face did little to cheer Pippa, and with a sudden return of panic she realised that she might never see the housekeeper's unattractive appearance again. Never see Mrs Purvis again – or Stephen. With a sickening lurch in her heart Pippa recalled her last words to him: *'I hope I never see you again.'*

It was almost as though destiny had heard and ironically obliged. Then a new thought struck her. By now Stephen must have heard of her accident. Perhaps he would forget those words and come to see her in hospital, perhaps even this evening.

Pippa sat up, running her hands over her hair. There were sticky lumps adhering to the strands – the adhesive used to secure the electrodes, no doubt – and they were decidedly stubborn to remove. Bit by bit she picked them off, tidying her hair as best she could.

Visitors began to trickle in. Pippa heard their steps passing her bed. There was no mistaking the slow, deliberate step of Mrs Purvis.

'Good evening, Philippa. I hope you are feeling better. I've brought your own nightclothes and toothbrush and all I think you'll need. I'll put them in the locker and you can ask the nurse later to give you what you want.'

'You're very thoughtful. Thank you.'

Stephen was not with her, evidently. Perhaps he would come later. There was the scrape of the chair again and the housekeeper's cool voice.

'Has the consultant given an opinion yet about your condition, Philippa?'

'Not yet. I've had tests. They'll know tomorrow.'

'I see. Well, let's hope for the best.'

Unbidden, the thought leapt to Pippa's mind, and she was instantly ashamed of it. Hope for *what* best? That Pippa should remain blind? But it was unkind of her to suspect Mrs Purvis, however cold and distant she was, of wishing her harm. She had always cared dutifully for Pippa over the years – and yet, along with Walters and Bainbridge and latterly, Stephen, she had not proved

127

herself an ally or a friend recently. But she was no secret enemy either. In any case, no one had caused Copper to throw her. That was the result of her own carelessness. She had ridden wildly, irresponsibly, and all because of that wretched scene with Stephen. If only he were here now.

Tentatively she put the question to the housekeeper. 'Where's Mr Lorant? Does he know about me?'

'He's gone. He left a note to say he had completed his work at Cambermere and was leaving the district. Most likely he's in London by now, or flown back to America for all I know.'

'Did he know about my accident?' Pippa asked incredulously. Surely he, of all people, could not be so hard as to leave her at a time like this? But he had spoken harshly at that last meeting, disowning all feeling for her because his work came first.

The housekeeper coughed and cleared her throat. 'No. He had gone by the time I got back from the hospital. That is, he didn't know from me, but Mr Walters might have told him, if they met.'

No, Pippa argued inwardly. He did not know or he would be here. Lost in this confusing darkness it was one reassuring belief she was determined to cling to.

The visiting hour dragged interminably. Mrs Purvis made small-talk about the amount of work still to be done on the London flat and the difficulty of her supervising the work in the present circumstances. Pippa barely listened. Her mind was far away, wondering just where Stephen was now and wishing that he knew she needed him.

After the bell rang and the visitors filtered out, the rest of the evening and the long night passed with inexorable slowness. Night in its dark mantle was no different from the day, save for the silence in the ward, interspersed only with snores and the rustle of papers where a nurse sat on duty. As she lay, restless, the same word kept hammering in her brain: *blind, blind, blind.* She longed for sleep and escape from the insistent horror of the word.

Pippa slept at last, a sleep of tangled dreams, no doubt due to the pills they had given her, but when the clatter of teacups awoke her, the same sudden alarm at finding herself still blanketed in darkness assailed her again. It was no awful nightmare, banished in the light of day, but a never-ending nightmare to accompany her for the rest of her days. God, but it was unthinkable to waken every morning for the rest of one's life in such a desperately lonely void!

'How's your head today, dear? I heard as you had a fall off a horse.'

It was a warm, motherly voice Pippa had not heard before, presumably either a nurse or another patient. Pippa sat up slowly, hearing again the chink of teacups. Her head no longer ached.

'Fine, thanks. It's just this not being able to see I can't get used to.'

The woman gasped. 'You mean you've gone blind, dear? Oh Lord!'

A nurse intervened. 'Miss Korvak must rest, Mrs Philips. Don't bother her with talking now. Here's your tea, Miss Korvak.'

Pippa took the cup gratefully and sipped. Distantly she could hear Mrs Philips, apparently now in conversation with another patient. 'Gone blind, would you believe! And her so young, too. What a shame!'

'Poor soul,' another voice murmured, and Pippa grew irritable. They were discussing her as if she were a child or as if blindness meant she was deaf too. Dear God, if she remained blind she would probably have to put up with even more humiliating treatment.

The blind man on the train; suddenly she remembered him, and his dog Shula. He had said something about able-bodied people not knowing how to talk to the disabled, about their embarrassment and often well-intentioned clumsiness. She remembered feeling uneasy at his words, recognising herself in the accusation. Grimly she realised that perhaps now she too was about to experience what he had spoken of, today, tomorrow — possibly for the rest of her life. Oh God! Would she have the strength to endure it, and alone too?

The ward routine of medication, temperature and pulse-taking preceded breakfast. Interspersed with the sounds around her, Pippa could hear snatches of Mrs Philips' conversation with some other patient, evidently also a newcomer, for Mrs Phillips was describing the recent extraction of her appendix in detail. By now she had evidently lost interest in Pippa's misfortune. By chance, Pippa's hand encountered the plastic headphones by her pillow, and she placed them over her ears. A radio announcer gave the time and said that the news would follow.

Pippa lay with closed eyes, feeling unaccustomedly weary. Suddenly the sound of her own name over the air arrested her attention: *Korvak.*

'He is at present in the Espirance Clinic in Los Angeles in a critical condition and fears for his life are mounting. Alexis Korvak made his name in the film industry in the 'fifties and was at one time husband of the film star Carrie Hope. His most recent films include *The Lorelie Legend* and *Passport to Frenzy.*'

Pippa started upright. As the newsreader moved on to other items she tore of the headphones and called out, '*Nurse! Nurse!*'

Measured footsteps came at once, swiftly but with calm authority. 'What is it, Miss Korvak? Is something wrong?' It was the cool voice of Sister.

'My father — he's dying in America! I must go to him!'

Pippa was already swinging her legs out of bed but Sister restrained her. 'Now what's this all about, my dear. Whatever the crisis, you're in no fit state to go anywhere yet. Your father dying, you say?'

'I've just heard on the radio — Alexis Korvak, the film producer — he's critically ill in Los Angeles! I must go to him!'

'Just you get back into bed, Miss Korvak. You've had nasty concussion and we've still to see about your eyes. You're not fit to go home yet, let alone to America. Critical doesn't necessarily mean he's dying, you know. Now Mr Hunter-Price will be along to see you soon, so just you settle back into bed until he comes.'

Sister tucked in the sheets so tightly that Pippa felt constrained and loosened them again as soon as her steps died away. She was right, of course; Pippa could be panicking unduly, and flying to the States was hardly feasible in her

state. Nevertheless, Father must learn about Robin —
before it was too late.

Hearing the young nurse with the warm manner at the
next bed, Pippa called to her. The nurse came over. 'Yes?'

'Please, would you do me a great favour if you've got a
minute to spare? I must write a letter to my father — he's
desperately ill in America.'

The nurse hesitated. 'Do you think it's wise to tell him
about your accident then if he's so bad?'

'It's not that — it's another terribly important thing he
must know in case — in case anything happens to him.
Please help me. It's very private and I can't ask anyone
else.'

'All right, then, if it's urgent. I'll be back in a moment.'

Until the nurse returned Pippa sat thoughtfully, mentally
phrasing, rejecting and re-phrasing how she should tell
him. By the time the nurse returned she was ready.
Five minutes later the letter was done and the nurse
addressed the envelope to the Espirance Clinic, Los
Angeles.

Pray heaven Father is not about to die, thought Pippa
fervently, but if he does please let the letter reach him first.
Perhaps by now he would be too ill to understand or to act
upon it, and she blamed herself for her delay.

It was not long before heavy male footsteps told Pippa that
the eye-specialist had arrived. She sat tense, eager for his
verdict.

'Good morning, Miss Korvak. Now let's have a look at
you. Drops, please, Sister.'

Pippa felt the cool liquid drip into her eyes. Hurry, oh
hurry and tell me the worst, she prayed inwardly, but the
specialist took his time, lifting each eyelid in turn and
breathing deeply while he examined her. Then there was
a brief, murmured consultation with someone else before
he came back to sit on the edge of Pippa's bed.

'Well, you really set us a poser and no mistake, Miss
Korvak,' he remarked. 'I can see no damage whatsoever,
no detachment of the retina, no lesions or haemorrhage or
any other injury. Moreover, the results of your tests show
that everything apparently functions perfectly normally.

Quite a mystery.'

Pippa held her breath, unable to decide if what he said was good or bad news.

Mr Hunter-Price went on: 'My colleague here and I are somewhat baffled, I have to admit. We can only advise you to be patient and take things easy.'

'You mean it will clear by itself? That my sight will come back? How soon?'

He sighed. 'I cannot promise that, I'm afraid. I can only say that there have been cases of blindness with no apparent physical cause, such as yours, though they are infrequent.'

'But what causes it, doctor?'

'It's hard to say. It's always of a psychological origin, usually a bad shock of some kind. Did you have such a shock, Miss Korvak?'

Stephen – that was it. The shock of finding he cared nothing for her. She remembered her rage and bitterness, how she had stormed out and gone off to ride Copper.

'Well, in a way, I suppose I did. You say it's psychological – you mean the brain shuts off sight, as though it didn't want to see whatever it was that caused the shock?'

'In a manner of speaking, I suppose that is it.'

'But what happens then, doctor? Does the blindness last only as long as the shock does? Do people recover their sight eventually?'

'Sometimes. Sometimes not. There is no clear prognosis, I fear. I'm sorry I can't offer you more encouragement than that, Miss Korvak, but your sight could suddenly return spontaneously just as swiftly as you lost it. It might return, or it might not. Another traumatic event could trigger it or it could happen while you're at rest. All I can advise is that you return home to Cambermere and live as normal a life as possible. Trying not to be too anxious – that wouldn't help.'

He rose from the bed. 'I'm sorry not to be able to promise more, my dear, but you are young and resilient and that is in your favour. Even if you do not recover you have the weapons to adapt more easily than the old. I'll see you again – we'll have you back for a check-up very soon.'

Pippa felt limp and empty at the prospect of facing

eternal darkness without Stephen, and perhaps with Father gone too.

Within an hour Mrs Purvis, summoned by Sister on the telephone, appeared to take Pippa home. Pippa refused help and dressed alone, but it was surprising how weak her legs felt as she stood by the bed. What was more, she ached all over but then she realised that she must be bruised after such a fall. No wonder she felt so tender and stiff.

'Let me lead you,' said Mrs Purvis when at last Pippa was ready, and Pippa felt her thin, cold fingers take hold of her hand to lead her from the ward. Pippa's instant reaction of resentment grew as the housekeeper turned her sharply left, then pushed her into the lift, and finally guided her down the steps out of the hospital. The steps were terrifying to Pippa. It was all very well to be told firmly, 'Here, now there are four steps,' but actually putting one's foot out into a void and the sensation of downward movement felt as if one was about to plunge into an abyss. Once inside the car she felt safe, and almost began to yearn for the security of the hospital bed again.

She must stop thinking about herself and examining her sensations and emotions all the time, she reprimanded herself. Self-absorption was not healthy. Blind people were capable of thinking about others beside themselves.

If only Stephen would be at the Hall when she arrived — then she felt she would be better able to cope with the frightening day ahead. But Stephen was the cause of her present plight and she ought to hate him. Indeed, because of his intention to torment her father even on his deathbed, she did hate him. But still she longed for him. The homeward journey passed in silence as Pippa battled to reconcile the two warring halves of her mind.

Mrs Purvis, driving the car with smooth dexterity, at last broke the silence. 'Mr Walters was most disturbed about your accident, Philippa, especially when he learnt that you were blind.' Pippa could not help noticing the way the housekeeper used the word boldly, with no attempt to spare her feelings. 'He rang to say he would like to visit you, and I suggested he should wait until you were back at Cambermere. Mr Bainbridge too was shocked and said he would call to see you.'

Oh no, thought Pippa. She had no desire to meet either. Hesitantly she asked about Stephen. 'Do you know whether Mr Lorant too came to hear about it from Mr Walters or someone else?'

'Not that I know of. Someone in the village may have told him if they learnt of it before he left Marlow. I really couldn't say.'

The tone of her voice seemed to Pippa to indicate that she really did not care either. Still, Pippa clung to the hope that someone had told him and that, despite everything, he would come to her. A chill thought struck her: she had no address either in London or America where she could contact him. He could be gone from her life forever. She shut the thought from her mind.

'I guess you'll have heard about Father,' she said to Mrs Purvis. 'About his illness, I mean.'

'Of course. I told you he was in hospital some time ago.'

'But I only heard today how critically ill he is. In other circumstances I'd have gone straight to him, but as it is . . .'

'Who told you?' The housekeeper's tone was crisp.

'I heard it on the radio. Didn't you?'

'Yes. But I didn't intend to alarm you in your condition. The doctor says no stress of any kind must be allowed to slow your recovery. It's a pity you had to learn about it yet.'

Pippa kept silent about her letter to the clinic. Some instinct warned her to hold her tongue. Poor Father, if he had never known about his illegitimate son it might be hard to accept on his deathbed; but it was possible that the news could bring him pleasure. In silence she prayed that Father would recover and that he would forgive her for her disclosure.

The sound of crunching gravel under the car wheels told her that they had reached the drive to Cambermere Hall.

'I'll drive round to the stables and then we can go in by the kitchen door,' said Mrs Purvis. She parked the car and came round to open the door for Pippa. 'Here, I'll take you inside.'

Pippa felt her fingertips under her elbow guiding her towards the door. One step, and she was inside. A succulent smell of roasting meat filled the air.

'Goodness, just in time,' said Mrs Purvis, and Pippa heard her open the oven door. Cautiously she moved forward, felt the arch of one of the wheelback chairs, and sat down.

'Shall I make some tea?' Mrs Purvis asked. Her tone was cool, polite rather than inviting.

Pippa shook her head. 'No thanks. I feel rather tired. I think I'll lie down.'

'Of course. Give me your jacket.' As she took it, Pippa heard her gasp with surprise. 'Philippa! Your arms are covered in bruises! Black and blue you are, and some of them turning yellow. What a sight!'

Pippa smiled ruefully. 'I imagine I have bruises all over judging by how tender I feel. Maybe a hot bath would ease the ache.'

'A hot bath would be the worst thing. But what about a spot of infra-red heat? That couldn't do any harm.'

'Is there a heat lamp in Cambermere?'

'Of course. Mr Korvak had a solarium installed as well as a sauna. It's on the same corridor as your room − come, I'll show you.'

Pippa rose and felt her way round the edge of the table. Mrs Purvis was evidently waiting by the door, watching. This time she made no attempt to take Pippa's arm and Pippa reflected that probably the housekeeper was right − she must learn to be independent, and after all, she was on familiar territory now.

Out of the kitchen she moved with care and along the short passage to the door leading to the vestibule. She knew when she had passed through the open door by the sound of her own footsteps, now ringing on the mosaic floor in the high-vaulted area. The marble columns − she must take care not to collide with them. She held out an investigating hand and eventually felt the cool smooth surface of a pillar. Here she paused.

'Which pillar is this, Mrs Purvis? I know there are seven here. Which one is it, counting from the left to the front door?'

'The fourth.'

Pippa moved forward a few steps. 'Then the door to the

east wing is about there? Between the second and third pillars?'

'That's right. And the staircase opposite.'

Pippa nodded. 'I'll soon learn. I remember meeting a blind man once, on a train, and he said the secret was to count everything. He knew what station we had reached because he counted every stop. I'll learn too.' And inwardly she resolved that she would. Blindness was a terrible blow, but it need not be the end of the world. God knew what she was going to do with her life now, how she would earn her living and act like normal, sighted people, but the first hurdle was to learn to fight back, to adapt and not to let tragedy and self-pity beat her down.

She turned and walked firmly in the direction of the stairs, but Mrs Purvis suddenly snatched at her arm and pulled her to one side.

'You'd have had yet another bruise, on your nose this time,' she said. 'You were heading straight into the pillar.'

She set Pippa squarely at the foot of the stairs, and as Pippa went up, hand on balustrade and counting, she reflected how easily one's sense of direction became confused in the dark. She could have sworn she had turned a full hundred and eighty degrees from the east wing to the staircase. The balustrade suddenly flattened out, just in time to warn her that she had reached the top step. Twenty-two.

The corridor was easy. Running her fingers along the wall she could count the doors until she reached her own room.

'Two doors further along to the solarium,' Mrs Purvis remarked. 'I'll show you how to use it and then leave you. Afterwards, you can rest in your room until dinner if you wish.'

She opened the door and Pippa followed her inside. There was carpet on the floor underfoot but the room had a hollow ring when Mrs Purvis spoke.

'It's a sunbed with an overhead lamp,' she explained. 'The lamp has both infra-red and ultra-voilet settings. I'll lower it to the right height for you and switch on. Then you can undress — there's a chair alongside to put your clothes on — and lie down. The infra-red is very soothing and relaxing so you might even doze there instead of on your bed. It won't do any harm.'

Pippa ran her fingers along the smooth surface of the sunbed and heard a mechanical noise as the housekeeper lowered the lamp. Pippa felt that too, long and smooth like the bed surface.

'Show me how to switch it on,' she said.

'There's no need. I'll switch it on and you can leave it when you've finished. I'll see to it later.'

The first surge of independence rose in Pippa. 'Show me just the same,' she said firmly. 'I'll have to learn to cope with everyday switches and things, or I'll end up useless.'

'Very well.' The housekeeper's cool hand took hers and raised it. 'Feel the large circular knob here? Turn left for infra-red, right for ultra-violet. Back to vertical to switch off.'

'And this knob?' asked Pippa, feeling another switch alongside.

'That's the timer. It's only used for ultra-violet, so you can forget that one. There, it's switched on now. Will you be all right?'

Pippa assured her that she could manage, and she left. Already warmth from the machine was caressing Pippa's bare arms. She undressed quickly and lay down on the sunbed's surface.

Despite its hardness she found the sunbed remarkably comfortable and after about ten minutes she began to feel drowsy. Above her there was a faint click, but she took no notice. Eyes closed and a velvety warm darkness all around her, she would have been asleep within seconds but for a sudden sound that made her jerk awake. A telephone bell was shrilling insistently in the solarium.

Pippa listened. It was probably an extension line and Mrs Purvis would answer it downstairs. But the demanding sound persisted, over to her right, and at length Pippa swung her legs cautiously off the sunbed, stood up, and walked carefully towards the sound. A smooth surface met her questing fingers and sliding along it, she found the telephone. Even as she lifted the receiver, however, the caller decided to hang up.

Retracing her steps towards the sunbed Pippa found it

easily and was about to extend her stiff limbs on it when a sudden, irrational impulse seized her. Reaching up towards the overhead machine which housed the sunlamps, very carefully so as not to burn her hands on exposed radiants, she found the switch on the edge. It was turned to the right. The right, surely, was ultra-violet if she remembered the housekeeper's words accurately. The switch should be turned to the left. Could she have remembered it wrongly?

Irritably she switched the knob off and began to dress. Mrs Purvis must have gone out, since she had not answered the telephone. Insidious suspicion returned. If the machine was set at ultra-violet, she would have been badly burned, especially if she had fallen asleep. Alarm seized her. It could have been accidental, of course; but if it was deliberate then someone, heedless of her disability, was still out to do her harm.

But why? What had she done?

10

All afternoon, lying on her bed, thoughts chased through Pippa's mind. Could Mrs Purvis have set the machine wrongly and if so, was it by accident or design? Or could she or someone else have come into the solarium surreptitiously, knowing Pippa could not see, to alter the setting? There had been a click, she remembered, but she had attached no importance to it at the time.

Mrs Purvis must have been out of the house or she would have answered the telephone. Then who else had access to Cambermere Hall? Carson was on holiday. None of the casual staff from the village appeared to be here today, though one of them could have a key. But why should he or she try to burn Pippa? The whole thing was so irrational and stupid that Pippa feared to mention the subject to Mrs Purvis when at last the housekeeper came to say that dinner was ready. Nevertheless Pippa told her hesitantly.

'Set to ultra-violet? Nonsense! I set the switch myself,' Mrs Purvis said shortly. 'You must be confused.'

'It was turned to the right, Mrs Purvis.'

'Indeed? I shall see for myself.'

'It's no use looking now. I turned it off.'

'I see. Then I only have your word for it. Will you come down before the soup gets cold?'

The soup could be no colder than the housekeeper's voice, Pippa reflected as she made her way downstairs.

Seated at table she mentioned the lamp again, politely but firmly: 'It was set to ultra-violet and I did not imagine it. If you did not set it so, then someone else did.'

She heard the sound of liquid being poured into her bowl. 'Someone else?' Mrs Purvis queried. 'Who, for goodness sake, when there's no one else here but you and myself? I tell you, Philippa, you are confused, that's all, and it's not to be wondered at after your concussion. You'll be all right in a day or two.'

Pippa fumed as she sipped the soup. The woman still had a maddeningly cool way of always putting Pippa in the wrong, making her seem stupid or forgetful, just as she did long ago in her nursery days. It was useless to argue with her.

'Did you go out?' she asked the housekeeper instead. 'The 'phone rang.'

'Did you answer it?'

'Eventually, but whoever it was hung up as I got there.'

'I expect they'll call again if it's important,' Mrs Purvis said smoothly. It was moments later that Pippa realised she had cleverly avoided answering whether or not she had gone out. Her next words drove all thoughts of further questioning from Pippa's mind. 'Oh, by the way, Philippa. I forgot to tell you earlier that I found a letter addressed to you in the hallway, presumably left by Mr Lorant.'

'From Stephen?' Pippa's heart leapt in hope. 'Where is it?'

'There, alongside your plate. To the right.'

Pippa felt the crisp paper under her fingertips, an

envelope but not sealed. It was both saddening and annoying that she could not take it away to peruse its contents alone. She was forced to forget her pride and ask the housekeeper, 'Would you read it to me, please?'

Mrs Purvis took it and cleared her throat.

' *"Dear Pippa, I am sorry that we must part with angry words but I want you to know that despite everything, I shall always think of you tenderly and wish you well. Though we may never meet again, God speed and bless you. Stephen."* '

Mrs Purvis handed the letter back across the table. 'There's a foreign word I can't say at the end. Otherwise, quite a charming note, wouldn't you say? I didn't know you two had words.'

'It's not important now.' Pippa's reply, murmured and spontaneous, made her realise how much she missed him. It was ridiculous really. Only two weeks ago she was swearing to forget men and tackle life alone, and now here she was desolate because of a man she hardly knew. The words in the letter implied he had gone forever — and gave no address where she could find him. She curled her fingers tightly about the letter in her pocket. The word Mrs Purvis had not been able to pronounce — that must have been one of the many Hungarian terms Stephen used to use, endearments which had sounded sweet to her ears though she could not understand. Now he was gone, she felt alone and cold inside.

Mrs Purvis refused her help with carrying the dishes to the kitchen, so Pippa made her way to the music room, the last place she and Stephen had been together. As she closed the door behind her, she felt tears begin to prick her sightless eyes. The room was still and silent, as though still shocked at the harsh, cruel words they had flung at each other.

'I never want to see you again!'

The tears sprang unbidden now, and she was conscious of the cruel irony that fate had taken her words literally. Even if Stephen were to walk in the door now, she would never see his broad shoulders, his blond head and gentle smile again. As Pippa lowered herself into the velvet seat of a large armchair, an indignant squeak met her ears. Puzzled, she reached behind her and found a cat, small and furry and with outstretched claws, half squashed beneath her weight. Pippa picked it up gently, murmuring comfort and apologies and stroking its back. It was only young, judging by its size, but its anger quickly vanished and it walked on to her lap, arching its back against her trustingly. Pippa's self-pity melted and vanished.

The touch of the cat, its soft fur and its bony little head cradling under her chin, began to ease her pain and she felt her coldness thawing. The kitten, so slender and fragile, forgot its vulnerability in its evident trust of her. Its tiny, rapid heartbeat in the warm, resilient little body stirred in her a sense of being alive, and of hope and trust, and she sat peacefully stroking the little creature until he went to sleep, purring contentedly.

Mrs Purvis found her later and expressed some surprise when, switching on the light, she saw the kitten on Pippa's lap.

'How on earth did that creature get into the house?' she exclaimed. 'It's a stray – I've seen it in the grounds. I'll bet it was because Mr Lorant made a fuss of it that it thought it was welcome here. Give it to me, Philippa, and I'll put it out.'

'Oh no!' Pippa's determination to keep the kitten was redoubled, if only the housekeeper knew it, by hearing that Stephen had fondled it too. It was one last link between them. 'He's not to be put out, Mrs Purvis. If he's a stray then I shall adopt him. I'll take him down to the kitchen and give him some milk. Would you please find a piece of blanket or something for a bed for him?'

'Keep him!' Mrs Purvis exclaimed. 'But Mr Korvak doesn't like animals in the house. And besides, it might have fleas.'

'No matter. I've made up my mind he is to stay, so please don't let's discuss it any more.'

She rose and made towards the door, aware that the housekeeper was obliged to step aside to let her pass. The kitten sat hunched under her arm, its little claws unsheathed in alarm at the sudden interruption of his sleep.

It was not difficult to find a saucer and the milk in the refrigerator, but less easy to pour the milk for there was no way of knowing when the saucer was filled. She put the kitten and the saucer on the floor and listened to its dainty, rapid lapping. Mrs Purvis brought a piece of blanket, sniffing her disdain audibly before leaving, saying she was going to bed.

The kitten seemed disinclined to settle in the spot she chose for him by the boiler, preferring instead to chase her as she moved about and to attack her ankles with its tiny claws. Pippa's heart swelled with affection for him, his obvious happiness and joie de vivre. She did not want to be parted from him. Managing to catch him at last when he pounced, she carried him up to her room.

This empty world of hers was always dark, and, it was unnaturally still in the old Hall at night, but the kitten's warm little body purring away like a miniature motor-bike on her pillow gave Pippa a measure of peace and reassurance. Its warmth and welcome friendship were just what she needed. A reminder of Stephen, she thought sleepily, before things went wrong.

The succeeding few days passed slowly; with no definition between night and day it was not easy to recognise the difference at first. Normal daytime sounds like birdsong and the distant clatter of dishes in the kitchen were clear signs, but the night with its deep silence and only the occasional hoot of an owl or bark of a dog was a nebulous, unnerving time. Cambermere Hall by night had been an eerie place even when Stephen was here, but now it was distinctly ominous. Whoever wished her harm was here still, and there was nothing Pippa could do to protect herself.

By day she kept to a normal routine, with the additional task of learning her way about unaided. Steps, doors, even paces across a room — everything had to be counted and memorised. It was an adventure, she told herself firmly, not to be compared to riding out on the fields, but that would come. She should be grateful that her handicap did not deprive her of all mobility; she was lucky compared to a paraplegic.

The housekeeper gave her grudging approval. 'You're doing well, Philippa. I'm so glad you didn't sit down and feel sorry for yourself as you might well have done. Now, what will you do while I'm out shopping this morning?'

'I think I'll go for a swim − is the sun shining?'

'No, but it's bright and warm. A swim will do you good. By the way, Marion is here to clean the bedrooms, so you can call her if you want anything.'

Marion was a woman from the village who 'obliged' twice a week. Pippa could hear her humming in the vestibule just after Mrs Purvis had gone out and Pippa was about to mount the twenty-two steps to her room to change.

'Oh, the postman's late this morning,' Marion commented. 'There's a letter for you, Miss Korvak, and it's got an American stamp on it.'

From America? Pippa's heart leapt in anticipation. It must be from Father! She took it eagerly, and then fingered it helplessly. She had not told Father of her accident so he could not know that she was unable to read. Someone would have to read it for her − but who? Not Mrs Purvis, she decided, and since no one else was available she had no choice but to ask Marion.

'I hate to trouble you,' she explained, 'especially as I think it contains matters which are confidential. Do you think you could read it and then forget what it says? I know that sounds silly but I really need to know what it says, and I don't want Mrs Purvis or anyone else to hear of it. If you'd rather not, then please say so and I'll find someone else?'

But who? Bainbridge and Walters were out of the question, Stephen was gone, and young Robin could not be allowed to see. To Pippa's relief Marion patted her arm.

'Don't you fret, miss. I can be as discreet as anyone. Of course I'll read it for you.'

She took the letter and Pippa heard her tear the flap. For a moment she paused. 'It's from a firm of lawyers in San Fransisco,' she said.

'Lawyers? Not Alexis Korvak?'

'No. But the letter mentions him.'

'Read it, please.' Pippa's heart was thudding. Pray heaven she had not written too late.

Marion began to read:

' "*Dear Miss Korvak, My client Mr Alexis Korvak instructs me to write to you on his behalf to say that he was both surprised and pleased to receive your news. Far from wanting to contest paternity of the child, as we advised, he is pleased and eager to recognise him. Though weak and seriously ill, Mr Korvak is perfectly lucid and instructed a new will to be drawn up at once and its contents to be notified to you.*

"Accordingly, the new will now instructs certain substantial bequests to his housekeeper for many years, and to one other legatee, the remainder of his estate to be divided in equal parts between yourself as his legitimate daughter and the boy, the latter's inheritance to be held in trust by you until the child attains his majority.

"We enclose a brief note from Mr Korvak, being all that he could write in his present circumstances. We look forward to hearing the name of your lawyers in England with whom we can process the matter in due course. Leo J. Engel." '

Marion sighed. 'There's a half-sheet of paper attached with a few scrawled words. It says, "*Thanks, honey. You've made me a happy man. Father.*" '

A lump came unbidden to Pippa's throat. It was clear her father was very ill, perhaps dying, yet the knowledge of his illegitimate son had brought him joy. Whether he was the wicked creature people said or not, he deserved to die happy.

'Thank you, Marion. I'm very grateful to you.'

'You're welcome, miss. And not a word to a soul, I promise.'

'Bless you.' At least the solicitor's letter had not mentioned Robin Walters by name, so perhaps even Marion did not realise the meaning of what she had read — though it was possible that it was common knowledge who fathered poor Nina's child.

At that moment the telephone rang. Marion picked it up. 'Hello? Yes, she's here. It's Mr Walters, Miss.'

A curious coincidence, thought Pippa as she took the

receiver. She would have some good news to tell him.

'Philippa? How are you now? I didn't know whether you were home yet. Are you all right?'

'Well,' said Pippa cautiously, 'I've recovered from the concussion, but perhaps you know from Mrs Purvis what happened?'

'I haven't seen her since that day. I did ring the hospital but they would only say you were comfortable, nothing more. What did happen?'

'The blow to my head — it did something to my eyes. I'm afraid I can't see.'

She heard his gasp, then there was a pause. 'You don't mean — that you're blind?' he said incredulously.

'They say it may go right again of its own accord, with care.'

'Oh, God! Oh, Philippa, I'm so sorry.' There was dismay and sorrow in his tone that she felt sure he was not feigning.

'But I've something to tell you that you may be glad to hear,' she hurried on.

'No, listen. I must tell you something,' Walters interrupted. 'I wasn't going to tell you, but in the light of what's happened . . . Listen Philippa, someone *is* out for your blood, I'm sure of it. Robin told me about someone locking you in the stable.'

'Well, yes, I'd almost forgotten that. Copper was very restive.'

'And no wonder. After the ambulance had taken you to hospital I unsaddled Copper. There was a thistle-burr under his saddle and his back was raw. That's why he was irritable, and no doubt that's why he threw you at the wall.'

'Oh!' Pippa digested the information slowly. 'But no one expected me to ride him,' she said reflectively. 'It was you who planned to ride him.'

'But someone locked you in with him, knowing he'd be in a vicious mood. Listen, Philippa, if you feel you should tell the police, I wouldn't blame you.'

'Too late now,' she replied. After all, the harm was done, she had lost her sight and the ill-wisher would leave her alone. And how could she be sure it was not Walters himself?

'It wasn't Bainbridge,' Walters was saying musingly. 'He

was with me and anyway, it's not like him to be devious. Whatever his faults, he's straightforward enough. Well, what was it you wanted to tell me?'

'My father has acknowledged Robin as his son. Robin will not lose out now.'

There was a silence at the other end of the line, and Pippa could sense that Walters was not pleased at the news. Then he asked, 'Who told him? Was it you?'

'Yes. I thought it only fair. You've probably heard on the news that Father is critically ill.'

'Yes. But Robin is my ward. I don't want Korvak to lay claim to him. He's mine, and he's all I have left. Now look, Philippa, I'm sorry for what's happened to you but I wish you'd kept your nose out of my business. I know you probably meant well – '

'Of course I did!'

'But Korvak has caused enough misery in my family. I won't have him giving orders to send Robin away to school or fetched to America. I won't have it! Nor do I want the boy to learn who his real father is – a man the world knows for a villain! How could you inflict that on Robin?'

His voice was so cold that Pippa felt wretched. Unintentionally she had hurt him and he would continue to believe that Korvaks always brought trouble. 'I'm sorry,' she faltered, 'I didn't think . . . '

'No more than your father did,' he snapped, and she heard him hang up abruptly.

About twenty minutes later, the telephone bell began to call insistently again. Knowing that Marion was now busy running the vacuum cleaner back and forth upstairs, Pippa felt her way out into the vestibule to answer it.

'Philippa? It's Arthur Bainbridge. God, what a terrible thing to happen! You wouldn't listen to me, would you?'

Pippa sighed. 'I take it you've been talking to Geoff Walters,' she remarked.

'He rang me just now and told me. Hell, I guessed someone would try something on, but I never guessed it would be that bad. Tough blow, that. I just wanted you to know it wasn't me – and I doubt it were Walters either.'

Pippa could not resist a smile. Her two neighbours were

gentlemanly enough to vouch for each other. 'I didn't think it was you, Mr Bainbridge.'

'Arthur,' he interrupted.

'In fact, whoever put the thistle under Copper's saddle could not have known I was going to ride him. I didn't know myself till the last minute. So if someone was being threatened, it wasn't me.'

'But Walters said someone locked you in with that horse in a nasty mood. You can't tell me that person wasn't gunning for you? You're a hard woman to convince, but I just wanted to let you know that, er, with your eyes, er, being the way they are now . . . ' He paused, obviously finding it difficult to phrase his words without hurting. Pippa decided to help him out.

'I know, Mr Bainbridge. In the light of my present circumstances you wish to say that you will not press me again with a proposal of marriage. I'm grateful to you, truly.'

'Nay, lass, that's not it at all!' Bainbridge bellowed. 'Just the other way about! Now that you must believe me at last, perhaps you'll admit that you need a protector! I'm your man, Philippa. I'll marry you as soon as you like. There's not a soul in Buckinghamshire or in all England for that matter as will dare to bother you once you're Mrs Bainbridge. Now, what do you say?'

Pippa swallowed hard. 'Mr Bainbridge, I'm very grateful to you, honestly, but I'm afraid the answer is still no, and will remain so. After all, I've lost my sight − why should any persecutor need to attack me now? Thank you, but I've no wish to marry, and especially now this has happened. That's my last word on the matter, Mr Bainbridge, and I'd be obliged if you would never mention it again. Goodbye.'

She hung up firmly before he could protest. He was a kindly man despite his roughness and she hoped she had not offended him. It was only as she was counting her way up the stairs that she remembered his proposal was not entirely altruistic, for he still wanted Korvak land. But marriage was not essential for that − he could always buy it. Then when the unwelcome thought suddenly leapt on her that perhaps soon the land might be hers, she thought fiercely that he need not buy the land — she would give it back to him.

On the landing a small, furry body suddenly thrust itself between her feet and began polishing her ankles with its arched back. She smiled and bent to pick up the young cat, cradling it tenderly. It purred loudly, pushing its bony head against her cheek. The distant hum of the vacuum cleaner stopped and Pippa heard Marion's quick footsteps approaching.

'Hello, miss. The bedrooms are all done now. Shall I give pussy the meat Mrs Purvis left for him before I go? It's ready in the kitchen, and she told me it was for him.'

'Oh, thank you.' Pippa handed over the kitten reluctantly, feeling its claws fasten into the sleeve of her shirt as if he too was unwilling to go. She was mildly surprised that the housekeeper had had such concern for him.

'She's left your lunch ready too,' Marion added. 'Would you like me to bring it up on a tray?'

'Oh no, don't trouble to come up again — I'll come down,' Pippa replied quickly.

'No trouble, miss. I've got to come up again to collect the polish and dusters and that. I'll bring it to your room.'

She was a cheery soul, a shaft of light in an otherwise cheerless day, thought Pippa. A pity she was on her way home now. She brought up the tray, but Pippa left it untouched on the table and sat instead in the window, feeling the sunlight on her face and staring out into the same blank void that confronted her wherever she looked.

Nothing. Black velvet. She sat alone in the Hall. Marion was gone and the place was deserted. Pippa longed at that moment for sight, to be able to gaze out over the tranquillity of Cambermere's grounds in the warm afternoon sunlight, to gain peace from just looking . . . Never to see sunlight again, or moonlight, never to see the tall grace of trees and the vibrant colour of flowers — it was too terrible to conceive. If only one knew, when sighted, just how fortunate one was. People felt no gratitude for sight, or health, they just took it for granted, as she had done. If only she could see now, she would never take it for granted again.

The dark night of the soul enveloped her for a few

seconds, and then angrily she thrust the feeling of self-pity aside. She must think positively, she reminded herself, not allow herself to wallow in negative gloom.

As she held out her hands to cross the room towards the table for her lunch tray, she heard the sound of the telephone once again. She would have to answer it herself. Groping her way out of her bedroom to the top of the staircase took time, and then she remembered the extension in the solarium. By the time she had retraced her steps to the second door beyond her room the bell had ceased its shrill call.

A sudden thought leapt to her mind: Walters and Bainbridge had already rung, so the caller was unlikely to be either of them. It could have been Stephen, anxious to make peace at last now sufficient time had passed for tempers to cool, or simply giving an address or number where he could be found. She went into the solarium, found the telephone and stood anxiously over it for several minutes, willing it to ring again, but the instrument failed to oblige. Disappointed, Pippa turned to go back to her room.

An unexpected sound arrested her. Down below, in the hallway, there was the sound of a light cough.

'Marion? Is that you?' Surely she had heard the door closing earlier as Marion left. There was no reply. 'Who's there? Is it you, Mrs Purvis?' she called.

Still there was no answer. Pippa felt her way along the wall until she reached the head of the stairs. Leaning over the balustrade she had a clear impression that someone below was looking up, watching her, but there was no sound.

'Who's there? Why don't you answer?'

She was positive she faced an intruder, but perhaps he might not know she was sightless. She walked with apparent poise to the stairs and began to descend slowly, her heart thumping inside her. What she would do when she reached the bottom she had no idea.

He was lightfooted, but she caught the quick sound of movement, and he could not disguise the click of the door closing. She recognised it as the door to the kitchen. Resolutely she went towards the hall telephone. An emergency call to the police would either deal with the intruder or, if he heard it, frighten him away.

Receiver in hand, Pippa had to search her memory to remember the order of the numbers. Did nought come first or last? Last, after the nine. Her fingertips felt for the last hole, then moved back one to the nine. Twice she dialled nine when the front door suddenly opened.

'Philippa! Who are you calling?' asked Mrs Purvis's surprised voice. Pippa replaced the receiver.

'Oh, Mrs Purvis! I'm so glad you're back! There's someone in the house — I heard a cough here in the vestibule.'

'Marion, probably. Had you forgotten it was her morning?' the housekeeper replied smoothly. 'You mustn't let things excite you so, Philippa.'

'No, it wās after she'd gone. And then I think he went through to the kitchen — I was just about to ring the police.'

'The kitchen? Wait here.' Pippa was amazed at the woman's calmness as she walked past and opened the kitchen door. A click, and she was gone. Dismayed, Pippa made to go after her, fearful lest the intruder should attack. But when she reached the kitchen she could hear only the rustle of paper.

'I've got some lovely tomatoes from the nursery,' Mrs Purvis remarked. 'Just feel how firm they are.'

'But the man . . .'

'There's no one here, my dear. You heard something you *thought* was a cough, that's all. Don't worry. It's probably just your highly fertile imagination working overtime — I shouldn't have left you alone in an empty house knowing how excitable you are. I won't leave you again.'

'I'm not excitable, and I didn't imagine it! I heard the cough, and I heard the door close. Mrs Purvis, there *was* someone here! Hadn't you better check that nothing of value is missing?'

'If it makes you feel happier', the housekeeper replied, and Pippa grew angry. It was evident she was humouring her charge. Pippa moved across to the door leading to the stable yard. The key was still turned in the lock.

'Satisfied, my dear?' said Mrs Purvis smoothly. 'Now, how about a nice cup of tea?'

Pippa shook her head forlornly. Whatever she thought was going on here she could not understand it. Now she knew only too tragically what being in the dark meant. She felt confused, disorientated, and in need of closeness and companionship.

'Is my kitten here? Marion brought him down to feed him?'

'No. He's not here. Perhaps he went out with her. I shouldn't rely on him coming back, Philippa. He's only a stray, remember.'

That was true, but he had seemed to welcome her friendship just as she had his, as though they sensed the need and loneliness in each other. He'd be back soon, she was sure.

'He's eaten all his dinner anyway,' Mrs Purvis remarked as she clattered dishes in the sink. 'Not a scrap left. He's probably sleeping it off somewhere. Did you eat your lunch?'

'No. I'll eat it later.'

'Too highly spiced for you, perhaps. I made the pâté myself.'

'I wasn't hungry, that's all. I'll eat it for dinner and you won't need to cook.'

The housekeeper sighed and went out. She returned a few minutes later and Pippa heard her clatter the tray down on the counter. Then she heard the sound of scraping. Mrs Purvis was throwing the meat away in the waste-bin. She was evidently annoyed at what she considered was Pippa's rejection of her cooking.

'I said I would eat it,' Pippa ventured.

'Not after it's been exposed to flies all this time,' the housekeeper snapped. Pippa bit her lip. There was no point in trying to apologise in her present mood. Pippa's best plan was to leave her alone.

Out in the vestibule again, Pippa lifted her head, her ears caught by a faint sound. It sounded like the kitten's mew, muted and distant.

'Here, pussy, here,' she called persuasively, but no little body brushed against her legs. For several minutes she called, opening the door to the music room where she had first found him, eager for the warm soft touch of him, but to no avail.

Dinner was a dismal affair. Mrs Purvis was still in a taciturn mood, only replying to Pippa's attempts at conversation with monosyllabic answers. As soon as she decently could, Pippa escaped from the table. Aimlessly she made for the music room. Perhaps it was the memories that this room held — of Stephen, and the kitten — that brought her here. Perhaps it was the piano. She found the stool, raised the lid and let her fingers drift over the keys in a haphazard collection of half-remembered chords from days long ago.

It was no use. Sombre music only served to enhance her loneliness and sense of isolation. In this dim no-man's-land she inhabited alone it was frightening to have no means of measuring time or space, a blankness without borders or definition. She shut the lid sharply and reached for the deep arm-chair.

There was something hard under her. Pippa stood up again to investigate. Her fingers encountered something hard and furry. She probed further.

A cry escaped her lips. At first her mind rebelled, refusing to acknowledge what she had discovered. It was the kitten — not warm and resilient any more, but stiffened and cold, its legs outstretched and neck arched from frail agony. It was the kitten, lifeless as a piece of stone.

11

It was not only the saddening recollection of the kitten's death that troubled Pippa as soon as she awoke next morning, but also the sickening thought that its death was unnatural. It had been lively and healthy earlier in the day, so its sudden death surely could not be the result of illness. It was an unnatural death, but whether by accident or design, that was the question.

The poor little thing had evidently chosen the armchair to lie down in when it began to feel something strange happening. It might have chosen her bed, where it usually slept if the door had been open. The thought of finding the stiff little body in her bed was even more heartrending than the shock of discovering it in the chair.

Tears filled her eyes, her heart swelling with compassion for the creature. Yesterday it had been so lively and capricious, completely ignorant of its approaching end. She was suddenly convinced that it had been poisoned — what other explanation could there be? But was it an accident, or had someone killed it deliberately?

Surely it was not yet another means of punishing her? Surely no one would be so petty as to try to get at her by killing an innocent kitten? A prickling fear tingled in her spine. If someone could be so inhuman, he was a deranged creature and the more to be feared.

But no, she was being silly, she reproached herself. Any such person, if he existed, must know she had already been punished, if that was what he sought. To harm her kitten gave him no advantage at all; it only robbed her of something she had treasured.

Pippa was reluctant to go down to breakfast. Instead she took a leisurely shower and examined her thoughts. She was disinclined to face Mrs Purvis, that was the truth of it, because the housekeeper was the only person who knew of her attachment to the kitten, the only person who knew how deeply its death would hurt her. It was stupid, Pippa told herself angrily. Mrs Purvis, however detached and cold she might be, had no reason to want to hurt her, none at all. And besides, Mrs Purvis had been out of the house most of the day. Pippa dressed and went downstairs at last.

Resolutely she pushed open the door to the kitchen, expecting the usual sound of dishes and the smell of cooking. Both were absent. The kitchen was deserted. Returning to the vestibule and calling the housekeeper's name had no effect. Pippa was alone.

The telephone rang. Pippa's heart thudded. Could it be Stephen ringing at last? As she lifted the receiver to her ear she heard Walter's voice and could not help feeling disappointed.

'Philippa? I just wanted to say I'm sorry. I shouldn't have snapped at you like that. You did the honourable thing and I should have thanked you.'

'That's all right. And if you've forgiven me for interfering, I'm happy. Incidentally, the news made my father happy.'

There was a pause before Walters spoke. 'How is he? Have you heard?'

'No, nothing, but I'm cabling the clinic to keep in touch. By the way, can you give me the 'phone number of your vet, Geoff? You must know a good one.'

He gave a number and the name Fletcher without query, and then went on: 'Would you like to go out for a drive with me this morning? Just to show there's no ill-feeling?'

She smiled. 'I'd be glad to.'

'I'll call for you at eleven. Okay?'

'That's fine, thanks. Goodbye.'

As soon as he had rung off, the idea flashed suddenly into her mind that she ought to check that the kitten's body was still there. She pushed open the music room door and groped for the chair. Its smooth fabric met her touch, but the seat was empty. Nonetheless, she decided, she would speak to the vet.

'Well, from the condition of the body as you describe it I would certainly suspect poisoning.' Mr Fletcher's voice said cautiously in reply to her query, 'although of course without actually inspecting the body it would be impossible to say for certain.'

'I understand. Thank you all the same, Mr Fletcher.'

That done, Pippa made another call, this time to the operator. Two minutes later she had sent her cable to the clinic where Alexis Korvak lay ill. The receiver was still in her hand when the door opened and Mrs Purvis entered. Pippa recognised her quick, light step.

'Telephoning someone, Philippa?'

Pippa was flustered. 'Geoff Walters has invited me to go out for a drive with him this morning,' she said hastily.

'Do you good to go out for a change,' the housekeeper remarked. Pippa wondered why she made no objection, when not so long ago she was warning Pippa not to encourage his friendship. Curious.

'My kitten is dead, Mrs Purvis. I think he was poisoned.' It took an effort to say it so coolly, and for a fraction of a second she could hear the housekeeper's silence, as though searching for a reply.

'Dead, my dear? How do you know? He went missing yesterday, strayed again, no doubt.'

'He was dead in the music room last night, all stiff and stretched out. I found him there.'

'Indeed? I know nothing of that – why didn't you tell me? I'll go and see.'

'It's no use because he's gone now. Did you move his body?'

There was silence for several seconds before Mrs Purvis spoke again. 'Gone, you say? Are you sure he was ever there? You know how you've been lately, Philippa, imagining all manner of things. Are you sure it's not just your concern for him that made you imagine it?'

'*Imagine.* That's all you ever say, Mrs Purvis! No, I did not imagine such a terrible thing, and I'm not ill. Why do you persist in trying to make me think I am? What have you got against me, Mrs Purvis? I want to know!'

'Oh, my dear child, you really are overwrought,' the housekeeper murmured in a maddeningly soft voice. 'I have nothing against you, you poor thing, and I never have had. But you really are ill, whether you believe it or not, when you say such things. And if the creature really is dead, you apparently imply that I had something to do with it. What nonsense! You prove my point, Philippa – you are ill and have no hope of a cure until you stop having all these silly paranoid ideas. I'll ask the doctor to come and see you. Perhaps he'll prescribe a sedative that will help.'

Infuriated, and knowing it would be useless to argue, Pippa turned, wishing madly that she could race up the stairs instead of being obliged to grope her way ignominiously. Her hand on the balustrade, she had a sudden change of heart. Anger and flight were useless. She must not let the housekeeper continue to treat her as a child; instead, she must challenge the woman's cold air of superiority. She turned slowly.

'Mrs Purvis, have you had breakfast? I haven't, and I fancy I'd like some bacon and egg today. I'll cook it myself

— shall I cook some for you too?'

She was already heading towards the kitchen as Mrs Purvis answered. 'Thanks, no, I've eaten. But I'll get the bacon and pan for you.' Pippa's ear could detect the tone of mild surprise in her voice.

It was not easy, although Mrs Purvis fetched all the materials she needed to fry the bacon and egg. Firmly she refused the housekeeper's offer to take over, but it was not pleasant trying to chase elusive bacon around the pan or to gauge when the egg was done. The fat spat every now and again, and she could sense that the housekeeper was keeping a wary eye on her. No doubt she feared the fat might catch fire.

'I've got to learn to do things for myself,' Pippa muttered defensively, but when at last the bacon and egg had been persuaded to leave the pan to sit on her plate, the resulting greasy bacon and half-raw egg made it clear she needed a lot more practice. Still, she told herself grimly, it might be necessary to fend for herself in the dark permanently. Sooner or later she had to begin to learn.

'I'm glad you seem so much calmer,' Mrs Purvis remarked as she poured tea. 'You had me worried when you flared up like that.'

'I was upset about the kitten,' Pippa replied levelly. 'Poisoning is a cruel fate. It was just my feelings showing, that's all.'

'Yes,' the housekeeper murmured, 'we would all welcome the opportunity to give vent to our feelings some-times, but the years teach us it is often wiser to learn how to hide them.'

Pippa looked up, across at where she imagined Mrs Purvis's face to be. She was curious about her remark but before she could ask her what she meant, Mrs Purvis spoke again.

'You're looking at my neck, Philippa. I know you can't see, but it's most disconcerting. I feel as though I have a dirty neck or something. Look up a little higher.' Pippa did so. 'That's better. Now you appear to be looking at me directly. It's something you'll have to practice so as not to draw attention to your disability. Odd how blind people always look down.'

Her tone was polite but her words hurt. Blind was a bare, brutal word, but what she said was true. One's instinct was to look down, as though watching warily for steps one could no longer see. Even seated and reasonably safe, one's eyes only rose half-way to the normal direct line ahead. Pippa reflected. Actors in films, supposedly blind, almost always stared up over their companion's head or looked as if they were inspecting the roofs of houses across the road. How false that was, she now realised, and then she recalled the frank gaze of the blind man on the train. He had stared fixedly at the direction of her belt, though his expression had been mobile. Practice, much practice would be needed, she thought sadly.

She was ready when Geoff Walters's car pulled up in the drive promptly at eleven o'clock. She opened the front door and called out a greeting, then heard his feet crunch on the gravel.

'Mind the steps,' he warned and taking her hand, he counted them slowly as her toe felt for each in turn. 'That's right. Hop in.'

The car sped smoothly down the drive. 'Any preference for where you'd like to go, Philippa? Reading or Maidenhead? Henley?'

Pippa suddenly remembered the letter from her father's lawyers. 'Can you take me first to a solicitor in Marlow, Geoff? I've got some business to see to.'

'Okay. I'll take you to mine.' He asked no questions, for which she was grateful. She was grateful too for the smooth way he persuaded the receptionist to allow Pippa to see Mr Hobbs there and then, without an appointment. Walters took her by the arm and led her into the solicitor's office, then murmured, 'I'll wait for you at reception.'

Pippa handed over the letter and explained. Mr Hobbs read it in silence, then agreed to handle the matter, and made a note of Pippa's name and address. If he knew the name Korvak he made no comment.

'There's just one thing I should add,' Pippa said as she rose to go. 'I'm afraid I can't see. I'd be obliged if you would ring me rather than write if the need arises.'

'To be sure I will.' Suddenly he was by her side, his hand

on her elbow, and a moment later she was back with Walters. She felt a warm glow. People could be so kindly and unobtrusively helpful.

As she came out of the solicitor's office with Walters, she felt the sun's rays on her face. Walters sighed. 'Heavens, it's hot. Shall we head for the river somewhere? Maidenhead is very pretty at this time — ' He broke off suddenly. Pippa realised he was embarrassed at his clumsiness.

'Please,' she said quietly, 'don't worry. If you keep trying to pick your words with care you won't be able to speak at all. I'd much rather you spoke naturally, as you would to anyone else.'

'I'm sorry. You're right,' he muttered.

She thought again of the blind man on the train. He had said something about handicapped people wanting and needing to be treated like normal people, and here was an instance of it. But at the same time she was aware of being jostled by passers-by who, unaware of her predicament, expected her to give way a little on Marlow's narrow pavements. Walters did his best, guiding her by the arm, but the pathway was barely wide enough for two.

As Walters unlocked the car, Pippa raised her head and sniffed. The heavy, sickly scent of brewing beer filled the hot, narrow street. Walters must have noticed her expression.

'That's the brewery just behind the shops,' he remarked. 'Powerful today, isn't it?'

There was another scent too, equally strong and more attractive. It was the delicious aroma of newly-baked bread. Pippa commented on it.

'That's the bakery along at the end of the high street,' Walters told her.

'I remember, at the corner where we turn off to Cambermere.'

'That's right, then turn right again at the pub.'

Pippa had a sudden idea. 'Geoff, would you mind very much if I asked you to leave me here? I have a sudden urge to try to find my way home alone. I'm sure I can do it. Would you mind?'

She was gazing eagerly at him, at where she believed him to be by the car. She heard his deep, contemplative sigh.

'Philippa, I can understand you wanting to fight back, to accept a challenge,' he said slowly, 'but are you sure this is the best way to start? There are roads to cross and you haven't even a white stick.'

'I've got my sunglasses in my pocket,' Pippa countered. 'I'll put those on. Oh, let me try, Geoff, please. It's the first time I've felt willing to try. You carry on, and let me do it alone, please. It's only half a mile or so.'

Walters was reluctant. He offered to follow and watch her, but Pippa refused. As she set off along the hot pavement she felt excited and only the least bit afraid. Around the corner she would have to cross the road but there was a pedestrian crossing outside the supermarket − it would not be too difficult.

She moved slowly and with great caution, and now passers-by seemed to recognise there was a difficulty and let her pass. When she reached the bakery the succulent smell of fresh bread was overpowering. Only a building society to pass now and the corner would be there.

She felt foolish running her fingers along the rough brick of the wall to discover the angle of the corner. But so long as one did not mind appearing foolish, independence would not be so hard to attain. The next problem was to judge how far to walk before trying to find the post which would indicate the pedestrian crossing.

She was lucky. Ahead of her she could hear a young woman's voice admonishing a child.

'Richard, hold on to the pram like I told you. We've got to cross here to go and get our shopping for tea. Hold on tight now. Wait till this car has gone.'

Pippa stood behind the voice and waited until she heard the pram wheels thud down on to the road. Then she followed. At the far side her ears again told her the pram was mounting a step. Judgement was needed to guess the distance to that step, but once on the pavement Pippa felt elated. She had crossed a busy road alone, unaided, with not even a stick to help.

She used her nose to discover the pub at the next turning. That was easy. The pub was open and laughing voices were coming out as she passed, and the open door emitted a powerful smell of beer and tobacco smoke. Beyond the pub, on this quieter road, the pavement became uneven and the scent gave way to petrol fumes. Of course, she remembered now, there was a garage on the far side of the road with a row of petrol pumps. The smell gave her an instant mental picture of the road. The lane up to Cambermere was not far now.

She discovered the lane by walking into an obstruction on the pathway. Rubbing a bruised knee, she explored the object with her hands. It was the post box on the corner of the lane. She turned up the lane with a growing feeling of achievement, and as she went she heard the faint purr of a car engine fading behind her. Curious, she had not heard it appoach. Then she smiled. She guessed Geoff Walters had been following her at a discreet distance after all, and now that the worst part of the journey was over, he had left her to it. Funny, she thought, only a few days ago she had believed him a threat to her, and she smiled to recall her terror in the labyrinth. Out here, in the warm sunlight, one could afford to laugh at one's foolish terrors in the dark.

She was still in the dark, in a sense, but climbing the last stretch of the lane towards the Hall she felt a quiet glow of triumph. She was not yet ready to accept blindness as a permanent state of affairs but as a temporary handicap she knew she could cope with it. It would have been easier with Stephen's encouragement, but there was gratification and pride in knowing she could do it alone.

Stephen. She wondered whether she kept penetrating his thoughts the way he constantly recurred in hers. She walked carefully along the edge of the grass verge, thankful there was no traffic, until the curve of the grass edge indicated the entrance to Cambermere Hall.

A tall stone pillar beneath her fingertips confirmed the gateway, and the crunch of gravel beneath her sandals kept her in the right direction. It was important to follow the snaking line of the drive with care and not wander off over the lawns, or she could end up in the lake. The sweet scents of wild flowers in the hedgerows gave way now to a drift of woodsmoke. It was the gardener, no doubt, making a bonfire of the hedge clippings. The drive seemed to go on endlessly, far longer than she remembered. Odd how one's sense of time and distance was distorted in the dark.

At last the drive curved sharply left to where the front steps mounted to the terrace. Pippa, remembering she had no key with her, decided to go round to the kitchen door rather than make Mrs Purvis answer the bell. She found the kitchen door at last, half-covered by the ivy on the walls. It was open, and there was no answer to her call of 'Hello' when she went in.

She crossed the kitchen and made her way out into the vestibule. She was about to call again, when her ear caught the sound of voices coming from the direction of the music room. Feeling her way cautiously around the marble pillars Pippa approached the door.

'I'm glad you came all the same,' she clearly heard Mrs Purvis's voice say. Her fingers told her the door was closed, and she hesitated. 'I must confess I've been worried about her. Not the accident so much – she seems to be coping with that very well – but her behaviour is decidedly odd.'

Pippa flushed. The housekeeper was evidently talking about her – but to whom? Hope leapt in her – could it be Stephen?

'Odd? In what way?'

Hope died again. It was a masculine voice but not Stephen's low-pitched, resonant tone. It was the higher pitch of an elderly man.

'Well, she seems convinced that someone is out to harm her, strange as it may seem. She thinks someone tried to trip her into the swimming pool and then burn her with a sunlamp – really, doctor, there's no end to what she's determined to believe. Why, I'll bet she even thinks the fall from the horse was no accident.'

'I see. That is rather unusual, I must admit. There really is no reason for such beliefs, you think?'

'Oh, I'm certain there's no foundation! Philippa has always been rather strange and secretive, but lately it seems to have become far more pronounced. Like yesterday, for instance – a stray cat appeared here and later it went. Philippa would have it that the creature had been poisoned on purpose to upset her! Really, doctor, I am beginning to become very worried over her, especially when one remembers her mother's last illness.'

161

'Ah yes – Miss Hope. Not my patient, but I recall the case-history. Paranoia and nervous debility, wasn't it? Yes, I can understand your concern and thank you for talking to me about it. As I was Mr Korvak's doctor while he was here, perhaps Miss Korvak will agree to see me. Would you ask her to arrange a convenient time for me to call again?'

'Of course, Dr Ramsay. She has been getting me very alarmed and it's a relief to talk to you about it. I mean, all this imagining there's someone in her room at night and even thinking she saw her mother's ghost in the garden. And talking to this imaginary friend of hers . . . .'

'Dear me, yes, I must see the young lady as soon as possible and see what we can do for her. In the meantime, don't worry, Mrs Purvis. I'll make arrangements for a social worker to call.'

Pippa stood there, stunned. Her first impulse was to cry out, to deny Mrs Purvis's accusation. But it was quickly replaced by fear. What Mrs Purvis had relayed was true, but the way she told it made Pippa sound crazy – and a furious outburst on her part would only confirm that view.

Pippa backed away from the music room as the doctor and Mrs Purvis came out. She felt for another door. As she opened it and hurried in, she realised it was the door to the east wing. Evidently Mrs Purvis no longer considered it necessary to keep it locked.

The voices in the vestibule faded away and Pippa heard the hum of a car engine. She emerged and called, but Mrs Purvis did not answer. She headed for the kitchen, and still Mrs Purvis did not answer. She must have gone out when the doctor left. Anger simmered in Pippa. She must indeed meet Dr Ramsay and endeavour to set him straight, but in her own time. He must be made to see that she was rational, not warped in any way, and that strange things really did happen here in Cambermere Hall.

It was in the vestibule that the frisson of fear tingled in her spine, the certain knowledge that she was being watched, just as once before when Mrs Purvis had stood watching from the head of the stairs. Pippa looked up.

'Who's there? Mrs Purvis?'

No sound disturbed the late afternoon stillness but the

song of birds in the garden. Pippa walked firmly to the bottom step. 'I know you're there. *Who are you?*'

Again, no answer, but seconds later Pippa could almost swear she heard a distant door close somewhere in the upper regions of the house. Pursuit was useless. At that moment the doorbell rang and Pippa hurried to the front door.

'Miss Korvak, Uncle Geoff sent me with these for you, and he told me to say congratulations.'

She recognised Robin Walters' clear young voice and felt the brush of foliage against her hand. He was offering her flowers. She took them and stood back to let him enter.

'Come in, Robin, and thank you. They're lovely.'

'How do you know? Uncle Geoff says you can't see. That's why he sent the flowers.'

'I know because I can smell them. There are carnations, aren't there, and roses?'

'That's right.' There was admiration in the boy's tone. 'We picked them in the garden because the ones in the shop are too expensive.' She could not resist a smile at his innocent candour. 'I took all the thorns off the roses so you wouldn't prick yourself,' he added.

'That was very thoughtful of you,' she replied gravely. 'Will you come and help me find a vase so we can put them in water?' She led the way to the kitchen, conscious of his curious gaze, and set the flowers down on the table.

'Tell you what,' she said brightly, 'we'll have a look in all these cupboards to find a vase − I'm sure there'll be one somewhere. And while we're looking, perhaps we can find some glasses so we can have a drink of orange juice. Okay?'

'Oh, yes,' he said eagerly, and she heard the cupboard doors open and close as he scrabbled in search. At last she heard a clink.

'Here are the glasses,' he said. 'I'll find the vase in a minute. That's a funny place to put a letter.'

'A letter?' she repeated. 'What letter?'

'This one here. It's not even been opened.'

'Whose name is on it?'

'Miss P. Korvak. That's you. Had you forgotten about it? Waiting for someone to read it for you?'

She recovered her wits quickly. It was not a letter from

163

Clive – that was upstairs and it had been opened. This must have been intercepted and held by Mrs Purvis. It could be from . . . She bent to the boy eagerly.

'Yes, that's it. I was waiting for someone to read it. Would you do that for me, Robin? Tell me the postmark first.'

'London. Seven-thirty p.m. Dated the fourth.'

That was last week, soon after Stephen had gone. 'Open it, then, Robin.'

She heard him tear it open and felt her heart thud in hope. London – it must be Stephen. Robin drew a deep breath and read:

' *"Dear Pippa, You meant what you said and so did I. But I hate to recall the angry words of parting and can't bear to think the cord is snapped forever. You must know why I have to go on. The enclosed may help to explain. If, after reading it, little pipistrelle, you feel you want to contact me, I shall be at the hotel until the tenth. If I do not hear from you, I shall know you truly meant what you said. Take care. Yours, Stephen."* '

Robin stopped. 'I'm not sure if I said that word pipistrelle properly,' he said thoughtfully.

'You did. You read beautifully,' Pippa said absently. *'Meant what you said,'* Stephen had written. That was about never wanting to set eyes on him again – she must ring the hotel and tell him she spoke in haste, in anger.

'There's a newspaper cutting here too,' Robin said. 'Shall I read that to you as well?'

'What is it about, Robin?'

'It's very old and yellow. It's from an American newspaper dated 1953. The headline says: "MORE DENUNCIATIONS IN McCARTHY TRIALS." '

Pippa was puzzled. Why should Stephen send a cutting of a rather unpleasant American episode of thirty years ago? There must be a reason. 'Yes, please Robin.'

' *"Yesterday further denunciations were made by Senator Joseph McCarthy's powerful Permanent Sub-Committee on Investigations of un-American activities.*

164

Those accused of Communist leanings included several well-known film actors and actresses, and the eminent physicist J.R. Oppenheimer, who directed the A-bomb project.

"*Public interest was particularly aroused by the arraignment of Jan Loran, Loran . . .* " '

Robin paused. 'I can't say it. Too many s's and z's. Somebody has underlined it and written the word "Father" in the margin.'

'Call it Lorant,' said Pippa. 'Go on.'

' "*Jan Lorant is not himself well-known — he is a technical operative in the Shearing film studio — but the fact that he was denounced by Alexis Korvak has stirred considerable interest. Both Korvak and Lorant are of Hungarian origin and were known to be close friends at one time. Someone close to Lorant claims that his denunciation was an act of vengeance on Korvak's part, in retaliation for an affair between Lorant and Korvak's beautiful wife, the actress Carrie Hope. Neither Korvak nor Lorant will confirm or deny the story.*" '

Robin paused. 'That's it, Miss Korvak. There's another cutting too, dated 1955.'

'Call me Pippa, Robin. Read that too, will you?'

'It's a shorter one. It says:

' "*Jan Loran — Lorant died, suddenly yesterday at his home in Los Angeles. His widow, Helen Lorant, told our reporter that she would never forgive Alexis Korvak, the film-producer, for bringing about her husband's death. It may be remembered that Korvak denounced Lorant in the McCarthy trials some time ago, and Mrs Lorant claims that Korvak's persecution led to her husband's excessive drinking, his loss of position in the film studio and his subsequent decline in health. Besides his widow, Lorant leaves one son, Stefan.*" '

'That's the end, Pippa.'

'Thank you, Robin. Here's your orange juice.'

As he drank thirstily Pippa thought of Stephen. He was right, she could see it now. His mother's determination to avenge her persecuted husband was a strong enough motive for Stephen to want to expose her father. But was Father really so ruthless? Had Mother really taken Jan Lorant as her lover? If so, Father too was to be understood, if not pitied. But it was cruel that passions so long dead could influence the present and drive her and Stephen apart. It was more than cruel — it was wrong, and she would not let it happen. She must get in touch with Stephen at once. When did he say he was leaving London? The tenth? Heavens! That was today! She might be too late!

'Robin, on the letter, is there a telephone number after the name of the hotel?'

'Yes, here it is.'

'Come into the hall with me and dial it for me, will you? Then you can have some more juice.'

Obediently he followed her out and dialled the number. Pippa took the receiver from him.

'The Argosy hotel? Is Mr Stephen Lorant there, please?'

There was a pause before a dispassionate voice replied. 'I'm sorry. Mr Lorant checked out this morning.'

'Oh.' Disappointment thudded like lead in her stomach. 'Do you have a forwarding address or a telephone number?'

'I'm sorry, madam. Mr Lorant left no instructions to that effect. We cannot help you, I'm afraid.'

She hung up dispiritedly. He had given her a chance to make peace and she had failed. Now he would believe she wanted no more to do with him. And she had failed because someone had hidden the letter — and that someone must have been Mrs Purvis. But why?

Obviously she must want to prevent Pippa and Stephen from continuing their relationship — out of jealousy, perhaps? Or did she know about Jan Lorant and her beloved Carrie all those years ago? And if so, why should that colour her attitude to Pippa and Stephen now?

Did she know and connive at that old affair, or did she hate Jan Lorant for it and so wish to prevent a relationship between his son and Carrie's child? The thought crossed Pippa's mind that Jan could almost have been her own

166

father, but for the fact that she was not born until after his death. If she *had* been his child, it might help to explain the housekeeper's attitude and even some of the strange happenings. Silly, thought Pippa, pushing the thought from her mind. All this wild speculation in the light of what the cuttings revealed was making her imagination work overtime again.

'I'll have to go home now, Pippa. It's nearly time for tea and I have to help Uncle Geoff to peel the vegetables and things.'

'Of course, Robin, and tell him I'm very grateful for the flowers. And thank you too for your help.'

'I like helping you. I put your flowers in the vase while you were on the telephone. They're on the kitchen table.'

'Thanks, every time I go in there and smell them I shall think of you. It'll remind me how glad I am of your friendship.'

She could have hugged his small frame, but instead she contented herself with ruffling his hair as they walked to the front door. Peel the vegetables, he had said. There was not enough money in the Walters household to afford domestic help, evidently. She wished she could assure the child that he would not always be poor, that one day, after Father's death, he would be a rich man in his own right.

'Flowers from your own garden mean far more to me than flowers from a shop, Robin,' she said impulsively. 'And one day you will reap your reward, I promise. You'll never want for anything, and especially not love.'

'Bye, Pippa.'

He was gone, his feet crunching rapidly down the drive in a hurry to return home. He was a delightful child, a source of much comfort to Geoff Walters, she was sure.

Before Mrs Purvis returned, Pippa had time to think. The McCarthy witch hunt of the 'fifties was something she had only read about in books. The senator's manic pursuit of all those he suspected of Communist sympathies at the height of America's cold war with Russia — intellectuals, writers, actors, scientists — had led to many of his victims losing their careers, even after they had been cleared. Stephen's father had evidently suffered and the family's hatred for the man who had denounced him unjustly was understandable. Had Father hated Lorant that much? And hated Mother too, for betraying him? He must have forgiven her, for Pippa was born later. Or had Father sought consolation in mistresses of his own? Pippa thought of Nina Walters, and the child Robin.

It was a curious coincidence that Mrs Purvis's conversation over dinner turned to the subject of Alexis Korvak's illness and his disappointments.

'He always wanted a son, you know, Philippa. It was a grudge of his that Miss Carrie never bore him a son.'

Although she could not see, Pippa could feel the housekeeper's bright eyes boring into her. Firmly Pippa kept her lips shut.

12

Pippa lay in bed wondering just how much Mrs Purvis knew about the past, and its effect on the present. Did she know that Stephen was the son of her cherished Miss Carrie's lover? The name Lorant bore some resemblance to the original Hungarian spelling Jan had used. And if Stephen looked like his father, Mrs Purvis had probably recognised him long ago. She must have known about Jan and Mother. Pippa could imagine the thin-lipped housekeeper moving heaven and earth to contrive secret rendezvous for her beloved mistress and her lover.

Strange, thought Pippa. If she had smiled on Jan Lorant all those years ago she certainly did not grant his son the same favour. In fact she had behaved very coolly towards him, apparently only receiving him on her employer's orders. Pippa had a sudden recollection of the openly hostile glare she had darted in Stephen's direction the night

Pippa and he had challenged her over the missing letter. Yes, Pippa remembered, she was lying then, denying the letter's existence when all the time it lay in the kitchen drawer.

Just as Stephen's letter lay there, unopened, until today. It would appear that once again the housekeeper was interfering with Pippa's mail — but why? What had she to gain by keeping back a message from Stephen? Why should she attempt to keep them apart? What had she to gain by alienating Pippa who, before long, might well become her mistress? And then only today she had been trying hard to convince the local doctor that Pippa was mentally unbalanced. It just did not make sense. And added to that, she had seemed to derive malicious pleasure from telling Pippa that her mother had not loved her but the other child, Irma, the one she had been forced to give up. Thank God Stephen had made Pippa read Mother's diary, which proved beyond doubt that she did love her younger child. Stephen had found that diary in a packing case in the east wing, the wing Mrs Purvis had tried to prevent Pippa from entering. The reason for that at least was clear — to prevent Pippa from reading of her mother's love for her.

Mrs Purvis must hate Pippa deeply to want to hurt her so, Pippa reflected. Was it because she really hated Alexis Korvak for his cruel treatment of Miss Carrie, and in his absence the hatred was diverted to his daughter? That was feasible. The housekeeper herself had reasoned that the local villagers would dislike Pippa simply because she was her father's daughter.

Well, then, if one accepted that reason, was the next step that the housekeeper should attempt to harm her? Pippa thought back over the now lengthy list of mishaps — the overheated shower, the oil on the pool steps, the ultraviolet lamp, the burr under Copper's saddle, and the agonising death of the little cat. Mrs Purvis had been around and could have made some of these furtive attempts on her life, but not all — and certainly not the thistle burr. That, Pippa decided, must be pure coincidence. The burr must have been accidentally transferred from a horse blanket to the horse's back and somehow overlooked when he was saddled. Since no one, not even she herself, had known she was going to ride Copper that day, no one could have planned that way of harming her. Mrs Purvis was certainly not to blame for that, reflected Pippa. Nor, surely, for any of the other mishaps. Then who could it be?

It was a double mystery to solve — both the identity of her attacker and the reason for Mrs Purvis's evident hatred. The latter, Pippa felt sure, was due to Father's behaviour over the years. It was sad to admit that he was less than the perfect gentleman she had always believed him, but in recent weeks a very different picture of him had emerged. Stephen had reason to speak so strongly of his hardness, his ruthlessness. Father had exploited his wife's charms, spurned her for many mistresses, and then punished her for her infidelity by ruining her lover's career and indirectly causing his death. That was why Stephen had called him a murderer. And he had raped Nina Walters and cheated Bainbridge. The truth, ugly though it was, had to be faced and admitted. Father was far less than perfect, but he was a dying man.

Pippa was grief-stricken. It seemed such a futile way to die, of alcoholism, just as Jan Lorant had been doomed to die. She was glad Father found comfort in knowing about Robin — the son he always wanted. But her heart was heavy. With Father so ill, Stephen gone perhaps for ever, and Mrs Purvis obviously resenting her so bitterly that she wanted to brand her a neurotic, the world was a dark place. She was alone, with no one to whom she could turn. Lying there in bed in what was once Mother's room, Pippa began to feel apprehensive. With night and blackness all around, she felt as though she were marooned on a tiny island in a sea of limitless gloom. She had a strange sensation of being completely disorientated, disembodied almost, and the atmosphere of Cambermere Hall cloaked her in claustrophobic silence.

That scent: it was there again, faint at first to the nostril but growing in intensity every second. Pippa lay still, tense and fearful. If someone was there in the room, they moved in catlike silence. Not a sound reached her straining ear except the whisper of the trees in the grounds. The sweet fragrance of Californian Poppy forced its way into her lungs, nauseous and powerful. She could bear it no more and sat upright in bed.

'Who's that? Is that you, Mrs Purvis?'

No answer came, and somehow she had expected none. No one had opened the door and there was no movement in the room, only that insidious scent growing now so powerful that it made her feel sick. And more than that, frightened, for if that perfume was being spread by no human hand, then it must be supernatural . . .

'Mother?' she ventured softly, half-afraid and half-annoyed with herself. 'Mother?'

There was the tiniest sound, a flutter which could be the echo of a laugh or the brush of curtains against the window sill in the breeze, then the perfume began to fade. In a few moments it had gone, only the least suspicion of it still lingering in the cool night air. Pippa lay still and sleepless, wondering fearfully whether she had imagined the menacing potency of the scent and that mocking, lilting laugh, or whether the housekeeper's suspicions regarding her sanity were indeed well-founded.

She must have slept well after all, for she awoke at last to the sound of china clattering on a tray and the dull, insistent patter of rain against the window. Whether it was Marion or the housekeeper bringing the tray Pippa could not be sure until, with a swish of curtains, Mrs Purvis spoke.

'It's a perfectly dreadful morning, Philippa. Raining cats and dogs. Not a day for going out at all. Did you sleep well?'

The question was posed in her normal cool and detached manner, but Pippa felt herself draw back, on guard. Whatever she told the housekeeper, she seemed to be able to use the information against her. She answered warily, 'Quite well, thanks. Did you?'

'Indeed, yes. I must have been exhausted, I think, for as soon as my head touched the pillow I went out like a light. As a result I'm all fresh and prepared for today's routine.' She sounded just as she used to in nursery days. 'Early to bed, early to rise, makes a girl healthy, wealthy and wise,' she would say, always in the admonishing tone of a governess. But, it struck Pippa, she was being more than usually chatty this morning. Was she trying to discover something?

171

'You were tired last night, then?' Pippa asked. 'Had you been extra-busy yesterday?'

'Oh, no more than usual, though it takes some effort to run a house this size. No, I think it's just the pure country air down here after the fumes of the city. It makes one sleep well.'

She poured out tea. Pippa could hear the gurgle and smell the refreshing aroma even before she handed her the cup. Then she still hovered in the room, as though curious. Pippa made a sudden decision. One thing she had learnt from this wretched blindness was that it sharpened the ears − failure of one sense seemed to heighten the perception of the others. She found it easier now to read people's intentions, their meanings, not so much in what they said but in the way they said it. Falseness or sincerity, decision or hesitation were far clearer. And added to that, a new kind of intuition came into play. Once she had watched a person's facial expression as they spoke to try to gauge their true intention, but now the voice revealed far more.

'Tell me, Mrs Purvis, I know how attached you were to my mother. You were with her before she married Father, weren't you?'

'Oh, yes, long before.' Already the housekeeper's voice had lost its sharp edge and softened with affection.

'Then you remember the days before she was a star. Did fame change her?'

'Not fame, nor wealth, nor adulation nor anything else. However sordid the world became she remained true to herself.' The voice was almost reverential now, the subdued tones of a tourist in a cathedral.

'Even in the dreadful days of the McCarthy witch hunt? Many famous film people lost their reputation and their jobs then, I understand. But a slur was never cast on her?'

'Good gracious, no! She never dabbled in politics. Others around her were tainted, but never my Miss Carrie! People like John Garfield were driven out of the studios, Joseph Losey the producer went into exile in Europe − many did fade into obscurity, but there was never a whiff of scandal about her.'

The indignation in the housekeeper's voice was threaded with a hint of anger, as though she was reluctant to expand on this theme. Pippa could guess why. Hints of scandal might be attached to Carrie Hope's name because of her affair with another man, who had been denounced as a Communist by his former friend. It was evidently an incident in her idol's life that Mrs Purvis would prefer to forget.

'I heard some of those discredited people were in despair afterwards,' Pippa went on as she sipped her tea. 'Driven to drink, some of them, and even suicide, I'm told.'

'I don't know about that,' the housekeeper said snappishly. 'Garfield certainly died young from alcoholism but I heard of no suicides. That's a morbid subject, Philippa. Don't let a miserable day like this throw you into a depressed mood. It's not healthy. What will you have for breakfast?'

Ignoring her question, Pippa challenged her. 'That's one advantage in my position, Mrs Purvis. Not being able to see the state of the weather I am hardly likely to be influenced by it. Only the sighted feel gloomy on a grey day.'

There was a pause for a moment, a silence in which the housekeeper's displeasure was evident. Pippa felt a small glow of achievement. For the first time in her life she had contested the older woman's unspoken domination, and the housekeeper seemed to be aware of her power slipping rapidly away.

'Will you have boiled eggs? Or bacon?' she asked quietly.

'Both, please,' Pippa replied calmly.

It was only after Mrs Purvis had gone downstairs that Pippa had time to consider whether she had been a little reckless. If the woman had been determined to have her classified insane and perhaps put away, she would be even more determined and more cunning, now battle had been openly declared. Her motive was still not clear, but her intention was.

Mrs Purvis denied that she had sprayed Californian Poppy in Pippa's room before, but Pippa suspected she had lingered in the bedroom this morning, slightly more affable than usual, waiting for Pippa to tell her that she had been almost overpowered by the choking perfume again. Then she could relay that information to Dr Ramsay as yet another sympton of Pippa's paranoid condition. 'Why, Philippa actually believes her mother's ghost returns to her,' she could almost hear the housekeeper tell him, 'to warn her that harm is about to befall her.'

No, thought Pippa firmly as she set the cup aside and got up out of bed, I shall not give her that satisfaction. Whatever happens now I must stay cool and in control and above all, not tell Mrs Purvis what thoughts are in my head. She had completely forgotten to tax the housekeeper about Stephen's letter being hidden in the kitchen, but on reflection she decided not to mention that either. Mrs Purvis must be curious to know where the letter had gone.

Stephen — if only he were here, the darkness would be so much more bearable! In his letter he had even called her pipistrelle, little blind bat — how ironic, in the circumstances. Stop that, Pippa told herself fiercely. You must shut him out of your mind, as you did Clive. You must not think of him again. He hated the name Korvak, and he was gone for ever. Forget him.

Yes, she could do it. Even if he telephoned now, she would not talk to him — would she? Uncertainty hovered. She might, just briefly, to clear up one or two things, but that was all, just to say she now understood the force that drove him on even if she could not condone it, that she would do the same in his shoes . . . But, that done, she would let him go.

It was the following day Pippa decided to test her position with Mrs Purvis further. In the meantime the housekeeper had remained distant but polite, not exactly subservient but certainly less positive than she used to be. If Pippa was to establish her new-found independence she must assert herself.

'That east wing,' she remarked casually as she helped the housekeeper fold the washing she had just brought in from the garden, 'the disused wing, I found that quite interesting.' She made no reference to the key and how difficult it had been to lay hands on it. Mrs Purvis made no answer. 'I should like to have another look around there. Will you come with me and tell me about the sets I have not seen?'

The housekeeper drew a deep breath. 'I am surprised it

174

interests you, Philippa, but for my part I do not care for it much. Apart from being busy, I would prefer not to go in there. Would you mind very much exploring on your own?'

That was progress. Instead of condemning the proposal and forbidding Pippa to go, she was actually excusing herself and allowing Pippa to go by herself.

'Very well,' she conceded. 'Then at least tell me what sets there are. I've seen a steamboat set, a Victorian drawing room and what seemed to be a sultan's palace.'

'Apart from those, there's only a medieval banqueting hall and a dungeon,' Mrs Purvis said coolly.

'Ah yes, I saw the dungeon. Then there's only the great hall left,' Pippa remarked. 'I can visualise that — straw-strewn floor, trestle tables, high slit windows and perhaps a minstrels' gallery.'

'That's right. Now, shall we take the laundry upstairs?' The housekeeper's tone had taken on an abrupt edge again. Pippa was curious.

'It all seems rather odd to me, either nostalgic or just plain egocentric, maintaining those sets for all these years. It seems almost like a mausoleum.' She was following the housekeeper up the stairs, one arm laden with linen and the other hand following the bannister. 'Downright unhealthy, in fact. Those sets ought to be stripped and the house brought back into use again. Rooms should be filled with living people, not become shrines to the past.'

'Not while your father lives.' The housekeeper's quiet voice drifted back down the stairs. Pippa caught her breath, angry with herself at her clumsiness. With Father so desperately ill it did indeed sound as though she were anticipating her inheritance already. It was not only stupid of her, but sounded callous too. Mrs Purvis had won that round in the battle.

In the afternoon the housekeeper declared that she was not going to stay indoors on such a glorious day but would take a pair of secateurs and go out in the garden. Some of the rose bushes could do with having dead blooms cut off, she said, and without inviting Pippa to join her she went out. She was probably glad to be free of her company. Pippa was debating what to do when she heard footsteps on the gravel outside and then the doorbell rang.

'Hello, Pippa,' said Robin's cheerful young voice. 'Can I read for you or something?'

Pippa's heart warmed. 'Thank you, Robin, no. Not reading, but you can take me for a stroll round the grounds if you like and see I don't fall into the lake.'

She loved the way his small, firm hand took hold of hers and guided her along the path below the terrace. Sunlight fell like a blessing on her upturned face. It was good to be alive, despite everything.

'Have you had a visitor today?' Robin asked. Pippa shook her head.

'No. What makes you ask?'

'Oh, I saw a lady by the gate. She asked me my name. And she asked if I knew you.'

'A lady?' Pippa was puzzled. She knew no woman except Mrs Purvis in Cambermere. 'What was she like?'

'Oh, quite pretty, really. She had lovely hair, all curly and shining in the sun, like our dog Rusty.'

A canvasser, perhaps, sounding out the lie of the land, Pippa guessed. 'Did she ask about me by name, Robin?'

'She said did I know Miss Korvak, that's all. I said yes. Then she went away.'

Curious, but not important. Most of the locals would know by now that she was Korvak's daughter. Robin let go of her hand, and she knew he was bending down. Then she heard him grunt with effort. A distant plop told her what he was doing: he was throwing gravel into the lake. She smiled. Such a simple action, and yet it rolled back the years for her. She could still recall skimming stones across the surface of the pool in the gardens of their Kent home, and Mrs Purvis jerking her arm and telling her to stop. Conduct unbecoming to a young lady, she had said. On an impulse Pippa bent and picked up a handful of gravel and began throwing pieces in the direction Robin seemed to be throwing.

'Further left, and throw harder!' he exclaimed, pleasure gleaming in his young voice. Obediently she changed direction and length and was rewarded with a gratifying plop. Robin cheered. 'Well done! That was clever, Pippa.'

After a while they moved on, around the house and across the lawns towards the woods. Robin was recounting how Uncle Geoff could throw a ball the length of a cricket pitch and knock down the middle stump at least twice out of every three goes, and Pippa derived great pleasure from his evident adoration of his uncle. Father would have revelled in this son if only he had known.

They came to the edge of the field. 'There's a fence here but we can climb over,' Robin said, and she could hear his shoes grate on the wooden rail. Suddenly he gasped. 'I think we'll wait a bit,' he said in a small voice.

'Why, what is it, Robin?'

'It's that lady. She's over there by the woods.'

'No matter, we can go on.'

'No, wait. She's talking to Uncle Geoff and he looks cross. He's all red and waving his arms. There, she's going — she's got into the van.'

'Van? What van?'

'A sort of caravan you can drive. She's gone in the back. Uncle Geoff is walking away. He hasn't seen us, but he looks very cross.'

So she was the owner of the Dormobile, Pippa thought. But what connection had she with Walters, and why were they arguing? The van was on Korvak land, not his. However, as the boy said, it was best to let him go without becoming aware of their presence, especially if he was angry about something.

She touched Robin's arm. 'Come on, let's go back. It's hot and we could get a nice cold drink from the fridge. There might even be some ice cream.'

Retracing their steps they approached the Hall from the back and made for the kitchen door. As they crossed the stable yard Pippa felt Robin's hand tighten on hers.

'There's a black lady by the door.' She recognised instantly whom he meant. 'I've changed my mind, Pippa,' he hurried on. 'I think I'll go home now and come and see you again soon.'

He relinquished her hand and fled. From his graphic description, she could visualise Mrs Purvis by the door, dark hair gleaming, black-gowned and probably still wearing proudly those jet earrings she treasured. She made no sound as Pippa approached until she was close to the door.

'I didn't know you were out, Philippa,' she said crisply. 'Was that the Walters boy with you?'

'Robin, yes. He took me for a walk. Do you know him? A delightful child.' Pippa was probing, and she sensed that the other woman knew it.

'I've seen him, that's all. Come along in and we'll have some iced tea.'

She led the way indoors. As Pippa entered, her nostrils were filled with the glorious, heady scent of roses. At first she thought Mrs Purvis must have cut some to bring into the house, but then she remembered Robin's gift of flowers. They filled the kitchen with their beautiful perfume, and her heart swelled for him again. She was lucky to have him as a half-brother.

Ice rattled in a glass. 'Philippa,' the housekeeper said calmly, 'I've been meaning to tell you. A letter came for you, from Mr Lorant, I believe. I kept it because I did not consider it good for you to continue the relationship with him.'

'What?' Pippa was astonished, not only by her admission of guilt but also by her presumption. 'By what right do you presume to make decisions for me, Mrs Purvis? As it happens I have the letter, but may I remind you it is an offence to interfere with the mail. And in any case, I am quite capable of making my own decisions.'

'I know, but I still think you naïve and unused to the ways of the world. I wanted to protect you.'

'Protect me? From Stephen?' Pippa's breath was taken away.

'Yes, from Stephen. He had more reason than most to hate you, though you could not know it. I know who he really is.'

But she was evidently unaware that Pippa knew too. Pippa decided to lead her on. 'Who was he, that you should think it safer to part us, Mrs Purvis?'

'He is the son of your mother's lover, the only man she ever loved. His name was Jan.'

'I see. But why should that make Stephen hate me?'

'Jan Lorant was a passionate man who adored your mother, and Miss Carrie adored him. I used to see to it that they met in safety. Though I did not approve at first, I had to see my Miss Carrie had what gave her happiness – she had too little with Alexis Korvak. For a time they were blissfully happy.' The housekeeper's tone mellowed to gentleness at the memory.

'And then?' prompted Pippa.

'Your father found out. He had Jan Lorant hounded and persecuted – those McCarthy trials you spoke of – and the man was ruined. He might have been competition to Alexis in the studios, so his dismissal was a double triumph for Alexis Korvak. Jan Lorant, a failure and ostracised by everyone, took to drink. Miss Carrie was whipped away to Europe and she never saw him again. She pined and became ill. When he died she almost lost her reason.'

There was bitter anger, quiet and controlled, in Mrs Purvis's voice. She stopped speaking, re-living the horror of those days. Pippa prompted her again. 'So you believe Stephen hates me for what my father did to his? I can't believe that.'

'Oh yes, he does. At first I did not know who he was when he came here with a letter of introduction from your father. But the American accent, the similarity of his name to Jan's – it soon dawned on me. Not that he looks like his father, but I knew.'

'And you did nothing? You did not tell me?'

'Why should I?' Mrs Purvis's tone was fierce. 'It was obvious he wanted to discredit Alexis Korvak, and why should I stop him? Korvak had made Miss Carrie's life a misery, and I'd be glad for anyone to punish him. He's a vile, callous man, a man everyone hates and no one loves!'

'You haven't explained why you intercepted my letter from Stephen,' Pippa said quietly.

'I thought I'd made it clear. He hates you because you're Korvak's daughter. He set out to harm you. He must have been the cause of all those events you told me about – the sunlamp, the pool, the shower. He was here in Cambermere when all those things happened.'

'No, no, that's monstrous!' Pippa protested hotly. 'He wouldn't stoop to devious things like that!'

'No? Then why is it that nothing has happened to you since he left?' the housekeeper retorted calmly. 'You're a very gullible child, Philippa, as you always were. And for that reason and because you're Miss Carrie's child, however unwanted, I feel it my duty to look after your interests. You should be grateful, though I don't expect you to be able to realise that. I'm going out now, down to the village. In the meantime, think over what I have said.'

The door closed sharply behind her and Pippa was left clutching her glass and shaking with anger. Not for a second would she entertain the dreadful suspicion the housekeeper was trying to plant in her mind. Not Stephen, no, emphatically not Stephen!

It was curious the way the shrewd housekeeper could turn her own deceit in the matter of the letter into a seeming virtue, claiming it was protection. She was a cunning creature indeed, one to be watched warily. Somehow, once again, she had made their encounter into a victory for herself. But whatever she did or said, she was not going to poison Pippa's mind against Stephen. If she had known the contents of that letter she delayed, she would have known its tone showed his concern for Pippa, not hate.

After supper Mrs Purvis referred to the subject again.

'Philippa,' she said tentatively, 'whatever he has written to you, I hope you are not going to see Stephen Lorant again. I honestly believe it will do you no good.'

'Then you can set your mind at rest,' Pippa retorted before she took time to think. 'He's left the country. I don't know where he is.'

She could hear the housekeeper's sigh of satisfaction and could have bitten her tongue. She should have kept silent and played a wary game just like Mrs Purvis, instead of blurting everything out. In that at least Mrs Purvis was right — she was naïve.

As Pippa stretched her arms and made a move to go to bed, Mrs Purvis chose that moment to hurl her final salvo — but carefully disguising it as concern.

'Never mind, Philippa, my dear,' she said soothingly as Pippa reached the door, 'although it's hard to acknowledge that you're alone and friendless now with your young friend gone abroad and everything, don't be too downhearted. We have to find inner strength at a time like this. I'm sure your solution will be to talk it over with Gwen. Sleep well, Philippa.'

Controlling her irritation, Pippa left. It was not easy to retort when one could find no words of defence. She lay sleepless far into the night, fighting to keep at bay the feeling of loneliness and disorientation that threatened to swamp her. It was bleaker than ever, now that warfare with the housekeeper had been tacitly admitted on both sides.

Lonely, vulnerable, fearful again of the night's silent menace, Pippa yearned for Stephen. Then, forcing herself to recognise that he was gone from her life, she curled under the blanket and chewed her fingernail. Half-asleep, she found herself murmuring, 'I don't believe her, Gwen, she's lying because she resents my friendship with Stephen. I'm sure it's envy, Gwen, truly I do. I won't believe evil of him — he was so gentle and understanding and, Lord, how I wish he were here!'

Troubled, she rolled over. It was hot and sticky in bed. She stretched her arms out of the blanket and up into the black void, vast and limitless and empty of hope.

'Stephen!' she called softly. 'Oh, Gwen! Where are you? I'm so lonely!'

She stretched her fingertips into the still night air, groping for hope, for release from this terrible isolation. There was a movement, and then a million volts seemed to crash through Pippa's body as she leapt in terror. Her hand, outstretched before her, was held in the cold grip of another hand.

13

Pippa lay rigid, shock and fear combining to render her speechless and unable to move. The seconds seemed to stretch into an eternity as cold sweat broke out all over her, then Pippa felt the hand slide away from hers. She lay there, numb and terrified, waiting for a sound to betray that the hand was human and not the cold touch of a spirit from beyond the grave.

No sound came, only the rustling of the trees, but just the faintest trace of that familiar perfume came to her nostrils. Could it really be Mother, come back again as she did the night she danced by moonlight? Pippa trembled. No, no, it could not be. There was no love or tenderness in that cold touch.

Minutes must have passed. Pippa shook from head to foot, then as no sound or further movement disturbed her, she began to grow calmer. It was a living creature, no ghost, she told herself firmly. Someone was here; someone who wanted to frighten her. She sat up quickly and reached for the bedside lamp. Even if it could not illuminate the room for her it would cause the intruder to start in surprise.

The switch clicked. Still there was no movement in the room.

'What do you want?' Pippa demanded sharply. If it was a stranger, he would not know she could not see. No answering sound or movement came. She swung her legs out of bed, trying to look confident despite her thudding heartbeat. The bed creaked as she stood up, and it could have been her imagination that there was the faint click of a door closing.

The room was empty. Pippa felt angry with herself for her recent fear. Some living person was playing a trick and she was foolish to allow it to terrify her. She groped for her robe and put it on, then marched firmly to Mrs Purvis's room. She knocked sharply on the door. Instantly she heard movement inside and then the housekeeper's voice.

'Philippa? Is that you?'

Grasping the knob Pippa turned it and went in without waiting for an invitation. A pity she could not see, she thought, for there was no way of telling whether Mrs Purvis was already dressed or genuinely disturbed by her knock.

'Mrs Purvis, are you up? Were you in my room just now?' Pippa demanded. 'If someone was trying to play a prank on me I am not amused. I've had about enough of someone's idea of a joke. Was it you, Mrs Purvis?'

There was a rustling sound which could have been the

housekeeper pulling on a dressing gown. 'What are you talking about, Philippa? No, of course I wasn't in your room. And what do you mean by joke? What happened?'

'Never mind that. Come with me and we'll see if there is anyone there now, though I doubt it.' Pippa walked out, hands outstretched before her. Mrs Purvis followed.

'This is nonsense, Philippa. It's not the first time either.' She opened Pippa's door. 'There, you see, there's no one here.'

'Then he's somewhere in the house. We'd better check.' Pippa was turning to go but the housekeeper barred her way.

'Now look here, there's no one in the Hall but you and myself and I have no intention of getting into a state of hysteria like you over some imaginary intruder. What happened, anyway, that you look so pale?'

Pippa hesitated. If the housekeeper continued to insist that the house was empty then the story of a hand in the dark would sound insane. But Pippa's fingers could still feel that cold, hard touch. It had been no dream or hallucination.

'I shall call the police and ask them to come and check,' Pippa said, but she could sense the housekeeper's thin body still blocked her way. 'Will you move aside, please? I'll ring from the solarium.'

Mrs Purvis hesitated and then moved. 'Very well, but remember this, Philippa. You are going to look very foolish indeed once they've spent an hour investigating the house and grounds and find nothing. Very foolish indeed.'

She was right, of course, Pippa had to admit. And the tale of the night's incident would be strong confirmation to Dr Ramsay that his patient was indeed paranoid. She heard a door close and knew that Mrs Purvis had returned to her room. It angered Pippa to think that the woman was so sure of herself, but what could she do?

All right, if there was no intruder in Cambermere Hall it could only have been Mrs Purvis who took her hand. But the hand, cold as it was, was not so bony as the house-keeper's. Slim-fingered, yes, and ringless, but not angular. It was smooth and supple, more the hand of a woman than a man.

But what woman would come to the Hall — except Carrie Hope? Puzzled and unwilling to believe anything so superstitious, Pippa returned to bed.

In the morning she awoke to the distant sound of church bells drifting across the fields. Pippa realised she must have slept late. She lay listening to the sound, so distinctly English and summerlike, visualising sunsoaked meadows and cricket on a village green. It all seemed so serene and secure after the fears of the night. Sunday. There was something reassuringly normal about an English Sunday with all its connotations of morning service and then a family stroll or a drink at the local pub before the roast beef. How could one believe in nightmares and ghosts on a day such as this, so steeped in tradition and normality?

The day passed quietly. Mrs Purvis decided to spend some hours on bringing her accounts up to date. Monday, as if having made up its mind to start the week with activity, proved more eventful. It was still only mid-morning when Mrs Purvis found Pippa in the music room and announced that she had a visitor.

'Miss Fenton, from the Social Services Department to see you, Philippa,' Mrs Purvis said. 'Do sit down, Miss Fenton.'

The door closed and Pippa knew she had left them alone together. She felt ill at ease, unable to determine whether the other woman was old or young, and knowing she had been sent by the medical authorities.

Miss Fenton spoke first. 'Miss Korvak, I understand you've recently had an accident. I've been sent to see if we can help you in any way. How are you coping?'

The voice was young, cool, capable. Pippa guessed her to be thirtyish, poised and efficient at her job. 'Quite well, thanks, in the circumstances,' she replied.

'Problems with cooking and so on, I expect?'

'Not really. Mrs Purvis sees to all that.'

'Yes, now I'm not quite sure what your circumstances are here, Miss Korvak. According to my papers you live and work abroad. Is that so? What do you do?'

'I'm secretary to a university professor in Paris. That is, I was until . . . ' It was the first time it had occurred to her

184

that now she could not possibly go back to Professor
Garnier at the Sorbonne. She would have to hand in her
resignation, and then what would she do? Miss Fenton's
cool voice was speaking again.

'So you will probably remain in England, I take it. Is this
your home?'

'My father's — Alexis Korvak. He's in America and my
mother is dead.'

'So you're here alone. And Mrs Purvis?'

'She's my father's housekeeper, both here and in his
London flat.'

'So she is taking care of you until your father returns to
England,' Miss Fenton surmised. She had evidently never
heard of Alexis Korvak or of his illness.

'So your own income will of necessity be stopped,' she
remarked. 'You're not married?'

'No.' Pippa could see where she was leading. No income,
no supporting husband — she might be in financial need.
'But there is no need to worry,' she went on quickly. 'My
father is wealthy and I am in no need.'

'I see.' Pippa could hear the sound of her pen on paper.
'Still, I'm sure we can help you. You must not allow your
disability to turn you into a recluse, you know. We can
arrange classes in mobility for you, to learn how to use a
long white cane to get around alone. And when you're
ready you can have lessons in braille-reading and — well, I
was going to say touch-typing, but you were a secretary.'

Pippa could not help the angry lump that constricted her
throat. *Were* a secretary, in the past tense? The implication
was that her useful life was over. From now on she could be
taught merely to endure life by means of braille dots or
basket making. The thought made her bristle.

'Thank you, Miss Fenton. I don't want to learn braille or
how to use a long cane,' she began tartly.

'Well, a collapsible white stick then, and you can keep it
in your handbag. Just to enable you to get out and about,
you know, and not feel cut off,' Miss Fenton said cheerfully. She was clearly accustomed to the natural hostility of
the newly-handicapped and knew better than to react
angrily.

'I do get out and about,' Pippa snapped. 'I walked back

185

here from Marlow unaided, and I can do it again.'

'That's splendid, Miss Korvak, and shows the right spirit. I can see you've come to terms with your problem already and are going the right way about meeting it. I'm very glad But if there is any way in which you think I can be of help to you, don't hesitate to contact me. I'll leave you my card and telephone number. Good day, Miss Korvak.'

She left the room, brightness and competence radiating about her. Pippa felt deeply sorry that she had treated the young woman in such a bad-tempered way, making her the butt of her own anger and resentment and fears. It was too late to hurry after her to apologise and thank her for her good intentions. Pippa slumped in the chair. Dr Ramsay and Miss Fenton might treat her blindness as a permanent condition but she herself was never going to admit that it could dog her all her days, or the fight would be over. White stick? Never! To carry that stick would be for her tantamount to an admission of defeat, a white flag of surrender.

It was useless to stay in the music room, idly picking out chords on the piano as she had been doing before Miss Fenton came. Pippa made up her mind to go for a swim – in the pool, at least, one could move about without a cautious hand to ensure that the way was clear. As she came through into the vestibule she was surprised to hear that Miss Fenton was still there. Her silvery voice, though gently modulated, echoed in the marble vault.

'I see, and thank you very much for the information, Mrs Purvis. It does help so much to have a clear picture of the situation. Good day to you.'

Suspicion leapt into Pippa's mind. What had the house-keeper been telling her, she wondered. No doubt the same exaggerated picture of Pippa's mental imbalance that she had drawn for Dr Ramsay. But before Pippa could question her the telephone rang. She could hear Mrs Purvis's quick, light step as she came from the door, and Pippa hurried to reach the telephone before her.

'Hello? Who? Hobbs, Sharp and Ridler? Ah yes, the solicitors. Yes, Miss Korvak speaking.'

Mrs Purvis's footsteps lingered close. The lawyer's voice sounded warm and Pippa remembered it – Mr Hobbs, whom Geoff Walters had taken her to see.

'I have some details now from your father's solicitors in the States,' he told her. 'There's just one question — two other beneficiaries are named — Mrs Purvis, who I understand is your housekeeper?'

'That's right.'

'And a Mrs I. Starkey, last known address in Nottingham. Can you tell me that lady's present address, Miss Korvak?'

'Starkey?' Pippa repeated slowly. 'No, I'm sorry, I can't help you, Mr Hobbs. I'm afraid I don't know the name.'

Mrs Purvis was instantly at her elbow. 'Who is that, Philippa? What do they want?'

Pippa spoke into the receiver. 'Just one moment, Mr Hobbs. Perhaps Mrs Purvis knows.'

'Knows what? What's this all about?' The housekeeper's voice was cold, demanding.

Pippa covered the mouthpiece. 'The solicitors dealing with my father's affairs. They need to know the address of a Mrs Starkey, last heard of in Nottingham. To do with Father's will, I believe.'

'Give the 'phone to me.' Mrs Purvis snatched it unceremoniously from Pippa's hand. 'To whom am I speaking? Ah, Mr Hobbs.' She paused for a moment, obviously listening. 'I see. Yes, well as it happens I do know the address. Yes, 32 Yewtree Close, Bramley, Nottingham. Not at all, Mr Hobbs, glad to be able to help. Goodbye.'

A click indicated that she had replaced the receiver and she began to move away quickly. Pippa hastened after her.

'What was that about? Who is Mrs Starkey?'

Mrs Purvis began to hum to herself quietly. Pippa persisted, 'Who is she, Mrs Purvis?'

Mrs Purvis sighed. 'Oh, no one of importance to you, my dear. She was a member of your father's household years ago, long, long ago.'

Of course, thought Pippa. Housekeeper perhaps in the days when Mrs Purvis's position was nanny. Another faithful servant whose service Father wanted to acknowledge at the end. He was not so thoughtless after all, to remember two of his employees in his will. Satisfied, she went to her room and changed into a swimsuit and robe.

Out on the terrace she had to feel her way gingerly around the sunchairs and tables. She was quite unaware that she was being watched until she heard the housekeeper's voice calling out, 'A swim will do you good, Philippa, but I should take care not to hang about afterwards. There's a chilly breeze about now. You could sunbathe on your balcony though, where it's sheltered.'

Pippa stepped forward carefully, feeling for the edge of the pool with her toes. Having found it, she sat on the lip and slid into the water. She was taking no more chances with slippery steps. The water was cool and caressing and it was a comforting sensation to abandon herself to it, gliding and floating, freed at last from the tension of walking. It was only now that she could realise just how tense she had been, her muscles permanently flexed and her brain always alert for signals of danger. It was bliss to lie on her back, supported by lapping water and feeling the sun's warmth on her face. After twenty minutes or so Pippa swam to the edge, felt her way round to the steps and climbed out.

Mrs Purvis was right, there was a nippy breeze blowing. Pippa shivered. It was too chilly to lie on a sunchair to dry off so she wrapped the towelling robe about her and went indoors. Perhaps a sunbathe on the balcony, out of reach of the breeze, would be pleasant.

As she crossed the vestibule she heard voices coming from the direction of the music room, so subdued that it was unclear whether a man or a woman was speaking. She hesitated, and then made for the staircase. It could be no one who wanted to see her or Mrs Purvis would have called her, and in any event she was not dressed to receive guests. As she reached the top of the stairs she heard a door open. Mrs Purvis must have caught sight of her.

'Ah, finished your swim? There's a deckchair on your balcony, Philippa, and a rug over the balustrade if you should need it.'

'Thank you. Is there someone with you, Mrs Purvis?' Pippa called out.

'With me? No — why do you ask?'

'I thought I heard voices.'

'Ah, the radio probably. I was listening to a play. I'll

make tea in an hour.'

The door closed, and Pippa went on to her room. She could feel the sunlight streaming across to her before she reached the open french window. Facing south and out of reach of the breeze, the balcony was a suntrap.

All the same, before the hour was up Pippa decided to dress. The deckchair was not so comfortable as a sunbed, and it was growing cooler. As she struggled up out of the deckchair she felt something brush her arm. Alarmed, she stretched out a curious hand, and then smiled. It was only the rug Mrs Purvis had spoken of, draped over the rail of the balcony. No wonder she had felt cool — its shadow had lain across her.

For a moment she stood there, her hand lightly resting on the rail while she looked out unseeingly across the grounds. She felt calmer now, though no less lonely than before. Calm acceptance, that was what she must cultivate — the ability to resign herself to destiny and not be frustrated by her limitations. At the same time, she must fight back and make what she could of life, with or without Stephen Lorant, and find the strength to be complete within herself.

She gripped the rail firmly as she made this private avowal, and turned to go inside. As she did so, there was a crunching sound as the rail slithered down from her hand and the rug fell across her feet. Then there was a metallic clang. Startled and mystified, she stood stock-still, and then heard running footsteps on the terrace below.

'Philippa! My God! What happened? Are you all right? Mrs Purvis's voice rang out. 'What on earth did you do?'

'Nothing. Why, what is it?' Pippa moved a foot cautiously forward and held out her hand. Nothing was there, no balustrade, only the rug on her feet. She stood, tense. 'Mrs Purvis? Has the balustrade fallen?'

'Yes, it has. You'd better go inside carefully.'

Pippa turned, puzzled. How could a whole metal balustrade just fall away like that, with no pressure to speak of? It didn't make sense — but then, nor did any of the other strange incidents which had occurred since she first came to Cambermere Hall. And the footsteps running just before Mrs Purvis called out — now she thought about it and heard the sound again in memory, she could swear there had been more than one pair of feet. If so, who was the second person, and why didn't she speak? Pippa remembered hearing the voices in the music room, and Mrs Purvis's denial.

She dressed quickly and went downstairs. Her nostrils had distinctly detected the smell of toast and she was led to the kitchen.

'Philippa, there you are! Tea's just brewed and I've got some lovely hot muffins for you, you used to love them on Sundays in the nursery.'

'Never mind the muffins, Mrs Purvis,' Pippa said firmly. 'Just tell me what's going on here, and why.'

'I don't know what you mean, my dear. Oh, the balustrade. Yes, I must get that seen to tomorrow. Such a mercy you weren't hurt. The railings can't have been checked for ages, since your father never gave orders to do so. Redecoration, yes, but maintenance is another matter. Perhaps I should have thought of that myself. So much for one person to do alone, you know, caring for two homes.'

'You're being evasive again,' Pippa persisted. 'That balustrade must have been tampered with, just like the pool and the sunlamp. No,' she went on as the housekeeper tried to interrupt, 'don't tell me again it's paranoia. I may be incapacitated in one way but I'm not stupid. Slow, yes, but I can see now that someone is out to harm me, even if I don't know the reason. But I suspect you do.'

'You think I would try to kill you?' The older woman's voice was harsh, challenging. Pippa tried hard not to subside before her cold strength.

'You are the only person around, so far as I know, and I know you lie to me.'

'Lie? What about?'

'You say we're alone, but I swear I sense another presence. That's one thing about blindness, you know, it gives you sixth sense, and I'm certain there's someone else. The door to the yard there closes when I come in, footsteps on the terrace beside yours just now, and I know I heard voices in the music room.'

'I explained that,' the housekeeper said with a patient sigh. 'The radio, remember?'

'And you interfered with my mail — twice. That too is deception. So is trying to convince the doctor I'm mad. I do not trust you, Mrs Purvis, though I cannot for the life of me understand why you do it. Would you care to explain?'

She heard the housekeeper draw a deep, quiet breath. 'Philippa, I could explain though I doubt you would appreciate my concern for you. The letters I thought would only unsettle you when you were in a sensitive enough condition already. I felt the doctor should be made aware of the chance you might inherit your dear mother's instability . . .'

'You always swore she was perfect, faultless in every way,' Pippa said angrily.

'So she was,' the other woman retorted icily, 'until your father drove her mad. Quite mad. She killed herself because of him.'

'*Killed herself?* You never told me that!'

'Killed herself, here at Cambermere, out of her mind after all he'd done to her. And how do I know you won't do the same?' the quiet voice went on. 'You're just as unstable now.'

'*No, no!* You're still doing it, Mrs Purvis! Either it's you who threatens me, or you're in league with someone else who is! And now you're trying to plant the idea of suicide in my mind, lying about my mother, but it won't work. It's you who are mad.'

'And you're not? Then why do the doctors call yours a hysterical blindness?' she asked mildly.

Pippa flared at her. 'For God's sake tell me why you hate me so!'

Despite the vow of calm confidence, Pippa could not help her outburst.

'Shall I pour you more tea, my dear? I think this first cup has gone cold. Help yourself to the muffins — I've already buttered them.' The swift change in Mrs Purvis's tone from icy rage to cool politeness was breathtaking. This time Pippa was not going to be thwarted so easily. In equally controlled tones she addressed the housekeeper. 'Why should you hate me so, Mrs Purvis? After all, I am Carrie Hope's child.'

'That's so, but Alexis Korvak's too. Her first child, Irma,

inherited all her looks and temperament, but her second child had the bad blood — the evil that was in Korvak. Irma was to be loved, but Philippa to be feared and hated.'

She spoke the words in such a sunny way, referring to Pippa in the third person as if she were not there, that Pippa recoiled in horror. There was no doubt of it — robbed of her adored mistress and first baby, the housekeeper was demented, but in a way that was not obvious to the world. So much the more dangerous, thought Pippa, and it was impossible to reason with a mad woman. She would have to think about how to handle this situation.

Over the rest of tea, Mrs Purvis made polite conversation as though nothing had happened. And Pippa found that even more sinister.

Later that evening the telephone rang. Pippa waited, but no one seemed to be going to answer it. Mrs Purvis must be out again, she thought. Pippa walked quickly from her room to the solarium, but as she picked up the receiver she heard a click.

'Hello?'

'Oh, Pippa! I was about to ring off.' She felt her heart thud in surprise and delight — it was Stephen's voice. 'Listen, Pippa,' he said urgently. 'I know you have no time for me but I'm at the airport now and I couldn't leave without speaking to you when I heard the news.'

'News?' she repeated, wondering if he could have heard about her blindness. 'What news?'

'You haven't heard? It was on the radio — Alexis is sinking fast. I'm sorry, Pippa.'

'I should go to him,' were Pippa's first words, a choke in her throat.

'Too late, I fear. You wouldn't make it in time. Listen, Pippa. There's little time — my 'plane leaves very soon. I know you never want to see or hear of me again — '

'Stephen, I — '

'No, listen. I had to contact you, just once, to tell you I'm not going to do that book.'

'You couldn't find all the material you needed?'

'On the contrary, I found it all. I found he did let your mother die — '

192

'You said he was a murderer.'

'So I believed, for he was there when she killed herself and he did not try to stop her. Now I know. He was mesmerised, horror struck. He did love her, despite her instability and unfaithfulness.'

'So you've forgiven him,' Pippa said acidly.

'I had no choice. From his sick bed he wrote me a letter, clearing my father's name, explaining he had acted out of revenge, and giving permission for me to publish the letter or use it any way I pleased. I'm afraid I under-estimated him. I just wanted to say I'm sorry, *galambom*. I know you hate me, but I was very fond of you. Forgive me. Be happy, little one — let things flow over you and you'll be happy.'

She grew alarmed for he sounded as if he was about to hang up. She could not let him go like this, believing she still hated him and unaware of her plight. 'Stephen, listen a moment,' she began.

'Oh, and one thing more — I nearly forgot. Your half-sister, Irma. She's not dead, after all, as we thought — '

There was a sudden crackle on the line and then total silence. Pippa rattled the receiver rest anxiously. 'Stephen? Stephen, are you there?' It was no use; the line was completely dead.

Replacing the receiver, she returned to her room and sat on the edge of the bed, numb with disappointment. She could not even ring the airport back since the line was dead. She did not even know which airport he was at. In minutes he would climb into an aircraft and disappear from her life, and there was nothing she could do about it.

And Father was dying. He too was cut off from her. Mrs Purvis was out, and Pippa could not drive. She was helpless to reach or contact him. Tears pricked her lids and began to flow. Poor Father, so maligned and reviled. Thank heaven at least Stephen's view of him was happier now and that dreadful book would never be written. Father had undoubtedly committed many sins, but he had done his best at the last to atone, admitting Robin as his co-heir with Pippa and clearing the name of a man he had dishonoured all those years ago.

She climbed wearily into bed, determined not to think any more about her problems. Tomorrow she would feel fresh and more able to plan how to cope. Right now, with Father and Stephen about to leave her life, she would prefer to sink into the oblivion of sleep.

But sleep would not come readily. For an hour she lay, trying not to think, but small insidious thoughts kept creeping into her mind. The news about Father was on the radio. Mrs Purvis had been listening to the radio, or so she claimed. Could it be that she already knew the end was near and had deliberately kept the news from Pippa?

She pushed the thought aside and tried to concentrate on pleasant things — light and flowers and butterflies — oh, why did one's thoughts always have to centre on the visual?

Mrs Starkey. For no apparent reason the name of the legatee in Father's will came to mind. Mrs I. Starkey. What could the 'I' stand for? That was a good exercise to send one to sleep, like counting sheep. Ivy, Ingrid, Irene. There weren't very many female names beginning with I. Isabel, Ida, Iris — and that lovely but unusual one, Imelda.

Sleep was still not approaching. Work through the alphabet, she told herself, like doing a crossword. Imogen, Inez, Isadora.

Irma! She sat upright in bed. Of course, Irma Starkey. Stephen had told her that Irma was not dead after all. Irma Starkey was her sister, alive and in Nottingham.

14

Irma — Pippa was sure of it. The name Starkey had meant nothing because she had never known the name of the man her sister married.

Yes, it fitted. Mrs Purvis had been quick to supply the Nottingham address to the solicitors because she had kept in touch with her mistress's child. What was it she had said when Pippa asked who Mrs Starkey was? A 'member of the household', she had said, 'many years ago'. Pippa's lips curved in an ironic smile. It was a part-truth, at least.

But why did the housekeeper lead Pippa to believe that her sister was dead? Why so many lies and subterfuges? There must be a reason, and yet for the life of her Pippa could not see it.

Mrs Purvis was undoubtedly in touch with Irma; after all, she had made it clear that she loved Miss Carrie's first child and hated the second. Pippa wondered if she had told Irma about the accident.

In the morning Mrs Purvis knocked and came in with the tea tray, which she set down on the bedside cabinet. She crossed to draw back the curtains: Pippa heard the swish.

'Good morning, Philippa. Another beautiful day,' the housekeeper said in her usual crisp, confident voice, as though they had never crossed words.

Pippa sat up. 'Is there a radio here? I know my father is nearing the end.'

'There's no change,' Mrs Purvis said crisply. The sound of liquid tinkled into the china cup.

'Has there been a message? A 'phone call?'

'No. The telephone appears to be out of order. I shall have to go to another telephone to report it.'

'Then how do you know?'

'It was on the news earlier.'

'Mrs Purvis, why didn't you tell me that Irma was alive and that you knew where she was?'

'Do you ask out of concern for her? You hardly knew her and haven't seen her in twenty years. Life has not been easy for her, if you care to know. Far from it, with a faithless husband who finally left her.'

Pippa sipped her tea, wondering. 'But caring for her as you evidently do, Mrs Purvis, why didn't you go to her instead of staying in my father's employ? You've made it clear you cared nothing for him.'

'I told you once. I know which side my bread is buttered. Your father gave me a free hand in managing his two houses and from his allowance I could see to it that she never starved. She's been good to me too, bless her.

Always a little gift when we meet, like these earrings she knew I longed for.'

The jet earrings; Pippa remembered how pleased Mrs Purvis was when she came back from London. A gift from a friend, she had said.

Without being prompted further, the housekeeper began talking again, softly, as if to herself. 'Yes, she's had a raw deal, poor lamb, just like her lovely mother. It's a cruel trick of fate, the two of them alike as two peas, beautiful and yet doomed to hardship. But I wasn't going to let it happen again. I promised my Miss Carrie I'd see to her child. All these years I've bided my time to see she gets what she deserved. She'll come into her own yet, or my name's not Emily Purvis.'

Pippa heard her move to the far side of the room, to the dressing table. 'Don't you fret, Miss Carrie,' the housekeeper was murmuring, 'I'll not fail you. I'll keep my vow, my angel.'

Pippa was stunned. It was clear the woman was in a private reverie of her own, talking to her dead mistress, still bearing an unhealthy obsession for her and her child and a heart full of hate for Korvak and his child. There was no doubt of it now, she was plainly mad.

In a moment Mrs Purvis picked up the tray and left the room. Pippa sat hugging her knees, deep in thought. Mrs Purvis had promised to care for Carrie's child – but which child? It was more likely Mother had begged her to look after little Pippa than the grown girl who had already fled the home. It was Mrs Purvis's deranged mind, probably, which had in its own strangely twisted logic transferred the vow to Irma.

As she showered and dressed Pippa's mind was racing. How did the housekeeper propose to see that Irma came into her own'? An inheritance from Father, no doubt. She had been quick to supply Mr Hobbs with Irma's address. But the legacy, however generous, would be unlikely to be so vast that it warranted twenty years of planning and hatred. It was all very puzzling.

So were the accidents, mishaps, attempts to harm or even to kill her that had happened since Pippa came to Cambermere. A sudden stab of apprehension pierced her.

Was it possible that there was a connection, that Mrs Purvis was indeed behind all those accidents, attempting to kill Pippa so that Irma could benefit? Pippa hated to admit it, but there was a kind of cruel logic in it — kill off the hated child in order to benefit the beloved one.

Pippa trembled as she finished dressing and put on her sandals. Loth though she was to admit it, she knew that Mrs Purvis's insane devotion to Miss Carrie and Irma could render her capable of anything. A mind warped by hate and revenge, fostered over so many years, was desperately dangerous. From now on Pippa realised she must tread warily, taking even more care than just counting the steps and measuring the paces. She must treat the housekeeper in her normal manner, without showing her suspicion, but it would not be easy. It still gave her a shiver to think of her addressing the empty chair at the dressing table as if her cherished mistress still sat there. For Mrs Purvis that bedroom was a shrine, and while she adored her idol she was unaware of any other human presence. It was sick, unhealthy — crazy.

Halfway down the stairs Pippa remembered Stephen's call, and realised that there would be no more calls from him — or anyone else — if the 'phone was dead. She crossed the vestibule and lifted the receiver. Total silence. Then, her fingers followed the curled length of the cable until it reached the wall, she discovered why: the cable had been wrenched clean out of the wall. Mrs Purvis had obviously been listening in and had heard Stephen tell her that Alexis was dying and that he had found out about Irma. Then she must have decided that he'd said more than enough.

The first thing Pippa decided to do was to have the telephone line restored. Geoff Walters was the nearest person with a 'phone so that was where she would go, now. But stealthily as she descended the stairs, the housekeeper's ears must have been alert; as Pippa was crossing the vestibule, arms outstretched to avoid the pillars, a voice made her jump.

'Where are you going, Philippa?'

'For a walk, Mrs Purvis. I'll be back soon.'

It did not take long to reach the riding stables. Pippa felt the rough wood of the five-barred gate warm under her fingertips. Before she reached the cobbles of the yard Walters' voice hailed her.

'Hold on, Philippa! There's a bale of hay and a fork in your way.' Running footsteps, and then he was beside her. 'What brings you down here?' he asked.

'The 'phone's out of order. Would you ring in and report it, please, Geoff? My father, you know . . .'

'Oh, yes, of course. There's no more news then?'

'Not yet.'

'Do you want to ring the hospital from here?'

'You're very kind, but no thanks. I'll hear soon enough. But you could do something for me — find out the times of trains to London.'

'You're leaving?' His tone of surprise was genuine, but then, he did not know of all the strange happenings at the Hall. Or did he? For some unaccountable reason she thought of the woman in the Dormobile and Walters together, apparently in heated argument, according to Robin's description. She decided to take the bull by the horns.

'Geoff — what connection do you have with the woman who has been camping near here in a van? You seemed to be arguing with her the other day about something. What was going on?'

'The redhead? What do you know about her?' Walters' tone was decidedly on the defensive. Something clicked in Pippa's brain: *red hair*. A lot of lovely shiny hair, Robin had said. Like Carrie Hope? No — wait! Like Irma — with whom Mrs Purvis admitted she was in touch? It could not be — it was far-fetched in the extreme. She must learn more.

'Yes, the redhead. Why were you quarrelling?'

Walters grunted. 'I didn't know you knew. Well, the truth of it is, she wanted me to help her drive you away. Because of Nina, I agreed at first. Then I began to feel uneasy. I didn't like the gleam in her eyes — she talked wildly and I thought the whole thing might get out of hand and I honestly didn't wish you any harm, Philippa. So I told her it was off. I'd found out by then that despite being a Korvak you were really quite nice. Robin was getting fond of you too — that was another thing. Then you told me about writing to your father and getting Robin acknowledged as his son. She tried again to get me to help in some madcap scheme and I refused point-blank. That's all.'

'What madcap scheme?' Pippa asked. Daylight was beginning to dawn: Irma, with or perhaps without Mrs Purvis's help, had been behind some of the recent events – but which?

'She didn't spell it out because I wouldn't listen. I said I had no interest in avenging Nina now because you had made everything right. She seemed furious at that.'

'It was Irma, wasn't it, Geoff? Irma Starkey?'

'That was the name she told me. She said she was your half-sister, not a Korvak, and that she too had a grudge to settle against Korvak, just as I had. I must have been choked with hatred for your father even to listen to her, but when I saw the way things were going . . . ' His voice tailed away.

'I think my father hurt several people once, but he's a dying man now,' Pippa pointed out gently. 'Forgive him, Geoff.'

'I can, but only because of your generosity of heart, Philippa. You have more than atoned,' Walters replied quietly. 'Anyway, she's gone now. The Dormobile is no longer in the woods.'

Pippa felt a surge of relief. Nevertheless, she knew she must get away from Cambermere and the strange house-keeper. She told Walters of her plan to find a hotel in London for the time being and leave word with the solicitor, Mr Hobbs, where to find her. She added casually to Walters, 'And if anyone should come looking for me or want to reach me, tell him to contact Mr Hobbs. He'll know where to find me.'

Just in case, she thought. It was foolish to hope, but wilder dreams had come true. It would be terrible if, some time, Stephen did decide to try and trace her and found only a dead end. She walked back down the track to the lane and up towards the Hall.

She only stumbled once on the homeward journey – a pothole in the lane she could swear was not there before. By the time she reached the Hall steps her ankle was beginning to ache and she realised she must have given it a worse wrench than she had thought.

Mrs Purvis made no attempt to hide her concern. She was waiting in the vestibule. 'Where did you go for your walk, Philippa?'

'To Geoff Walters. He'll arrange to have the 'phone fixed. And you tell me something, Mrs Purvis — has Irma been here in Cambermere Hall? And whereabouts did my mother die, and just how exactly? Why didn't you want me to know about Irma? What harm have I done to either of you?' Pippa realised she was blurting out far more than she had meant to say and wished she could learn to control her impetuous tongue.

The housekeeper seemed not a bit disturbed. 'Shall I pour your tea? You do ask a lot of questions, don't you? Your curiosity about your mother is understandable, but Irma is no concern of yours at all.' How possessive she was, thought Pippa, about Irma as much as her beloved Miss Carrie. 'So I shall tell you what you want to know about your mother. She died in the east wing, in one of the film sets. She stabbed herself.'

'*Stabbed herself?*' Pippa was shocked. 'But you led me to believe my father was responsible?'

'So he was,' the housekeeper went on imperturbably. 'His treatment over the years had quite unbalanced her poor little mind. After he broke up her affair with Jan she was distraught, but after Jan's death she was overcome with a feeling of guilt. Her poor brain confused it with a role she had played in a historical drama some time before, until it became so muddled she could not distinguish between real life and fantasy. She would spend hours in the east wing, saying her lines over and over on the set.'

'What set? What part was she playing?' Pippa's question was no more than a whisper. She did not want to remind the housekeeper of her presence, for the woman was evidently only remembering aloud.

'The great banqueting hall. She played the medieval lady of the castle, the beautiful Lady Alys, whose lord has been away on a crusade for years and is now at last to return. Lady Alys is forced to part with her lover Peiral before he comes. Nevertheless she is torn by the conflict of love for

200

Peiral and loyalty to her lord, knowing she had betrayed him. As Lord Hubert enters the castle, eager to see his lovely wife, she takes a dagger and kills herself.'

There was love, compassion and pride in the housekeeper's voice as love for her dead mistress combined with proud recollection of how well she played the memorable role.

Pippa was sickened, horrified. 'And Alexis?' she asked.

'He came into the great hall looking for her, just as my Miss Carrie took up the knife. She had acted it out a hundred times before and I never dreamed she would really plunge the knife into herself. He watched, and did not stop her.' The hard edge of hatred crept back into Mrs Purvis's voice.

Poor Father. He had no more expected it to happen than the housekeeper had. The fading, forgotten actress, out of her mind with grief and the knowledge of her infidelity, probably never planned to do it at all. As Mrs Purvis had said, she was no longer able to distinguish between real life and dramatic fantasy.

The housekeeper suddenly averted to everyday practicality. 'I'll go up and change the beds while you finish breakfast, Philippa.'

There was a clatter of dishes, a brisk movement, and she was gone. Pippa pushed her plate aside. She had lost interest in eating. How she hated Cambermere Hall, she thought; outwardly it was so gracious and beautiful, but its whole atmosphere exuded sadness and grief. It was haunted by tragedy; suffering permeated its very stones and marbled magnificence. She would be glad to leave it behind. One day, perhaps, it could be exorcised and cleansed by other people and happier events, but not yet . . .

Yet it was not wholly evil, she reflected. There had been love in this house. Father undoubtedly loved Mother despite his lapses, and Mother had loved her children. Mrs Purvis's strangely twisted adoration of her mistress was love of a kind too. And it was here that Stephen had brought a new, stirring, wildly intoxicating sensation to Pippa — she knew now, beyond a flicker of doubt, that she loved him as she could love no other man. So much love in

201

this house — it had an element of redemption in it already.

There was a tap at the yard door. Pippa rose and felt her way around the table, wincing at the throb in her ankle. She expected the caller to be a delivery man with groceries or on some similar errand, and was surprised to hear Bainbridge's gruff voice.

'Ah, Philippa, I'm glad you're here. Hoped it wouldn't be that housekeeper woman. Funny soul, she is. Can I come in — only for a moment?'

Pippa sighed. One more proposal from Arthur Bainbridge would be the last straw. 'Come in. Would you like a cup of tea?'

'No thanks. I only came to say as I'm sorry. I realise now I was harassing you. I learnt how you'd been stricken and I shouldn't have pressed you like I did. So I've come to say — forget all about it, and I'm sorry if I vexed you.'

His speech, evidently carefully rehearsed, was gruff and stiff but Pippa was quick to recognise his magnanimity. She smiled. 'There's nothing to forgive. I appreciate your concern and I value your friendship, Arthur.' She could feel his tension ease as she used his first name. 'And what's more, I shall see to it that your land is restored to you, very soon now.'

He cleared his throat, understanding her unspoken words, and groped for the right phrases. 'Ah, yes. I heard about your father. Very sorry, Philippa. If there's aught I can do . . .'

'You're very kind. I shall be leaving Cambermere soon, but I'll be back. I look forward to seeing you again then.'

She felt her hand seized in a strong grip. 'And I look forward to that too, lass.' Abruptly, he was gone. Pippa felt a sense of warmth. One old axe was buried at least — two, she corrected herself, now that Geoff Walters' ancient hurt over his sister Nina was healed. She could be satisfied that her visit to Cambermere had achieved something after all.

It was time to pack. Pippa left the kitchen and went up the stairs. Twenty, twenty-one, twenty-two. She turned the corridor where her bedroom lay, and then stopped short. There were voices. As she strained her ears, she recognised it was one voice — the housekeeper's, but in a lower, softer range than she was accustomed to speak — and the sound was coming from Pippa's room. Pippa approached the door quietly.

Mrs Purvis was murmuring soothingly: 'There now, my lovely, there is no more need to fret. Alexis Korvak is nearing his end. There is not much time left, then all will be well. Oh, how your hair gleams in the sunlight! Glorious hair, so soft and abundant!'

Despite all her dislike and distrust of the woman, Pippa could not help feeling compassion for her. There she was, in her dead mistress's room, addressing her as though she still lived. It seemed almost sacrilege to disturb her, alone with her prayers in her shrine. Pippa turned to move away unobtrusively and heard the last quiet words: 'Are you ready, my precious? There is so little time.'

Poor thing, thought Pippa. She was trying to prepare her Miss Carrie for Alexis's arrival in the other world. It was all so sad and distorted. Pippa left her to her orisons.

For a little while Pippa walked in the rose garden, savouring the heady scent of the blooms until her aching ankle forced her to sit. She sat on the terrace, the sun warm on her face, and reflected how vastly her life had changed over the past few weeks. A month ago – was that all it was – she had still been busy working for Professor Garnier, unaware of Clive's imminent departure from her life, unaware of the details of her mother's tragic death and of her own half-sister in Nottingham, unaware that she was soon to lose her sight, and unaware of the existence of the man she loved with a hopeless longing. Who would believe that life could change so dramatically in so short a time?

A sound like a distant voice distracted her from her reverie and she looked up sharply. An ironic smile curved her lips; it would take a long time yet to grow used to being sightless. The voice, high and shrill like a woman's or a child's, did not come again. She could have been mistaken; it might have been the squeal of a rabbit or a startled bird.

Pippa was never able later to pinpoint the moment that day when she began to be filled with a growing sense of unease, the kind of inner sixth sense that warned that all was not quite as it should be. It might have been when Geoff Walters appeared in the gardens looking for her to tell her that the London trains ran hourly, except on Sunday.

'By the way, have you seen Robin?' he asked. 'He hasn't been around since breakfast.'

'No. He hasn't been here.'

'Just thought he might, knowing how fond he is of you. I wonder where the little monkey's got to.'

Or the unease might have originated with Mrs Purvis's non-appearance at lunchtime. Normally so meticulous in seeing that there was at least a snack, today she was nowhere to be found. Pippa made good use of her absence to limp upstairs to pack. The task took far longer than she had anticipated. It was not easy to gather all one's belongings by touch. The drawers were a simple matter − it was easy to distinguish her own things from Mother's because the scent of Californian Poppy lingered in Miss Carrie's. Finding her suitcase gave rise to some delay until her fingers encountered it in one of the cupboards in the dressing room.

As she packed, she thought of Irma's promise to Walters that Robin would benefit, in return for Walters' help in driving Pippa away. But Irma herself only stood to inherit a limited sum. Perhaps she thought she and Pippa were joint legatees. That would certainly account for Mrs Purvis's promptness in supplying Irma's address to Mr Hobbs. And by getting rid of Pippa, Irma could inherit it all. Pippa blanched. Getting rid of someone could mean driving them away or, if they proved stubborn, taking more drastic measures. Was that what all the recent strange happenings here at the Hall had been aimed at? Had Irma been making those attempts on Pippa's life, with the help of the half-crazed housekeeper?

But Irma was gone now, according to Geoff Walters. Either she had given up, or some other factor had changed her mind. Was Father already dead, perhaps, and they were keeping the truth from her? Or, more likely, had Irma learnt that she had little to gain by Pippa's death or disappearance?

It was only when the doorbell rang that the new fear entered her mind. She opened the front door to hear Geoff Walters' voice.

'Philippa, have you seen anything of Robin since I saw

204

you? He still hasn't come home and it's almost teatime. I wouldn't have bothered you but your 'phone's not working yet.'

It was then she felt the sick feeling. 'He hasn't been here, Geoff, so far as I know. Has he got a friend he might be with?'

'I've tried them. No one's seen him today. I'm worried, Philippa. He's not a secretive child; he hardly ever goes off alone. He's usually with the horses, but the stable lads haven't seen him since breakfast either.'

She could hear the deep concern in Walters' voice. 'I'll go and call around the grounds and up to the woods if you like,' she ventured. 'Do you think you should ring the police?'

'It's a bit early for that, but I am worried. Okay, you go uphill and I'll look down towards the village. Someone must have seen him.'

Walters hurried away. Pippa had forgotten about her wretched ankle until she began crossing the lawn and the throb returned to remind her.

'Robin! Robin!' she kept calling. 'Where are you?'

Her way was suddenly barred by something which pricked her face. Her hands told her it was a hedge, and further groping along it revealed a gap. Of course, it was the maze. She hesitated. If Robin had gone in there he could have become utterly lost, but surely he would have called for help? Suddenly she remembered the sound she had heard earlier in the day from the rose garden, the sound she had taken for the cry of a bird or animal. Could it have been Robin? Was he still in there, possibly asleep from exhaustion?

'Robin! Are you there?' she called loudly. 'It's Pippa — can you hear me?'

She listened intently but heard no answering sound. She hesitated. If she were to go in there in search of him, she too could become lost. Stephen flashed into her mind. What was it he had said about finding one's way through a maze? Something about marking the right hand wall with chalk. It would lead one to the middle and out again, if she remembered rightly. Perhaps if she kept her right hand on the hedge, following it continuously wherever it led her, the result would be the same.

'Robin! Robin! Are you in there?' Her cry echoed and died away across the grass. No, she decided, she would not venture in. The whole process could take an hour or more, and that hour could be better spent searching elsewhere. She cupped her hands around her mouth and drew a deep lungful of air for one final call.

'*Robin!*'

As the sound died away she caught her breath. Was it her imagination, or was there a faint, far-away cry, just like the one she'd heard in the rose garden? She turned slowly. If there was, it came from behind her, from the direction of the Hall and not from the maze or beyond.

The nearest point of the Hall was the east wing. Pippa limped towards it as quickly as her ankle would allow. Nearing it she felt the sun's warmth on her face suddenly turn cool and knew she was in the shadow of the wing. She stopped.

'*Robin!*'

This time there was no doubting it: it was an answering cry, high-pitched and shrill — the sound of a frightened child. Poor little thing! He must have got himself accidentally locked in, in one of those bewildering film sets.

Pippa hobbled along the front terrace until she reached the front door and went inside. To her surprise the double doors to the east wing were unlocked. He must be hurt, she thought, and was calling for help. Pippa hastened along the corridor calling his name, but this time there was no response.

She flung open the first door. 'Robin?' Hearing no answer she limped quickly to the second door. That room too only echoed her voice hollowly. Then she heard a whisper much further along and hurried towards it. At the fifth door, the set she hazily remembered was the dungeon, she hesitated and listened. There was clearly a muffled sound within. She opened the door.

'Robin, is that you? I've been looking for you everywhere!'

A sound like whimpering or subdued sobbing came to her ears and she moved towards it anxiously. At the same time a vaguely familiar aroma came to her but she took no notice. 'What is it, Robin? Are you hurt? Come now, it's me, your friend. Don't be frightened.'

She was holding out her arms towards the sound, concerned lest he was injured, but no small hand met hers. Instead she heard a click behind her and recognised the sound of a key turning in the lock. Bewildered, she turned.

'Robin, are you playing a trick on me? Come on, Robin, you have me at a disadvantage, you know. Tell me what you're up to. You're not hurt, are you?'

The whimpering sound returned, subdued at first and then growing gradually in volume − until she realised it was no whimper but a laugh. And it was not Robin's laugh. It was not the laugh of a child at all, but that of a full-grown woman.

'Mrs Purvis? Is that you? What are you playing at?' Pippa demanded.

The chuckling subsided. 'Oh yes, it's me, Philippa. And your precious Robin is safe − for the moment. We haven't done anything to him yet, have we, my precious?'

The tinkling laugh resumed and Pippa wondered whom the housekeeper was addressing. Her words were sinister, and Pippa's bewilderment suddenly gave way to tingling fear when she recognised the haunting perfume of Californian Poppy.

15

Pippa was momentarily bewildered. Mrs Purvis and that perfume, now associated in Pippa's mind only with darkness and menace, combined to fill her with fear. The housekeeper spoke to her beloved mistress as though she were here, and Pippa was convinced that the woman had finally lost her reason completely. Then another thought came to her. Up to this moment she had not wondered which film set was in this room. Now she could guess: it must be the one where Carrie Hope took her life – the banqueting hall of the medieval castle.

Pippa had no idea of the room's layout, so she remained stock still. It must be next door to the dungeon set. Mrs Purvis was making purring noises like a contented cat, but there was no sound of Robin. Yet she could swear it was a child's cry she had heard from the gardens.

'Mrs Purvis, Robin Walters is missing. Do you know where he is?' she asked timidly.

Amused laughter rippled round the room, and Pippa realised with horror that it was not the housekeeper's voice but that of a much younger woman. She clenched her fists, feeling the perspiration damp in her palms.

'Robin?' the housekeeper echoed. 'He's not missing, my dear. He's here, safe with us in the next room.'

With *us,* thought Pippa? But something in her refused to accept that the spirit of Carrie Hope really was there. She existed only in Mrs Purvis's warped mind, didn't she? Then whose was the soft laugh?

Realisation dawned even before the housekeeper spoke: only one other person claimed Mrs Purvis's loyalty – a woman who might have reason to keep Robin Walters from his uncle.

There was patent pride in Mrs Purvis's tone. 'Really, Philippa, you really are rather slow just as you always were. Not like my quick little Irma, so like her lovely mother. If you could see her now, Philippa, the same glorious hair and figure. A pity you never reached stardom, Irma, like Miss Carrie did. The whole world had an opportunity to adore her.'

'It's not my fault if I never graduated from repertory to the West End,' a woman's mellow voice answered snappishly. 'I did my best.'

'I know, my love. You just didn't have luck on your side, that's all,' Mrs Purvis soothed. 'You had none of the advantages that were showered on Philippa. But your time is coming, my precious. We've waited and planned for years and soon the world will be yours.'

Pippa listened in horror, taking in the full implication of her words. Irma had been cheated, she believed, by Korvak, but she could still inherit his wealth if — and it was this thought that appalled and frightened Pippa — if Pippa was not in the way. They meant to do her harm, to remove her permanently from the scene, and she was like a powerless, fragile butterfly in their hands. And Robin — he too stood between Irma and the inheritance. Pippa realised with dismay that it was she herself who had put him in danger when she told Geoff Walters he was to inherit jointly, and Walters in turn had passed the information on to Irma. What a blind, stupid fool she had been!

But was her half-sister really so obsessed with this crazy idea as Mrs Purvis was? There was a chance she had only been coaxed into the scheme by the doting housekeeper. It was worth trying to appeal to her better nature.

'Irma? Is it really you, after all these years?' she asked quietly.

That musical chuckle again. 'Oh yes, it's me, Pippa. Twenty years older and wiser, but it's me. You haven't changed since I last saw you in the nursery. Still mousy and insignificant. I recognised you at once when I came to your room. I was curious, but I needn't have bothered.'

'So it was you who came to my room in the night — soon after I arrived here?' Pippa breathed.

'As I said, I was curious, so I came at once when Mrs Purvis told me you were here. I couldn't stay here, of course, because you had that young journalist fellow here.'

The van. And that was why Mrs Purvis kept coming and going quietly from the Hall, to see Irma. Things were beginning to become clearer.

'The perfume — that was you too?'

'Yes. Mrs Purvis likes me to wear it constantly because my mother did. And to be frank, I liked the way you reacted to it and thought it was Miss Carrie's ghost, so I continued to use it.'

Pippa shivered, remembering how that perfume had terrified her, choking in her nostrils to the point of nightmare. She was wrong about Irma: she had evidently enjoyed tormenting Pippa as only a cruel, twisted person could.

'You had to go, there was no doubt of that,' Irma's pleasant voice went on smoothly. 'You stood between me and comfort, and after the wretched life I've had I deserve some comfort now. I'm thirty-six, you know.'

'The same age as your dear mother was,' Mrs Purvis murmured, 'and you look just as magnificent as she did. How that husband of yours could walk out on you passes all comprehension.'

'He was slow and stupid, just like Pippa here, and anyhow that was a long time ago,' Irma remarked. 'What matters now is getting her out of the way before Korvak dies — and the boy too.'

'Everything is ready,' Mrs Purvis said. 'I've only to fetch the boy.'

Pippa's mind raced. Whatever they planned, there was little time. She spoke to her half-sister again, playing for time. 'Then it was you who changed the sunlamp to ultra-violet and oiled the pool steps?' she asked.

'Oh yes, in an effort to drive you away. And later it was I who loosened the balcony rail.'

'And the hand in the night?'

Irma chuckled. 'That was funny. I hadn't planned that but it appealed to my sense of the theatrical. You couldn't see I was standing there watching you, feeling just a little bit sorry for the silly, helpless creature lying there so completely in my power, and then suddenly you cried out for Stephen and then for Gwen and held your hands out. I couldn't resist it. It was hilarious to see the expression on your face!'

'It was cruel, and you know it,' Pippa retorted.

'But you ask for it with your blind trust and simplicity! You're a fool, Pippa, and easily taken in, so it serves you right if people trade on it. I learnt long ago to trust no one and care for no one, then you can't get hurt.'

'Except for me, my precious,' Mrs Purvis interjected. 'You always trusted and cared about me. You bought me these lovely jet earrings only the other week, remember. You do love the one person you know cares for you.'

'As you're so fond of saying, Mrs Purvis, I know which side my bread is buttered,' Irma snapped. 'But we're wasting time. That Walters fellow will be back by dusk when he hasn't found the child.'

'And it was you who locked me in the stable with Copper?'

Irma laughed shortly. 'That wasn't planned, just an opportunity I couldn't miss. I'd seen Walters leave before you arrived, then I saw the boy go into the house, and no one else was around.'

'One more thing,' Pippa burst in. 'You say you look very like my mother – was it you, then, who danced in the garden one night by moonlight? You had me completely fooled then, I confess; I really thought it was her.'

There was a momentary silence and Pippa sensed that the two women exchanged looks. 'Danced in the garden?' repeated Mrs Purvis. 'When?'

'Soon after I arrived, before I fell off Copper. Irma does look exactly like those old stills of Mother, doesn't she?'

'She does,' Mrs Purvis admitted slowly.

'But it wasn't me,' Irma cut in. 'I have many talents, but dancing isn't one of them. I inherited many things from Mother but not her talent for dancing. Sorry, Pippa, but it wasn't me you saw. That must be your imagination. Mrs Purvis, give me the matches and fetch the boy.'

Alarm leapt in Pippa. She could see it all now – they had somehow brought or lured Robin here and used his cry deliberately to lure her to this set too. Matches – did they really plan to set fire to the place and leave her and Robin to perish? Irma was right. They were completely at her mercy. The set, no doubt composed mainly of chipboard and hardboard, would go up like dry kindling.

'Pippa!' Robin's thin little voice echoed across to her.

'Robin? Come here to me.'

'I can't. My hands are tied up and Mrs Purvis is holding me.'

She could hear the bewildered fear in his voice and she grew angry. 'Let him go, Mrs Purvis! He's done nothing to you,' she commanded.

Irma's laugh rippled out again. 'Let him go? And lose all we've worked and waited for? You're crazy, little sister. I won't tie you up – there's no need. You can't see and the door will be locked. There's no other way of escape. I believe it's quite quick really. You'll know nothing once the

211

smoke has made you unconscious.'

She talked as calmly and coolly as though she were an anaesthetist reassuring a patient, and Pippa could visualise Mrs Purvis standing by with an approving smile. They were demented, the pair of them, planning to execute a woman and a child so cold-bloodedly. Impractical ideas for escape tumbled into her brain and out again. The door was locked; she had heard the click. She could not rush at the house-keeper to grab Robin because she could not tackle Irma at the same time, especially as she had only a hazy idea of where they stood. Irma was moving about now, her shuffling footsteps mingling with metallic clangs. Then there was a splashing sound, and moments later an even more pungent smell overlaid Irma's familiar perfume. Pippa lifted her head and sniffed. *Petrol!*

She rushed forward impulsively towards the sound. 'Irma, what are you doing?' she cried, groping wildly to find the woman and restrain her. 'The set is inflammable enough already − you'll only succeed in burning down the whole wing, maybe the entire house!'

'What do I care?' the voice taunted. 'I hate this house, these loathsome sets, and you! I don't want Cambermere Hall! If I know Alexis Korvak, he has the place heavily covered with insurance and the money will be of far more use to me! Keep still, you fool − out of my way if you don't want to be soaked in petrol!'

'Take care where you're flinging it, Irma my love,' Mrs Purvis said anxiously. 'You don't want to splash yourself or me.'

'I know what I'm doing. Now stand back, near the door, Mrs Purvis. I'm going to strike the match.'

Pippa held her breath. If Robin was still being held by the housekeeper, then he was near the door − but where was the door? She had lost her sense of direction.

'Robin! Where are you?' she cried.

'Here, Pippa, by the door!' Even as she turned towards his voice she heard the scrape of the match behind her, and she hesitated. Should she leap for Robin and the door, and face the housekeeper − or should she turn back to try to stop Irma throwing the match? A click told her that Mrs Purvis had unlocked the door, ready for escape.

A hiss and a crackle behind her made up her mind. The pain in her ankle forgotten, she leapt forward, her hands outstretched, and encountered the boy's shoulders. Pushing him sharply to one side she groped for the housekeeper's angular body, but met only thin air.

'Watch out!' Irma cried. 'Don't let her reach the door!'

Instantly bony hands seized hold of Pippa, and with amazing strength Mrs Purvis forced her back. At the same time the housekeeper cried out: 'Take care, Irma! You've spilt petrol on your frock! Edge round the blaze towards the door!'

Pippa wrestled with her, trying to release herself from the woman's vice-like grip. Close behind her, so close, she could feel the heat, flames sizzled and roared. Pippa heard Robin cry out: 'Pippa, the pillar's on fire! The balcony above you is all in flames!'

With every ounce of her strength Pippa tore at the housekeeper's hands until she finally broke free, then sent the older woman flying. The crackling heat all around her made her break out into a sweat and at that second she heard a rumbling sound overhead.

'*Pippa! Jump!*'

Robin's warning came too late. She felt a sharp crack on her head and stumbled forwards, momentarily dazed by the blow. Then suddenly Mrs Purvis began screaming: '*Irma! Oh, my God! Irma!*'

It was then the miracle happened. In the black void before her Pippa suddenly saw a glow, a dull red glow which began to grow and gather colour. Then she saw a strange and terrifying *tableau vivant*: a thin, gaunt figure in black staring with wide, terrified eyes at a column of flame: and a small boy crouched with his hands behind his back beside a long trestle table. She stared, transfixed. It was not her imagination – she could see. Only hazily, but she could see.

Mrs Purvis screamed again and leapt forwards, directly into the column of flame. And then Pippa realised that the flame was not static but veering wildly from side to side. With a sickening rush of horror she saw red hair flying and hands beating at it, and Mrs Purvis beating her bare hands against the body. It was Irma, completely engulfed in fire.

213

'Irma, my precious! I told you to take care with the petrol!' Mrs Purvis was shrieking. 'Oh, my darling! What have you done?'

Pippa stared around. There was no water, no drape to quench the flame, only straw on the floor − and that was burning fiercely. She raced to Robin and seized his shoulder.

'Poor lady,' he was whimpering. 'Poor lady.'

'Outside, Robin,' Pippa commanded. 'Mrs Purvis, out! Get blankets!'

But the housekeeper seemed deaf, crazed with hysterical sobbing and feverishly tearing at Irma, who screamed and fell to the floor. Mrs Purvis crouched over her, still shrieking and sobbing. Pippa wrenched the key round in the lock and flung the door open wide. Robin scuttled out.

'For God's sake, Mrs Purvis!' Pippa yelled. 'Get help! Fetch blankets!' The figure of Irma screamed and then lay still. Mrs Purvis stared for a second and then, straightening, she turned a look charged with hate towards Pippa.

'You bitch!' she cried, unaware of the flame licking around her. 'You'll die for this!'

Like a cat she leapt, black and sinuous and swift as an arrow. Her slender body felt like a ton weight when it cannoned into Pippa, and they both fell heavily on the floor. Over the housekeeper's shoulder Pippa caught a flashing glimpse of Robin's terrified little face through the smoke.

'Go − fetch help!' she gasped, but as she rolled over and struggled to rise she could not see whether he obeyed. The housekeeper leapt on her again, her dark eyes glittering and her nails outstretched to rake Pippa's face. They were enveloped in smoke now, in the centre of the great hall, and Pippa was choking and gasping for air. The draught from the open door was fanning the flames and the minstrel's gallery overhead was blazing fiercely. Soon it must fall, and perhaps the roof too.

Mrs Purvis's hands found a hold on Pippa's throat. Pippa kicked and lashed out as hard as she could, but the older woman was amazingly powerful, and her adversary out of condition after spending so long as an invalid. Pippa was growing desperate. Air no longer reached her lungs. She was choking and the world was going black again. Irrationally it flashed into her mind that it was her nightmare all over again — darkness, and the perfume choking her nostrils, only this time the smell was petrol and smoke, not Californian Poppy.

But this time the nightmare was not going to defeat her. As Pippa gathered the last ounce of her strength to fight back she felt the vicious grip about her throat begin to loosen. Encouraged, she battled even harder. The hands let go, and she gulped in a lungful of smoke-filled air. Dimly she was aware of the housekeeper scrambling to her knees and then she vanished into the smoke. Pippa too began to scramble up, filled with determination. Mrs Purvis must be caught and dragged to safety. Just as she stumbled upright, there was a rumbling, wrenching sound and something hit her, sending her flying. It was not Mrs Purvis making a renewed attack, she realised, but a great beam, charred and smouldering, which pinned her helplessly to the floor, like a butterfly pinned to a display board. She lay there, unable to move, desperate with fear. A blackened, immobile figure lay beside her. Inches from her head, a tower of flame was consuming the trestle table. Its heat was singeing her hair.

It was ridiculous, she thought. Suddenly and for no accountable reason she could see again, only to watch helplessly as she and her sister were burnt to death. The incredibly magnificent colours dazzled her. The blue and grey of the smoke, the scarlet and vermilion flame, were a garish kaleidoscope of colour which seared her eyeballs so long accustomed only to blackness, with an intensity no less than the fire. To behold a world of beauty in colour as she was to die was unbearably tragic. She struggled with every muscle to move, but it was hopeless. She was trapped. Smoke was filling her lungs, burning and choking — was it the nightmare realised at last? The hissing and spitting flames came nearer. Pippa choked, gasping for life, but she could feel the blackness of oblivion beginning to close in on her . . .

'*Pippa!*'

It was a dream, an overwhelming nightmare. It seemed to her dazed mind that a powerful male voice rang through the smoke-eddying rafters – Stephen's voice. Dimly she wondered whether she had already crossed the threshold to the life beyond. She was aware that the crushing weight across her body was suddenly gone, and then strong arms held her close. She felt herself being lifted and carried and then moments later there was pure, sweet air. Coughing and gasping, she gulped it in with desperate gratitude.

'Pippa, Pippa *babam,* are you all right?'

Unbelievingly she stared up into anxious blue eyes and her heart swelled with happiness. It was Stephen, alive and here and holding her tightly as he hastened along the corridor.

'Irma – and Mrs Purvis,' she managed to gasp.

Stephen shook his head. 'Too late for Irma. Mrs Purvis has gone – she was running out as I came in. She's all right. Let's get you out now.'

Over his shoulder Pippa could see smoke billowing from the room they had left and flames licking round the door. Stephen was running, and she could see the ash in his blond hair. Suddenly they were out in the open, and the air had never smelt so clean.

'My God!' she heard Stephen mutter. Dazed though she was, she could not fail to note the horror in his tone.

'What is it?'

'Mrs Purvis – oh, my God!'

With effort Pippa turned her head to look. At the foot of the flight of steps from the front door of Cambermere Hall lay a black, prostrate figure with a crimson halo.

'What happened, Stephen? Is she hurt?'

Stephen turned away so that Pippa could see no more. 'She's dead, Pippa. Stabbed in the neck.'

'*Stabbed?*'

'Yes. Her earrings. One of them has pierced her neck. It must have severed a carotid artery.' He strode quickly away from the building. 'Ah, thank God! Here comes the ambulance and the fire engine.'

Afterwards, Pippa could remember dimly being carefully lifted into the ambulance, the murmured, soothing words, and Stephen's hand in hers as she lay numb and stupefied. After that she must have sunk into oblivion.

Later, how much later she had no way of knowing, Pippa came slowly to her senses. For long moments she lay there, staring into the darkness and trying to recollect the nightmare that had so recently overwhelmed her mind. Gradually she began to recall taunting voices, a child's cry of fear, flame, blood . . . The isolated images that drifted back were so terrifying that it must have been a nightmare more hideous than she had ever experienced before. The only memory of it that filled her with disappointment was the belief, in the dream, that she had somehow miraculously regained her sight.

But was it a dream? Even now it seemed as if she could discern a faint light some yards away — and yes, beneath it a head wearing a white cap. Was she dreaming now of hospital after she fell from Copper? After all, even blind people probably dreamed. As she lay there, perplexed, the white cap rose and came towards her.

'Ah, you're awake, Miss Korvak. How do you feel?' It was a young nurse, but not one she recognised. She stared at her hazy face. 'Still a little sleepy, are you?' the nurse went on. 'Don't worry. That's the sedative the doctor gave you. Quite a nasty shock you had, wasn't it? Still, you were very lucky. Only a sprained ankle and your hair will soon grow again.'

Pippa raised a hand to her head and felt the short, crisp ends of hair. It had been no dream; dreams don't singe one's hair away. Her heart leapt. Then if it had all really happened, what had become of Robin and Stephen?

'Stephen . . . ' she murmured. The nurse smiled.

'Is he the young man who sat by your bed all night? He's still here. I don't suppose Sister will mind if he comes in — it's nearly time for the morning bell.'

Suddenly he was there, tall and broad, his fair head surrounded by a halo of golden light, and as he bent to kiss her cheek Pippa felt warmth and life flow in her veins. 'Stephen — '

'Don't speak, my love,' he whispered, laying a finger to her lips. 'I'm so glad I listened to the promptings of my heart and not my head or I'd never have reached you in time.'

'The 'plane to New York . . . '

'I let it go. There was something in your voice on the 'phone when I rang you, nothing you said, just a tone of helplessness, fear even. I stayed the night at the airport hotel trying to decide whether to go, or to defy you and come back. Thank God I came back. I should never have left you. I'll never leave you again, Pippa.'

He was covering her hands with kisses, muttering brokenly, 'I've thrown away the book. My father's name was cleared and I realised I wanted you more than I wanted revenge. I didn't realise how much danger you were in, that Irma was crazy. Oh, my little pipistrelle, I was nearly too late!'

'Robin?' Pippa murmured.

'He's safe, and unhurt. Irma died, I'm afraid. And Mrs Purvis. Strange thing that, being stabbed by her own earring.'

Strange, and ironic, thought Pippa, since the earrings had been a treasured gift and a memento of her beloved Miss Carrie. Ironic too that her pet child Irma had died in the same spot as her mother.

'Cambermere?' she asked.

'The fire's out. The east wing was gutted but the rest is safe. Don't worry.'

She was not worried. Indeed, she was glad that the east wing with its grisly film sets and unhallowed memories was gone forever, and with it the reminders of Miss Carrie's tragic death and Father's past misdeeds.

Stephen said in a low voice, 'I've only just learnt of your blindness, Pippa, and I'm amazed at your courage. You never told me or cried out for help. And yet, as I carried you out, I could swear you looked at Mrs Purvis as she lay there. But never fear, my darling, I'll always be here now to love and guide you.'

She would tell him the glorious news later, once the memory of that dreadful night and the two sprawled black figures circled in scarlet had begun to fade. There was time enough, she knew, to tell him of the miraculous blow on the head in the midst of the fire which had restored some hazy sight: and time to tell him she had never meant to blaze at him, to banish him forever, because she too loved him with all her heart. With his hand tightly gripping hers and his gentle voice murmuring words of love, there was all the time in the world.

'I discovered how your mother really died from the coroner's inquest, poor soul, and how your father kept the truth a secret so that her fans would never know she had lost her reason. Instead he put it about that she had gone into a decline and died in a sanatorium. Then I traced Irma to Nottingham,' he was saying softly. 'She was not there, but her talkative landlady told me a lot. She took me for a relative, I think. She said Irma had expectations of great fortune once she had got rid of an importune sister. That worried me. I kept thinking of the things that had happened to you — the oil on the swimming pool steps and all that — but I couldn't bring myself to believe that she could be behind it. Now I see she must have been, probably with Mrs Purvis's help. Forgive me, *galambom,* for not taking your fears seriously and for leaving you to face danger alone. I see now that all those odd things must have been her doing. I should have stayed by you, whatever you said.'

Pippa stroked his bent head. His hair too was singed. Yes, my beloved, she thought. All those strange events have at last been explained away — except one.

Irma had sworn, in that great hall which was to become the blazing inferno where she was to die, that she had not danced in the gardens of Cambermere Hall by moonlight. Who, then, had been the enchanting, ethereal figure that glided from the trees and dipped and curtseyed with such lissom grace? Pippa raised Stephen's face and cupped it between her hands, seeing dimly the gentle curve of his lips and the tenderness in his eyes. She might never speak of it to him, but deep inside she was convinced that figure was the shade of the woman who wrote so lovingly of her child in her diary, the doomed, unhappy Carrie Hope. From her grey limbo world she had come back to ensure that child's safety and escape from darkness into the bright world of love and hope.